IAN *and* ANTON

A NOVEL

ROBERT BECKSTEDT

Copyright © 2024 Robert Beckstedt.

Cover Design: Robert Beckstedt
Technical Support: Katharine Beckstedt Randall
Interior Formatting: Ashleigh R. Benedum

All rights reserved. No part of this book may be reproduced, stored, or transmitted by any means—whether auditory, graphic, mechanical, or electronic—without written permission of both publisher and author, except in the case of brief excerpts used in critical articles and reviews. Unauthorized reproduction of any part of this work is illegal and is punishable by law.

This book is a work of fiction. All names, characters, locations, and incidents are products of the author's imaginations. Any resemblance to actual persons, things, living or dead, locales, or events is entirely coincidental.

ISBN: 979-8-89419-401-1 (sc)
ISBN: 979-8-89419-402-8 (hc)
ISBN: 979-8-89419-403-5 (e)

Because of the dynamic nature of the Internet, any web addresses or links contained in this book may have changed since publication and may no longer be valid. The views expressed in this work are solely those of the author and do not necessarily reflect the views of the publisher, and the publisher hereby disclaims any responsibility for them.

One Galleria Blvd., Suite 1900, Metairie, LA 70001
(504) 702-6708

BOOKS BY ROBERT BECKSTEDT
ON AMAZON.COM

I Murdered Your Mother, I think?

The Great Great Aunts from Prussia

The Tributaries of Alex Beckham

THE DEDICATION

To find God on his spiritual level of consciousness, one must listen in one's own silence, then actively seek it by questioning, not by unconditional acceptance of a human interpretation. Only by following his lead, stepping outside the physical structures, and walking his path, will you find what you are seeking.

—Robert Beckstedt

"The world reveals itself to those who travel on foot."

—Werner Herzog

INSPIRATION

"I have a deeply hidden and articulate
desire for something beyond the daily life"
—*Virginia Woolf*

The Lord said, "Go out and stand on the mountain in the presence of the Lord, for the Lord is about to pass by." Then a great and powerful wind tore the mountain apart and shattered the rocks before the Lord, but the Lord was not in the wind. After the wind there was an earthquake, but the Lord was not in the earthquake. After the earthquake came a fire, but the Lord was not in the fire. And after the fire came a gentle whisper. (1 Kings 19:11-12)

I urge you, brothers and sisters, to watch out for those who cause division and put obstacles in your way that are contrary to the teachings you have learned. Keep away from them. (Romans 16:17)

"Within you there is a stillness and a sanctuary
to which you can retreat at any time and be yourself."

—Hermann Hesse

PRELUDE

As the story begins, the main character is set on a path by the catastrophic events of September 11, 2001. His past prepared him for a journey he could never have foreseen, one which made the experiences in his life to this point seem random. The dots were unconnected, like a puzzle with a thousand pieces but no box cover. Ian described the path to which he was drawn as an 'invisible undertow' or 'a hand in his back'. It pushed and pulled him to a vortex, like a star pulled into a black hole, the other side remaining unknown.

As the book continues, it raises the ancient debate between Predeterminism and Free Will. Is it possible for Ian Roberts to eject himself from this force drawing him inward; does he have that option? Is his path predetermined by some metaphysical answer? Is it God's omnipotent power predetermining Ian's path, so he has no choice? Or can Ian make any one of an infinite amount of decisions every day of his own free will?

Ian impulsively volunteers to travel to a Black township in South Africa during the height of the country's AIDS epidemic with only a vague mission statement, 'Start a business that will kick off profits to fund the operations of an AIDS Hospice and create jobs." As an entrepreneur, he was qualified. And as an entrepreneur, he was used to starting with no business plan, and only the capital from his own pocket. That was his first hint. He was chosen for a reason.

As his journey continues, people teach him to believe he has choices. He can choose to ignore the hand in his back and avoid the pain and confrontation coming his way, or he can accept his calling and follow the philosophy of 'Yes'. Challenged by his church in America, his mystical mentors, Anton and Esther, teach him to listen to God's instructions through his silent meditation, and to trust his growing faith in the Lord.

In the end, the story concludes the way it was supposed to. Ian learns to listen in the silence. He accepts what is expected of him, yet he realizes he can choose to make his own decisions and accept the consequences. He understands God will suggest where and when he needs him next. God will erase the blackboard and give Ian a clean sketch pad, but it will be up to Ian to pick up the pencil.

Buddhism says man is meant to suffer. Human life is hard, physically and emotionally. Since Buddhism believes in reincarnation, they believe in free will. They believe our next life is determined by the actions of our current life. But predeterminism believes we cannot make our own decisions for it has been scripted by data placed in our personalities by our ancestors since the beginning of time. So, I will leave you with a quote by Stephen Hawking:

> *"I have noticed that even people who claim that everything is predestined, and that we can do nothing to change it, look before they cross the road."*

I hope the book entertains you. I enjoyed writing it.

—Robert Beckstedt

TABLE OF CONTENTS

1. An Invisible Undertow 1
2. On the Third Day 9
3. Your Time has Come, Mr. Roberts 13
4. The Arrival in South Africa 20
5. Let us Come Together 24
6. The Mission Trip 31
7. Mr. Roberts, Welcome to Church 40

   Part 1 40

   Part 2 47

8. Morning has Broken 53
9. Miriam 59
10. The Christening 63
11. A Silent Declaration of Loyalty 70
12. The Dedication of the Hospice 81

    Part 1: The Return of Jordan 81

    Part 2: The Tour 87

    Part 3: The Battleground 92

    Part 4: The Victory Lap 96

    Part 5: The Dedication 99

    Part 6: The Finale – The Awakening 110

13. Cape Town Dining 119

    Part 1: 'Confess your weariness to the Lord,
           And he will send you Comfort' 119

    Part 2: 'He who has ears to hear, Let him hear' 133

14. The U.S. Army 146
15. The Cape of Good Hope 153
16. And He Ascended into Heaven To see the Lord 166
17. Botswana 173
18. Campaign Interference 178
19. Credence has Needs 180
20. Remember September Mr. Roberts 185
21. The Compound Compounded 192
22. Trip to Mozambique 198
23. Return from Maputo 202
24. And the World Turned 211
25. The Churches Part Ways 218
26. Fare Thee Well 221
27. Returning Home to the Wasteland 224
28. The Message 231

AN INVISIBLE UNDERTOW

As the autumnal bliss approached in early September, the heat of summer was pushed aside by cool breezes and deep azure skies. Ian Roberts was unaware of his new life which was approaching, a life that would change his view of God and humanity, a life putting all his experiences into perspective. A chilly winter would force him inward, but by Springtime, the seed silently planted inside him through his meditation would take root. Maturity and wisdom would begin to grow. But with that growth, both joy and pain would be felt, and many tears shed. Ian Roberts would never be the same.

* * * *

Ian snaked his way through the parking lot, but like a stream in a sudden deluge, it filled rapidly. Ian found himself in grid lock. The lot hit its saturation point. Everyone was here for the same purpose; to attend a church service on this unique Sunday morning. A small group of men in yellow vests waived traffic past the lot's entrance, while others directed those trapped in the quagmire out the same entrance. The overflow drained slowly into the street. Ian considered passing on his mission, predictable knowing his more than occasional impatience. But something inside compelled him to stay the course. He circled the surrounding neighborhood. Three blocks from the lot he found a spot. It appeared to be a driveway to a garage, but no more. The driveway was walled off at

IAN AND ANTON

the property line. It was as if the spot was created just for him. He parked the car, looked upward, and mumbled, "Thank you, Lord."

Ian was familiar with the neighborhood. It was an affluent area of well-groomed homes. Its residents consisted of the professional elite in this growing city of Charlotte, North Carolina. Ian grew up a few miles away, but in a different environment. His neighborhood was a blue-collar manufacturing district with small worn houses and multiple-family dwellings. The creek he played in as a boy changed colors daily depending on the chemicals dumped by the factories. Ian felt blessed to learn from those who struggled, his parents included. And even though he was now educated and financially successful, he valued the ethics and morality of the working class.

As Ian came nearer to the church, he became cognizant of the smell, a smell marking the end of another summer and an approaching fall. He could see the building. It was not a church; it was a private grade school. He made his way up a set of spiraling stone steps to the doorway. A line of casual but well-dressed people methodically entered the building. As Ian entered, he observed a hoard of people; most of a similar age, race, and stature. It was Generation X, vanilla, but with an occasional sprinkle of color. It reflected the neighborhood.

Now only a droplet in this sea of people, Ian could do nothing but shuffle his feet forward with baby steps. Again, he felt an unexplained force tugging him in, like that of ocean undertow. Ian did not like crowds, but turning back was not an option. The droning of a hundred voices filled the air, but not one distinguishable word. Ian wondered whether that is what God hears when everyone prays at the same time on Sunday mornings. Now in gridlock for the second time, Ian waited patiently for the flood waters of people to recede.

"You look perplexed, sir. I'm assuming this is your first time at Credence Community Church?" A young woman of college age stood toe to toe with Ian staring up, like a puppy waiting for a biscuit. "My name is Sara. All of us with red badges are greeters." She extended her hand. Ian took it with a smile. "Can I get you a cup of coffee, sir?"

"You can try, but in this crowd, we may never see each other again." Ian's grin was a nervous grin this time. Sara smiled back.

"Stay right here. I will find you again. Don't move."

Ian did not feel comfortable. "Wait, that is kind of you, but I think it best I follow you. How much do you need?" Ian reached for his wallet.

"No sir, it's free and you may take it into the auditorium during the service." Ian thought about his youth when it was all he could do to keep his eyes open during Pastor Hofer's sermons, a sweet man, and a magnificent mentor, but not overly exciting to a sleepy teen.

"What a smart idea, Sara. Coffee before and during the service."

Ian followed as Sara parted the crowd like Moses parted the Red Sea. Weaving through the masses, they came upon a cart in the middle of the room. It contained six commercial coffee brewers. With organized precision, a team removed and replaced the brewers continuously. As a systems analyst, Ian was impressed with the organization of the process. It was designed well. Sara went to the cart and quickly returned with a cup of hot coffee.

"Sorry sir, they are out of cream and sugar."

"That's fine. I'm a purist." Sara did not know what Ian meant, but he seemed satisfied.

"Those people are working hard. I've never seen a crowd like this." Sara handed Ian his coffee. "You have questions for me? You have not given me your name, sir."

"My name is Ian, Ian Roberts."

"Well, very nice to meet you, Mr. Roberts, ask away."

"First, the sir and the Mr. are not necessary. I appreciate the respect, but you are an adult and I find titles only valuable in a formal work environment."

Sara looked at Ian with a forced smile and thought, *'This is not work for you, but it is for me.'*

Ian noticed an obvious generational difference between himself and those surrounding him. He also sensed the cultural difference between them and his blue-collar background which went unnoticed.

"Is this church associated with any particular denomination, Sara? And is the auditorium large enough to handle all these people? I parked three blocks away and people were still searching for a place to park."

"The answer to your first question, Credence Community Church has no affiliation with any denomination. They opened a year ago and are independent. Secondly, we anticipated an influx today, but nothing like this."

"The terrorist attack in New York is what prompted me to attend. People are frightened. They want to gather together in the name of God."

"Have you attended other churches in your life?" Sara opened a notebook. Ian saw it but found it irrelevant until now. She began to take notes.

"I was raised Lutheran. When my three children were young, we attended a small nondenominational church north of the city. My close friend was the pastor. We mentored and confided in each other. I taught his High School Sunday School class for years."

"You are Protestant and a strong believer in Jesus Christ," she stated.

"I have studied many religions and traveled to Nepal, India and Thailand."

"Where exactly is Nepal?"

Ian did not want to get in a discussion, and she was now the one seeking information about him. "You have other questions for me?"

"Why did you leave your church and come to Credence? Sara had noted: fifty, grown children, Sunday School teacher, Protestant, travels a lot.

"My children left for college, so I moved back into the city."

"I am still curious about Nepal and the other religions." Sara seemed genuinely interested.

"Nepal is in the Himalayas. It is home to Buddhism and Hinduism." Sara took more notes. Ian knew he must stop. The next question would be why and what did he learn. This was not the time nor the place.

"Go on," Sara asked.

"You asked why I am here. I was referred by a friend and…" Ian was interrupted. He heard his name.

"Ian, over here." A hand was waving above the crowd.

"Mark, how are you?" Ian returned the wave and called back loud enough to rise above the buzzing.

"I'm good, Ian. I didn't expect to see you here. Let's talk next week." Mark smiled and returned to his conversation circle.

"So, you know someone here?" Sara was surprised a man of his age would know anyone at Credence.

"Yes, he is one of my junior partners."

"What do you do for a living, Ian?" Before Ian could answer, two others from a different group waved.

"Ian, how are you? We didn't expect to see you here." It was a tall man sporting a blonde toupee. "Did you play last night?" he asked with a friendly smile.

"I had a rare Saturday night off. Patricia next to you suggested I try this church, so here I am."

"Hi, Ian." Patricia waved. Ian waved back.

"I'll talk to you sometime when it is less crowded. We will play next Friday. I can talk to you then."

"You know a lot of people here, Ian. I have to ask again, what do you do for a living?" Ian realized; this was an interview. "I own a management firm for physicians, I sing and play guitar in a rock band, and I love to travel. That is where I know these people." Sara interrupted.

"Would I know the name of your band? Have I seen you in concert?" Sara waited for the answer and Ian thought the question was cute, naïve but cute.

"I doubt it, Sara. We are local and play classic rock, probably not your genre." Ian was making a prejudicial assumption.

"I love the Beatles and Pink Floyd, and I really love Stevie Nicks," Sara responded.

"You listen to them?"

"My parents do so I do. I'll come to see you and bring my parents. How many more people do you know here?" Sara was running out of time.

"Not a lot, I assume. Few people in my business world know I'm a musician. And few people in my music world know I am a businessman. And even fewer know of my spiritual life."

"Last question, why are you here today?"

"I'm in the process of finding a new church, one that matches my philosophy of life. I have not found it yet. I felt drawn here this morning and I do not understand why. There is something I need to learn here. I can feel it."

She looked at Ian and a warm feeling went through her. She never experienced sincerity emanating from a person like it was from Ian. She was speechless. Suddenly, her interview was interrupted.

"Can I have everyone's attention, please?" Standing precariously on a folding chair and holding a microphone, a young man, thin with a touch of premature balding, stood above the crowd. He appeared important but not someone in charge. Shushes spread through the room until only a few inattentive people continued to talk. They were quickly tapped on the shoulder. "Good morning, everyone. My name is Jim Bennet and I recently joined Credence Community Church as their pastor in charge of outreach programs. It appears our church expanded rapidly overnight. For those of you who have never attended Credence, we have twice as many people today as ever before. We just finished talking among the pastors. We want to ask; how many have attended today due to the tragedy Tuesday morning in New York?" Half raised their hands." It is sad and beautiful at the same time. We have come together in the name of God, in the name of Jesus Christ. However, we must announce the auditorium for the 10:30 service is full. We will be finishing that service at noon. We will have repeat services starting at 12:30 and continuing every ninety minutes until 5:00. We want to bless all of you with our fellowship in this time of grief. We know you will be patient. Let us hold hands and pray." The crowd held the hand of whoever was next to them, closed their eyes, and bowed their heads. Pastor Bennet began. "Dear Lord, thank you for bringing us together in the name of love and peace. Help us to live in your image. Let us pray for those victims and families killed and injured in this terrible act of Satan. Bless our leaders and protect all of us in the days to come. In the name of our Lord and Savior, Jesus Christ, amen." The room echoed the amen. People hugged and cried in sympathy and in fear of the unknown.

"Well, Ian," Sara said in an apologetic tone, tears welling in her eyes. "I'm sorry about this. None of us saw this coming. I hope you can stay for the noon service. Since you are a musician, they have an incredible music program."

"Sara, I would stay but I have plans. I will return. What was your last name?"

"I am not permitted to give my last name for legal reasons. Please come back next week. How do I contact you to let you know of our schedule and projects?"

Ian handed Sara his business card. "Sara, I have one more question for you. There were so many new people here today, but I did not see a lot of greeters. Why did you approach me and spend time with me rather than others?"

"I must be truthful. I am not a member of this church, although I find it interesting. I am Jewish. I am studying for my MBA in marketing. All of us with badges are in a master's program. Our professors assembled us to work on this project."

"And the project is?"

"It helps Credence recruit new members, specifically, the kind they prefer. We get credits for the project, and I assume our schools gets money."

"You are performing market research." Ian was fascinated. "You go home and send in your findings?"

"Not exactly. When the service begins, we meet in a classroom. Our project leader gives us survey forms to complete from the interviews we performed."

"Go on."

"When I saw you, you were not the typical new member. I thought it would be interesting to interview an older person. I don't mean to insult you, but I did use you. You were even more different than I expected."

"No, Sara, not at all. It sounds like Credence is as much a business as a church. And I assume it has a formal business plan. I am anxious to find what their religious philosophies may be."

"You have no idea how organized they are. The rumors are some big corporate executives are involved." Sara was peaking Ian's interest even more.

Ian belonged to small neighborhood churches where everyone knew everyone. This was different; non-denominational and professional. This market research was to grow them in the direction they preferred.

Ian left the building, descended the stone steps, and walked to his car. He understood overcrowded holy days. The September 11 tragedy was different. It was sudden and on a worldwide scale. Ian was pensive. A non-denominational church built with a corporate business plan by big business. Unlike Catholicism, Judaism or Baptist, it did not have the support and guidance of a large sect. He refused to allow himself to form an opinion. Churches were perishing as the elderly died. The culture of youth demanded entertainment. Ian wondered how they were attracting them. He would soon see. Rock bands, Jumbotrons, youthful messages; energy in the air. Perhaps this is God's new path. It was worth exploring.

Ian would return, but not for a lesson in business. He was being mystically and subconsciously pulled to another level of consciousness, one that would take him halfway around the world and all the way down. Its source emanated from the silence of his prayer room.

ON THE THIRD DAY

It was three days since the terrorist attack of September 11 flooded Credence Community Church with a host of fearful and confused souls. The staff of young pastors entered the meeting room. Electricity was in the air. Smiles, high fives, low fives, and fist bumps were passed freely. Then Jordan West, Head Pastor and Executive Director of Credence Community Church entered the room. The Board of Directors did a near perfect job casting this young man in his role as leader. He was strong in physique. He displayed handsome facial features and flaunted a captivating smile. In his early thirties, he was still without a blemish. He was married to a wholesome, educated woman, daughter of a successful corporate president in Charlotte. They had two small children and a Golden Labrador. Jordan received his undergraduate in Business and then received his Master of Theology from the Candler School of Theology in Atlanta. He was the right person for this experiment in modern religion, meshing young spirituality with entertainment, adding profit for investors, then parlaying it all into a megachurch. It had the potential of a win for all.

September 11th was like the destructive thunderstorm ending a lengthy mid- western drought. The fear that permeated through all Western civilization boosted attendance at Credence Community Church two hundred and fifty percent in one weekend. The pews were shoulder to shoulder for four straight services. And beginning the following Sunday, three services in total would be offered between nine and noon. With email exploding in popularity in the late 1990's, word spread quickly. Free cups of coffee were filled to the brim as were offering plates. The prayers of the Credence pastors, investors, and Board of Directors had been answered by an act of terror, an act that pulled the youth back into God's arms. The new pastors were ready. Today would be the first hint of long-term success and job security.

Jordan West began the meeting, "Let us hold hands and pray. Dear Lord, all our lives we have heard the worn cliché, the Lord works in mysterious ways. It has. As you had John the Baptist prepare the way for your son Jesus Christ, you have called upon us to lay the groundwork for your youth to seek and find him. The horrific events of September 11th pushed our mission to a new level. We now know why you named our church what you have. A credence is the small table on which holds the elements of the Eucharist, the body and blood of Jesus Christ, before they are consecrated. You have placed the body and blood of your son upon us. We waited patiently for those seeking meaning in their lives to arrive so we may do your work and save their souls. Now they are here. In the book of Isaiah, we are told "The Lord will take hold of you and not let you go." Satan cannot win this battle. His evil has resurrected your people. Our founder's plans have laid out our framework for the future. Dear Lord, continue to give us the wisdom to guide your flock onto this higher ground. In the name of Jesus Christ, our Lord and Savior. Amen."

The room repeated 'Amen' in unison and proceeded to hug each other. Tears were shed. The tables were arranged in a square. West took his place. They all sat.

"Well Professor, let us begin with your report on attendance. Your students must have had a busy Sunday. Tell us their findings."

"Jordan, it seems like our target demographics were the same, just more of them. Our observations were Caucasian at 85%, African American 8%, Asian 4%, Latino 3%. Age-wise it was what we want to attract: 20's at 20%, 30 to 45 at 65% and over 45 at 15%. It was hard with such a crowd, but that is close."

"What did you estimate to be our overall attendance, Professor?"

"We estimated 250% of historic attendance."

"That's what I thought, "said West. "Any interesting anomalies?"

"We had a Middle Eastern family visit."

"Any problems?"

"My students were tentative, but one student, Sara, approached them immediately. She has no fear, and her curiosity is stellar." The professor smiled.

"What did she find?" asked West.

"The father is one of our founder's employees. They have been here numerous times."

"You know, I do remember seeing them. With what just happened, I assume I am more observant. Anything else?" Jordan asked.

"Yes. Sara, also noticed more middle-aged people in attendance, one in particular." The professor looked at Jordan for a response.

"Go on, Professor."

"Sara talked with him at length. She said he seemed different somehow."

"In what way, Professor?"

"Well, he is divorced with three early adult-aged children."

"How many times?"

"She didn't say. She said he spoke briefly of his Lutheran upbringing; he taught a High School Sunday School class at his last church and has studied Buddhism in the Himalayas." *Divorce and Buddhism?* Jordan thought. "She also said he knew people in the church, both young and old. She used the term, 'kind of famous.'"

West wrinkled his brow. "Anything else?"

"And he plays music professionally."

"Symphony?"

"No, classic rock. She said she was going to take her parents to hear him. She said he was most entertaining to talk to." The professor stopped and waited for West's response.

"Did she ask him about his financials?"

"He owns a medical management firm with a few partners. That is all she said on financials."

"Of course, Professor, to her the financial part would be boring, but don't let them forget that part. It is important."

Jordan was puzzled. He thought, *the man is financially sound it appears. He could bring in an older, professional crowd which is always good for donations. His music might bring in a younger crowd. He seems free-spirited. How does his Buddhism fit with his Christianity? He is not married. The young student finds him charismatic and kind of famous. He is obviously a leader, but he sounds self-centered. And he sounds unconventional, possibly a rebel. We do not need any more leaders, especially ones with their own ideas. We need followers and we need donors.*

"Oh, and one more thing seemed peculiar."

"What might that be, Professor?"

"Sara said he was interested in your business plan." The Professor ended.

West looked around the room. "Anybody concerned? Could this man be a spy? Some people are referring to us as a cult."

Jim Bennet spoke." Well, we can't be too careful. Our mission is to bring young people to Jesus, and you are right, Jordan, some people do think we are brainwashing the youth for donations."

"I agree. Check him out for me, Jim. If he is for real, we must encourage him to support us. But we do not need strong leaders, we need resolute followers. He sounds like he loves power and attention. We don't want him behind the curtain. Thank you, Professor, and make no mention of our discussion to Sara, please."

The professor was dismissed. As he walked towards the door, West stopped him. "By the way Professor, what is his name?"

"Ian, Ian Roberts."

"Anybody know him?" No one responded. "Okay, let's continue with the meeting." The group of modern-day holy men and women made plans to handle this congregational explosion that found its way onto the table of Credence Community Church.

Regarding Ian Roberts, it was not an act of terror that brought him to Credence that Sunday. It was not the church's formal business plan, nor Ian's friends that would make him return. It was not even Ian himself. God rang the bell at the starting gate and Ian was off. Outside of his awareness, he was brought to this point in his life for a reason. And now there was a hand in his back that would push him where he was needed.

YOUR TIME HAS COME, MR. ROBERTS

Three years have passed since Ian Roberts first visited Credence Community Church. He attended consistently and remained unassuming. The church renewed his interest in Christianity, but he still felt something missing. The music was modern and inspirational. The messages were contemporary and relevant. The force that drove him to Credence was still inside him and as time continued, the force grew uncomfortably dormant.

Within the first two months of Ian's attendance at Credence, a retail warehouse went out of business. It was less than a mile from the grade school. With the financial strength of the founders, the building was purchased and transformed into Credence's worship facility. From purchase to first service took only eight months.

With the additional space and its popularity among young adults, the church grew rapidly. By January 2004, another building campaign was needed to expand the seating once more. And this time, the Board of Directors added a new twist. To encourage increased pledges from this young congregation, an informal partnership was formed with a Black South African church. Credence campaign would include funding for an HIV/AIDS hospice in a South African township. Footage of the area was produced, along with weak and dying AIDS patients. Projected onto the big screen in the Credence auditorium, the film was moving, especially to

Ian Roberts. After watching the short film on a cold Sunday in February, Ian Roberts went home, climbed the stairs to his studio, and without hesitation, drafted an email:

Pastor of the Credence Outreach Program

Dear Jim Bennet

My name is Ian Roberts. I have been attending your church since the tragic event of September 11. I am an entrepreneur and I have traveled extensively throughout the world. I have time on my hands, and I am not afraid of third world. If I can help with your South Africa project, I am available.

Ian Roberts

By noon Monday, his email was answered. A luncheon was set for Tuesday. The conversation was brief. In July, Ian Roberts was on a South African Air flight to Johannesburg, South Africa. He accompanied a Credence team of five.

"Ian, change seats with me please? Pastor Kristin wants you to sit next to her on our flight to Atlanta. She says she knows nothing about you. She wants to know more about all her team members." Brent's request was apologetic, his voice timid.

Brent Cooper was Ian's luncheon appointment in February. Someone inside Credence felt Ian's email was worth exploring. Brent explained the mission clearly and simply. Credence wanted someone to start a business in South Africa to create jobs and produce profits that would fund the ongoing operations of the Hospice. Ian was told the Pastor in South Africa listed job creation, and something called Black Empowerment, as his business priority. For Credence, this business would reduce or eliminate their responsibly once the Hospice became functional. And it was made clear this business start-up would receive no funding from Credence, no investment capital, no working capital, no airfare, no expenses. Ian would be on his own. And with that, Ian made it clear, Credence would have no ownership and no say in the operations. As an entrepreneur, it was how he liked it. He knew he was a good leader, but a terrible employee. To Credence, they had nothing to lose in this arrangement. It was agreed.

"Sure Brent, I'd enjoy getting to know her as well," Ian gathered his belongings. He made his way to the center aisle and sat next to Kristin. She was an attractive woman, mid- thirties with a wholesome and healthy appearance. She was married to a middle-school teacher. They had no children.

Kristin was from Alabama, an ordained Baptist minister. She was third in command at Credence. Her father, Charles Wik, Chairman of the Board of Directors at Credence, brought her and her husband to Charlotte right after the terrorist attack in 2001.

"Kristin," Ian said in a gracious and gentle tone. "It is good to see you again. I believe we met once before. Brent said you would like for us to chat on the first leg of our long journey." Ian extended his hand. Kristin received it with no expression.

"Get yourself situated, Mr. Roberts," she responded.

Ian sat, fastened his seatbelt, and stuffed his GQ in the seatback in front of him. Kristin took notice from the corner of her eye. She thought, *'I know he is divorced. I know he has not remarried. He dresses well and is attractive. His greeting to me seemed patronizing, and he is reading a sinful magazine published only for men. I do not feel good about this already." What is his motive, power, money, sex?'*

"All settled. This is an exciting venture." Ian had a peaceful aura about him. First, tell me about you, Kristin."

"You are correct, Mr. Roberts. We met once before at a brunch after our noon service. Everyone on this trip was there. Jordan, or should I say Pastor West, asked everyone what they expected from this mission. Everyone's answers were about their internal spiritual growth through helping others. Do you remember?" asked Kristin.

"I do, that was wonderful! That would be a win/win for all," answered Ian.

"But your answer, Mr. Roberts, was vague. Do you remember how you answered?" Kristin was waiting for an answer to prove Ian's insincerity.

"I do. I said I did not want anything. I said, this isn't about me, it is about them."

"What did that mean, Mr. Roberts? It sounded as if you were inferring spiritual growth for you is not necessary. It sounded arrogant to me."

"I'm sorry if it sounded like that to you. My answer was not planned. Like my first introduction to Credence, and my email last February, spontaneity happens, like I am being controlled."

"Let me ask again since time has passed and you have had time to think. What do you want from this mission? What is your personal motive? Something must be driving you."

"I still feel it is not about me, it is about them, and I do not even know who 'them' are yet."

"Go on."

"It is as if I have been trained for this moment in time; my travelling, my business career, my social skills, my religious studies."

"Are you telling me you are called here by God?" Kristin was not buying it. Ian had an agenda. He was not a man of God; he was a layperson. "Mr. Roberts, no one does anything without a benefit to themselves." Ian thought that to be a strange comment coming from a pastor.

"I'm sorry you do not believe me." Ian was calm.

"Let me be blunt. You want to create profits over there from this business."

"I do."

"So, you admit it is not about them, it is about money." Ian held steady as Kristin hurled her rocks.

"Profit is the goal of any business. Without it, there is no business. But all profits in this business go to their Hospice. I will receive no money of any kind. It is my agreement with Credence."

"Tax write-off, that's what it is." Kristin was sure she figured it out.

"If I lose money, yes, but how is that different than the tax write-off I get from my donations to Credence? My donation is just going straight to Africa." Ian was surprised he was handling the attack on his integrity so calmly. But why was she attacking?

Kristin was not going to give up. Turning her face directly at Ian's and leaning in, she stared into his eyes. It reminded him of a dog ready to bite off an ear. She then whispered, "Is Jesus Christ your Lord and Savior?"

Ian was jolted, not by the question, but by the ferocity. She could have asked calmly, but she attacked. He thought her inquisition ended after the business conversation. Ian knew the answer to this question would define his relationship with the powers at Credence, with the clergy and with their staff. He knew her father was Chairman of the Board. He also knew Credence employees were required to swear an allegiance to Jesus Christ and Credence upon employment. But Ian felt at peace inside, unusual for a man as passionate in his life as Ian. He took a breath, silenced his mind and like other times on this Credence journey, waited.

Kristin was uncomfortable in the silence. She asked again, "Mr. Roberts, I asked you a question. Is Jesus Christ your Lord and Savior? Your hesitation concerns me. Is he, or is he not, Mr. Roberts?"

"Kristin, where have you travelled in the world?" Ian responded.

"What does that have to do with the question?"

"I am curious."

"Charlotte is the farthest I have been from my home in Alabama."

"So, this is your first trip out of the country, even out of the South, correct?"

Kristin was irritated by the redirection. "Yes, this is my first trip out of the country. I went to seminary school then received my MBA. I studied the gospels and dedicated my life to Jesus Christ. I have had no time for travel. But I asked you a question, Mr. Roberts, and you are purposely avoiding answering."

"Have you ever experienced the poor, Kristin? I mean, the really poor."

"Of course, my father owned nursing homes and took me with him a few times. It was sad." Kristin was starting to get the drift.

"Kristin, I am speaking of the poor, not the underprivileged. I mean places where you might see someone dead on the sidewalk of starvation or disease. Places where people simply step over them. Or places where people go through garbage cans for scraps of food. Or they rob stores, not because they are bad people, but because they need to buy medicine for their children?"

"No, I have not, Mr. Roberts, but what does that matter? Our job is to give people hope by showing them the way to Christ and to eternal life in the comfort of heaven. The Hospice will allow us to pray for them and let them die with dignity and eternal salvation."

"We do agree on the purpose of the Hospice, Kristin. Have you been around many people of color? And what do you think or know about HIV/AIDS in South Africa?" Kristin forgot momentarily about her question.

"Where I grew up, there was a section on the edge of town where Black people lived, but they stayed to themselves. Credence is the first place where I have met and conversed with Black people, one-on-one." Kristin was proud of that. "As far as those with HIV/AIDS, I believe we must pray for their salvation. They contracted it from a mortal sin. They need to repent and be saved before they die."

"Have you met any Buddhist, Hindu, Islam, Jews? Do you have any non-Christian friends?"

"I do not, and I do not need to. Christ says in the gospel of John 14:6, 'No one comes to the Father except through me.'"

"Yes, I know the verse. I believe it starts with 'I am the way and the truth and the life.'"

"Oh, so you know some verses, Mr. Roberts, good for you. I welcome meeting someone of another religion, but only if I thought it could bring them into a relationship with Jesus Christ. I doubt if that would happen." Kristin was frustrated. "Do you believe the only way to the Father is through Jesus Christ?"

In a flash, Ian saw the faces of so many he befriended in his travels, people of different races, religions, ages, nationalities, and economic groups. Ian knew he and Kristin's view of the world was different.

Ian smiled. "Kristin, I do not support that verse of scripture in its strict Christian interpretation. I am unwilling to accept that the God I believe in would reject my non-Christian friends and their children and turn them away from heaven, if there is one. I am more spiritually broad."

Kristin loved that answer. "What? You don't believe there is a heaven and hell? Jesus was resurrected to sit at the right hand of God the Father Almighty. What are you saying?" Kristin was going to do what she could to take Ian down and get him banned from the project, hopefully from Credence.

"Kristin, I wish I had the strong faith so many of you have. I am envious. But I cannot be dishonest. God knows what I am thinking. He has not given me what you have, that wonderful gift of peace. The gift of acceptance. I doubt and I question. Perhaps God has sent me on this mission for a number of reasons." Ian fell silent inside once again. He felt a thought suddenly enter his soul.

Kristin looked at Ian with disgust. "I am glad we had this conversation. Now I know you are not a Christian, a seeker perhaps or an agnostic. I will label you a 'Do-Gooder' and treat you accordingly." Kristin made her judgement.

"Kristin, label me as you will. I believe in the philosophy of love and kindness as Jesus taught. I believe in a higher power that brings people together in caring ways. I want nothing for myself from this mission. I want nothing from Credence. I want nothing from you. This project is between God and me, not Credence and me. If you wish, you may call me a 'Christ Follower'."

"You realize I must report this conversation to Jordan West and my father. They must know who and what you are. You will not be trusted or supported by our church."

"Kristin, it's okay. I know what I must do. God has spared my life many times in the past. Now I know why. It is for this moment."

"Are you going back with us at the end of the week?" asked Kristin.

"No, I will be staying for three weeks to do my due diligence as to the area's human and technical resources. I also want to get to know the people; their wants and needs."

"Well, I will need to tell Pastor Anton in Africa of your lack of commitment to Credence and to Jesus Christ. It will be his decision whether he allows you to stay. I pray he does not.

For Kristin, they landed in Atlanta not a minute too soon. She made the others aware of Ian's lack of faith. She would do the same with Pastor Anton Nkosi. What she did not foresee was Pastor Anton Nkosi was different than her American colleagues. He was a Black pastor in a poor Black township. He had a vision and purpose for the future of his church and his people. It was different from Credence. He was a pure preacher and teacher. He would quickly see Ian Roberts as a spiritual piece of clay to be molded, not to be stepped on and cast away. Ian and Anton were about to meet.

THE ARRIVAL IN SOUTH AFRICA

Ian awoke to a single ding of the cabin bell. As he slowly opened his eyes, flight attendants scampered through the aisles, tray tables were raised, and seats backs brought to their upright position. And, yes, all personal items stowed under the seat in front of you. The routine was universal.

Ian gazed out his window. He saw nothing except a cloud illuminated by the lights of the wing. It was early evening in Johannesburg. Eighteen hours of flight coupled with a seven-hour time change saw the group landing close to the same time of day they left Atlanta. Brent and his wife Joanna appeared pale and unwell in the anemic light of the cabin. Kristin seemed distraught for reasons unknown. In the seat next to her sat Edward Bellamy, a large man, owner of a retail carpet company in the suburbs of Charlotte. He had the persona of a salesperson, with a projection of overconfidence. Credence paid for his trip. He was to evaluate the motives and competence of Pastor Anton Nkosi and his people. He was to evaluate Ian Roberts as well, but in his case, Edward only needed to agree with Kristin.

The plane touched down softly. It made its way to the concourse. With another ding, the passengers sprang from their seats and attacked the overhead bins. Standing in the aisles, faces smashed into overstuffed backpacks, no one was moving. Kristin spoke to her entourage. "We must all stay together. Don't lose me. Jordan has told me this is a crime ridden country, especially Johannesburg. He said people steal luggage right off the carousel, and if you wander off you could be kidnapped. Speak to no one. If you do, they will know you are an American and you will be a target." The group listened carefully. Ian smiled.

Ian was a seasoned traveler. He was perfect for the project. But Kristin and the rest of the team were not. Cable news and suburban neighbors were their source of education. Ian could see the fear in their faces. He remained silent. His input was unwanted and unnecessary, for the moment.

All deplaned and the race was on. They approached rows and rows of immigration booths. People of all ages, colors, and nationalities filled the lines. The fashion was intriguing, not sweat suits and gym shoes like the U.S. "Hold on tight to your belongings." Kristin warned. She turned to the group, shaking her head in disgust. "I thought Pastor Anton would get us around this mess. This will take forever." Kristin and the others did not realize this was normal for international travel. He wanted to tell them, but he continued his silence as he enjoyed the moment.

"Oh my," Kristin said in a worried tone. "I hope none of you have anything of value in your luggage. I doubt it will be there when we get to baggage claim."

Ian thought of soothing fears, but after his first encounter with Kristin, it would not be welcomed. Besides, anxiety was part of the fun of traveling.

The group reached the immigration officer sitting in his booth. He waved Kristin forward. Like a mother hen, Kristin turned and directed all to follow her. "Come, come, everybody. It's our turn. Let's go. Stay together." Everyone except Ian approached the desk.

"Whoa, stop people, stop!" said the officer. With that, another officer and a man in camouflage holding the leash of a guard dog came to the rescue. The other officer said, "Let's get back in line, people. Let's go, back in line. One at a time unless you are family. If you are family, you may approach together."

"No sir, we are not family, but you don't understand, we must stay together. We are Americans and came here on a Christian mission trip. Do you know Pastor Anton Nkosi?"

The officer responded. "Back in line, people."

IAN AND ANTON

Kristin panicked. She overestimated her power. Ian remained in line, holding back his laughter. Kristin whispered to Edward, "These people can't talk to me like this. I will report this behavior to Pastor Anton."

One by one the group obeyed the rules and officially entered the country of South Africa. They made their way to baggage claim. Ian smiled, remembering his first terrifying trip through immigration.

"Where's my luggage. I don't see my luggage. I knew it. Jordan warned me about this. These people are all thieves." Kristin had everyone frightened once more. Ian could hold his silence no longer. Chaos was about to reign.

"People, I see my luggage over there on a different carousel. And luggage is still coming out. They took our luggage to the wrong carousel, that's all. And it takes time to unload those big jetliners this time of day. Follow me."

Kristin looked across the room. "I still think someone could steal our luggage."

"Kristin, lost maybe, but steal no. Thieves cannot get past the customs officers into this area. Only international passengers are allowed." Kristin did not like Ian taking charge.

Everyone retrieved their luggage and proceeded to customs. "Oh, dear God, what now; another line? What this time?"

Kristin was ready to take her frustration out on somebody, but Ian wisely spoke up again. "At Immigration they checked your passport to see if your visas' are current and whether you are on a terrorists watchlist. This is Customs. They inspect your luggage for weapons, fruits and vegetables, and other illegal smuggling like money or drugs. I assume no one has any of those, correct?" No one did, but they all felt unwarranted fear, and they all looked guilty.

"Okay, that sounds reasonable," Kristin agreed, as if her approval were of any consequence to the South African government.

Ian pointed. "The dogs in front of us will be sniffing you and your luggage for contraband."

Joanna spoke in a panic. "I have prescription drugs, Ian. Are those okay?"

"Depends on what they are, Joanna."

THE ARRIVAL IN SOUTH AFRICA

"What if they are illegal here? How would I have known? What will happen?"

"They will either confiscate them or pull your passport, arrest you and put you in prison for the rest of your life." Joanna looked at her husband. Ian smiled. He could not stay serious. "Joanna, they will do nothing. They are prescription." Nobody smiled.

When they reached the dogs, a small beagle stopped at Ian's feet and stared at his backpack. Kristin was not disappointed.

"Sir, may I look in your backpack, please? Are you carrying any drugs, large amounts of cash, weapons, fruits, vegetables?" The officer was without expression.

"No sir, I have nothing." Then he held up his index finger and smiled. "I do, sir." The group was astounded at Ian's calm demeanor. What was he smuggling? "I have an apple." He took his backpack from his shoulder to retrieve the apple, but the officer grabbed his wrist.

"No sir, place your backpack gently on the floor and put your hands on your head." By this time, a man in camouflage with an Uzi was standing behind Ian. The officer rooted through the backpack and pulled out the apple. The dog lost interest. "Move on, all of you." Ian enjoyed God's sense of humor. He looked up and smiled. *I deserved that.*

Emotionally drained, the group made its way to the airport rotunda. Steel barricades herded them to the middle of the room. At the end was a sign. It read, "Credence Community Church." Eight Black Africans were there to welcome this band of innocent urban nomads to a quite different world.

LET US COME TOGETHER

Pastor Anton Nkosi and his entourage greeted the frazzled Americans in the vast rotunda of the O.R. Tambo International Airport in Johannesburg, South Africa. The rotunda was a Black and Indian assemblage with a sprinkling of White. It buzzed like a bee hive, and smelled like Africa. In his travels, Ian recognized each continent to have its own unique bouquet, and Africa was the most distinct. Ian was in his element. Women in long colorful dresses, others in burkas, Buddhist monks in bright yellow robes and Europeans in dark suits. It was like a painter's busy palette. Handshakes were engaged connected to warm smiles. Names were exchanged. The group from Credence felt loved and protected.

Pastor Anton led everyone outside where Ezekiel, his young bus driver, was circling the arrival zone. Horns honked incessantly and the spew of exhaust filled the air. Car doors slammed and security officers with whistles attempted to control and direct the rebellious traffic. Within ten anxious minutes, all were on the bus safely and leaving the airport. Silence presided over the coach, except for Anton and Kristin. She was already explaining to Anton how he could make the immigration process easier in the future if they did it like America. Of course, that was an assumption since she never reentered the U.S.

Ian loved the chaotic traffic of foreign cities if he did not have to drive in it. It was fascinating. With his face close to the window like a puppy dog, his eyes darted. Cars with short 'Beep-Beeps' communicated their location and their intentions. There was no road rage, no long angry blasts; just people avoiding hitting someone and avoiding being hit. It was a mechanical dance. The anarchy made sense.

Brent leaned towards Ian. "Kristin said we have about an hour bus ride." Joanna sighed. "Do you think anyone on this bus, other than Pastor Anton, speaks English?"

"I'm sure they do, Brent. South Africa, although becoming a Union in 1910, was still considered a British colony with its own White colonial government until 1961. English is their first language, but most Blacks speak multiple tribal languages as well. Then there is Afrikaans." Ian was interrupted.

"What is Africans? Sounds like it would also be a tribal language also." Brent was confused. Joanna stayed quiet.

"It's not Africans, Brent, it's 'Afrikaans'. It's a derivative of Dutch, but officially, it is its own language. It caused many problems here in recent history, and still does."

"How so?"

"In the mid-seventeenth century, the Dutch settled South Africa. They formed the Dutch East India Company to support trade with India around the Cape of Good Hope. But then gold and diamonds were discovered at the end of the nineteenth century. That is where the problems began."

"What problems? You were talking about the Afrikaans language. I'm confused." Ian continued.

"The Dutch Afrikaans were of the Dutch Reformed Church. Their theologians conveniently interpreted 'The Book of Acts,' to justify enslaving not only Black Africans, but Asians and Indians as well. They claimed God intended all races to be segregated and the White race to dominate."

"No way, Ian. Our Bible does not say that?" Brent was disturbed.

"It is historically documented, but I am always open to challenge." Ian nodded his head politely and smiled.

"Okay, but what does this have to do with the Afrikaans language?"

"The act of segregation became known as Apartheid."

"I am familiar with that."

"It was slavery. The Dutch were White Supremist and believed they were anointed by God. It lasted through the 20th century. It ended in 1994."

"You said the Afrikaans language was a problem."

"The rebellion took hold in 1976 in a small township called Soweto. The White British government reinstated the requirement for Afrikaans to be used in Black schools alongside English."

"Why?"

"To further control the youth in the Black townships. That was not popular at all. Afrikaans was considered the language of the oppressor."

"What happened?" asked Brent. He was gaining respect for Ian even though Ian was not the type of Christian Credence wanted.

"The children of Soweto left their classrooms and took to the streets, refusing to learn Afrikaans. They had enough of oppression."

"And?" Brent was waiting.

"The children were celebrating their own courage, singing, and dancing in the streets when the White British police descended on them with machine guns on the back of jeeps. They chased the school children and shot hundreds of rounds into their backs. In the end, the death toll was 176 children killed and four thousand wounded." Ian became serious.

"No way, the British did that? So, that ended Apartheid?" Brent was in disbelief.

"Not right away, but it received world-wide attention. It started the rebellion, and it wasn't until 1991 that a truce was negotiated."

"Why so long?"

"There was guerrilla warfare in the streets and country sides for fifteen years. But there was another reason Apartheid continued. What else happened in 1991, Brent?" Ian stared at Brent and after a brief pause, Ian blurted. "The fall of the Soviet Union."

"Why would that have anything to do with South Africa?" Brent was curious.

"South Africa is a freak of nature. It has the highest reserves of precious metals in the world, gold, silver, and diamonds. And it also has the largest reserves of strategic minerals on the planet."

"Go on."

"Chromium, manganese, tungsten, antimony; all used in building fighter jets, tanks, military equipment. And what is the only other country where these minerals are found?"

"The Soviet Union?"

"Correct, and until the Soviet Union fell, the West was in the Cold War with them."

Brent now understood. "So, the West could not let South Africa go Communist until there was no more Soviet Union."

"You got it. The West wanted to abolish Apartheid for civil and political reasons but couldn't take the chance." Ian finished his point.

"How do you know all this, Ian?" Joanna interjected. She still had her doubts as to his motives and did not want to go against Kristen and Credence by being friendly.

Ian smiled and responded, "I study places I'm about to visit, Joanna. The people will respect me more if I take time to learn about their culture and history. And it's fun. But be careful discussing Apartheid with Afrikaans. They are like our Deep South after slavery. Apartheid only ended ten years ago."

"Will we encounter them?" asked Joanna.

"Maybe. Just remember, they feel we are wrong in God's eyes to help Anton and his people, even the youth feel that way. Watch what you say."

Brent and Joanna would take heed. Ian continued, "Brent, you started by asking whether anybody on the bus speaks English. Let's find out."

"No, wait Ian."

Ian raised his voice to be heard over the bus's engine. "Excuse me, young lady." He called to a young woman wearing a red bandana and a long moo-moo dress.

She looked around and pointed to herself with a surprised expression. Her eyebrows raised. She smiled, "me?"

"Yes, please join us." Ian's smile made her feel safe. She moved to the seat across the aisle from Ian. Brent and Joanna sat in the row behind. "What's your name?" Ian asked.

"Mulenga Chepape, but please, call me Kathryn." She had a beautiful English accent with a twist of African tribal.

"Why don't you go by Mulenga? It's a beautiful name and so melodic," Ian asked. Brent and Joanna listened.

Mulenga returned the compliment with a sweet smile. "That is my Zulu name. Kathryn is my White name." She smiled again. It was innocently captivating.

"I don't understand, you say your White name?" Brent and Joanna felt uneasy. Ian was talking about her race. Americans don't do that.

"During Apartheid, White people could not pronounce our tribal names, the same as I have a challenging time with many Indian and Chinese names. So, they gave us English first names to make it easier on themselves. Our last names were unimportant to them. So please, call me Kathryn." She smiled politely.

"Well Kathryn, I am sorry, but I prefer to call you Mulenga if that is okay with you. It is Zulu? Does it have a meaning?" Ian was respectful. Mulenga was feeling respected.

"No, I was named after Mulenga Kapwepwe. She is an author and playwright and co-founder of the Zambian Women's History Museum. My father named me after her because she was one of few women who graduated from The University of Zambia in Lusaka during Apartheid. My family, and many of us here in South Africa, are from Zambia. Pastor Anton and his wife performed mission work in our village." Brent and Joanna's attitudes were changing quickly.

"Mulenga, my name is Ian, Ian Roberts. This is Joanna and Brent Smith. What do you do for Pastor Anton?"

I am attending the Ghandi/Mandela Nursing Academy in Pretoria and doing my field work with Pastor Anton in his HIV/AIDS ministry. Momma Mary is Pastor Anton's head HIV/AIDS nurse. She is training me. You will meet her at dinner." Mulenga was proud to talk about her education, especially to adults, but she did not want to sound precocious. Some Whites in South Africa did not respond well to an educated young Black woman. She was unsure about American Whites.

"Are your studies a two-year program?" asked Ian.

"No, I received my under-graduate degree at the University of Zambia. I will receive my master's degree in Pretoria. My masters is a three-year program. This is my last year. I am specializing in HIV/AIDS treatment."

"Why did you move here?"

"I met Pastor Anton as a child. He preached at my church. He invited me here and has helped me obtain financial grants from the government. He is becoming a very influential man in this country. He is wonderful, and such a pioneer in HIV prevention. He treats not only the body, but the soul as well."

"What do you mean by prevention, Mulenga? You mean abstinence?" Ian asked.

"That too, but he talks about condom use from the pulpit. Nobody did that in the past. It was unacceptable. He has been harshly criticized by the bishops and the government."

"Why criticized?"

"It is not considered appropriate to talk about sexual relationships from the pulpit and the government refuses to accept the true cause of HIV. There are some strange ideas floating around. But Mr. Roberts, I will tell you more about our AIDS mission tomorrow in the township. I believe we have arrived at the restaurant." Mulenga smiled. "I'm hungry."

Brent and Joanna did not know what to say. As most Americans, they assumed the rest of the world was slow and uneducated. Ian knew better and he picked the right person. "What is this restaurant, Melunga?" Brent asked.

This is Pastor Anton's favorite. It is a Native American restaurant called 'The Apache.' It is fantastic. You'll love the braised ox tail and pap." Mulenga looked out her window.

"What is pap? "Asked Joanna. She already tuned out on the oxtail.

Mulenga giggled. "It is the consistency of your lumpy mashed potatoes, but you may call it porridge. It is made from white corn. It is heavy in fiber and helps to fill you up."

So, it has a lot of calories?" asked Joanna. "It must be fattening."

"No ma'am, because of the fiber it can help control weight. It feels funny to eat if you don't like the consistency of oatmeal."

Ian extended his hand. She took it. "Mulenga, I look forward to learning more from you tomorrow. You have already taught us so much." Mulenga smiled one more time, but this time it projected a beautiful intelligence.

"I am going to return to my friends, Mr. Roberts. See you all inside."

"Bye, Mulenga." Ian turned to Brent and Joanna. "Brent, I think they speak English."

"Ian, I am embarrassed." Brent learned a lot since deplaning. "I was not expecting that sort of intellect from these people."

"Don't be embarrassed. It's part of the experience. God sent you here for a reason."

"Why did he send you here, Ian?"

"I don't know. I am taking one step at a time. I do know from my travels to learn as much as I can from others. Travel opens my heart to diversity, religion, culture, family. Soak it in, Brent. I think God wants the world to be loving and at peace. Only by knowing each other can that happen." Joanna sat back in her seat and stared out the window.

THE MISSION TRIP

The team awoke to near freezing temperature, both inside and outside. Heat was only for the fortunate few in the township, so due to the cold, the team limited themselves to the most essential of hygiene needs. Ian was the only one who packed appropriately for the South African winter in July. The rest assumed Africa was warm year-round. Their sweaters and light jackets were now wrinkled after being used as pajamas.

They shivered on their way to the main house for breakfast. Kristin led the group into the dimly lit kitchen. "Pastor Anton, how do people live like this with no heat. It is unbearable." Anton smiled at Kristin and responded, "Let us pray."

Forks shook in their hands as they devoured chunks of scrambled eggs and toasted bagels. The pap was left alone. Coffee flowed among the Americans; tea for everyone else. The team was exhausted from their eighteen-hour flight, but with only four full days in South Africa, there was no time to rest.

Making their way to the bus, Anton stopped everyone before loading. "We are going to visit a few of our HIV/AIDS patients in their homes. With you and your congregation's help, we will build an HIV/AIDS Hospice to care for these people. Today, you will see why. You will better understand why these people and their families need us. All of God's children deserve to die with dignity and in the loving care of our Lord." The bus loaded.

Sitting behind the driver was Momma Mary, a large South African woman pushing fifty years. She was widowed. Her husband died in a mining accident five years prior. She wore a thick woolen sarape, plain and tattered. She had a wool blanket across her lap. She looked tired. Dark circles lay heavy under her eyes. Anton made the introduction. "To all, this is Momma Mary. She is our head HIV/AIDS nurse and has been with me from the beginning. Feel free to ask her anything about our mission. She is a wealth of knowledge and God has been good to bless us with her." Ian was excited to get to know this hard-looking woman who had an aura of peace surrounding her. Anton tapped Ezekiel on the shoulder. With a grinding of gears and a heavy jerk, the bus was on its way.

Ian stared out the window. The landscape was sparse in vegetation. It was high desert with an elevation of a mile. It was void of vivid color. The main thoroughfare was paved. People walked on both sides balancing everything from baskets to mops atop their heads. Off the thoroughfare, the roads were unpaved, reddish brown and hardpan. Rainfall was meager. The cars and clay roof tiles were covered with a thin coating of fine dust. The houses were small, all constructed with monotonous reddish-brown brick. Between each house stood a six-foot brick wall topped with razor wire. The township pushed a million in population, including the informal settlement on the outskirts. The settlement was government land and allowed no private ownership. More than 350,000 inhabitants jammed into this field and lived in cardboard shacks and sheet metal lean-to shelters. As Ian observed the landscape, the others spoke amongst themselves.

The bus stopped and all got off. Ian saw a young girl, petite and weak in stature, sitting on a wooden vegetable crate. Her appearance exposed a haunting and lonely innocence. Holding her blanketed infant in her arms, her younger brother and sister stood behind her. She seemed physically frail and emotionally delicate.

Ian reunited with Mulenga as soon as he boarded the bus. He stayed close to her. He whispered, "Who is the girl?"

Mulenga responded with no emotion. "That is Pearl. She is fifteen. Her mother belonged to Pastor Anton's church when she contracted HIV from her husband. He contracted it from one of his mistresses, became infected, and passed it on. But when she was diagnosed HIV positive, he turned it around. He accused Pearl's mother of cheating on him. So, he left them all."

"Wait, he infected her then he left. She didn't kick him out?" Ian was puzzled.

"Mr. Roberts..." Melunga was interrupted.

"Melunga, from now on call me Ian, please."

"I cannot do that out of respect, sir, but how about Mr. Ian."

"Melunga, I find that respectful. Go on please."

"Okay, Mr. Ian, as I was saying, that is the norm here, but let us discuss this topic at another time. It is something our women keep to themselves." Ian nodded. "Mr. Ian, our government states we have 5.5 million people infected, making us the second most infected country in the world. But unlike HIV transmission in America, here it is predominantly transmitted heterosexually, not homosexually. We have a 21% positive HIV rate in our townships and 63% of those infected are woman. We have a promiscuity problem, Mr. Ian. We will talk more about that later, as well." Ian respected the delicacy of the subject.

"Where is Pearl's mother now?"

"She died a year ago leaving Pearl and her other two children on their own. Pearl became their surrogate mother at age fourteen. It was then that Anton took over the house. It belongs to her family and his church pays them rent. We supply the bare amounts of food and medical supplies. She then receives government assistance."

"What about support from the father?"

"He is required to, but he does not. It is unenforceable."

"The governmental assistance is because they are orphans?"

Mulenga uttered a frustrated chuckle. "Mr. Ian, according to UNICEF, South Africa has 3.5 million orphans, mostly caused by HIV/AIDS. That is 18.6% of all children in South Africa. There just is not enough government money to go around."

"Then who supports them?"

IAN AND ANTON

"First, 75% of our children in the township live under the poverty level."

"And what is that?"

"That is about $80 U.S. per month," Ian shook his head, "And 40% of our children die before they reach age five, two-thirds of those are in the first year."

"What from?"

"Most of the children are malnourished and weak, so about half die of HIV/AIDS related illnesses. You must realize, according to UNICEF, 2.5 million live in shacks in our informal settlements and another 4.5 million live in overcrowded homes. Most lack clean water and toilet facilities. And a quarter of those live without electricity." Ian felt sick.

"So, why the governmental assistance?"

"Because Pearl is HIV positive," said Mulenga.

"Wait, she could not have contracted it at childbirth. She is too old." Ian was confused, his anxiety levels increasing.

"Correct, but when her mother died, Pearl prostituted herself to feed herself and her siblings. That is what she says anyway, but probabilities are it was her father that infected her, and she is protecting herself from his violence."

"His violence?"

"Yes, Mr. Ian, the Department of Social Development estimates 83,000 children are assaulted sexually or physically each year. And the overcrowded conditions do not help. Many beds need to be shared. Either way, she became HIV positive and with child." Ian was shaking his head as he closed his eyes. Mulenga continued. "There was and still is a sinister rumor here in South Africa. It says if a man has sex with a virgin, it can rid him of HIV." Mulenga stayed unemotional as she looked to the ground.

"No way, that is primitive. Who came up with that?"

"Sir, you seem like an intelligent man, so I do not want to insult you. You cannot figure out how that started and the motive?" Mulenga looked sheepishly at Ian to see his reaction.

Ian felt embarrassed, not insulted. "Oh Mulenga, I am so sorry. Yes, I do understand, but that is wretched. I tried to block it in my head. Is the baby...?"

"Yes, she is."

"During pregnancy?"

"Probably. But if not, then from Pearl's breast milk. Either way, antiretroviral treatment is virtually non-existent to our babies in the township. She will not live to be a year old." Ian was holding back his emotions as he observed this family of little children in front of him. He could barely speak.

"Okay, you say she gets financial assistance for being HIV positive?"

"Yes sir, they both do. But it is complicated. If a person suspects they are infected, they must be tested by a government agency, not a private lab, and those testing facilities are spread out. That is the first problem. Many of our people in their late stages of AIDS are too weak to get to a testing facility. And many family members still do not understand how it is transmitted. They become afraid to go anywhere near a testing site; like a leper colony in the past."

"Okay, let's say they go to a facility and test positive."

"There are four stages of HIV/AIDS. If you are healthy, you have CD4+ cells. These are the cells that fight infections from opportunistic disease."

"Opportunistic disease?"

"Like tuberculosis, pneumonia, cancer, things like that." Ian nodded for her to continue.

"If healthy, your CD4 count is between 500 and 1600 cells per microliter when the HIV virus first enters the blood stream, either by blood transfusion or exchange of bodily fluids like semen, lesions or breast milk."

"Got it so far."

In Stage 1, the CD4 count is still above 500. A person goes through a period of minor illnesses like colds or influenza. This stage is also called seroconversion. But although these illnesses are usually mild, this is when the virus is most transmissible."

"Okay."

The next stage, Stage 2, is called asymptomatic. A person's health appears to be fine, but this is when the virus begins to rapidly copy itself. The HIV cells begin to attack the CD4 cells, and these cells reduce to between 350-500.

"Then what?"

"The HIV virus continues to copy itself and the CD4 drops to 200-349. This is Stage 3. The body can only fight off attacks for so long. If left untreated with antiretroviral therapy, the count goes below 200 and acquired immunodeficiency syndrome sets in, Stage 4."

"AIDS."

"Exactly, and the person eventually dies of cancer, tuberculosis, pneumonia, something of that sort. Our government has some strange views on treatment, some quite primeval, but the real treatment is antiretroviral drugs, and they are not available in the quantity necessary for our poor here in the townships." Mulenga stopped.

"So where is Pearl right now?"

"She reached the end of Stage 3, the copying stage, and entered Stage 4. Her baby has as well. Pearl will not live past twenty and her daughter will die soon. So, they both recently qualified for government assistance. That means they receive barely enough money for food, nothing for lodging. If we can keep her and the baby fed well and sheltered, it will slow down their deaths, maybe long enough until antiretrovirals are available or a cure is found. We can only pray. Pearl's case is typical."

"What is life expectancy here?"

"Ten years ago, life expectancy was sixty-four. Today, in 2005, it is forty-nine. Estimates in 2015, 41."

"That low?"

"40% of deaths among adults 15-49 are from AIDS."

"How is your health care system?"

"We do not have universal health insurance. We have private plans and a public program, but the public care is ranked 90th in the world. It takes weeks or months to see a doctor. Much of our health care is performed by social workers, even minor surgeries."

"What kind of surgeries?"

"Minor things like stitches, broken bones, cataracts."

"Social workers cut on people's eyes?"

"My aunt, like many older people in this country, is blind in one eye. Look closely. During Apartheid, social workers did cataract surgeries on our parents."

"Why blind in only one eye?"

"Mr. Ian, would you let them do your other eye if they blinded the first one?"

Ian and Melunga moved closer as the team gathered around Pearl. Momma Mary cradled Pearl's baby to her breast. Jim Bennet embraced the siblings on each side of him with outstretched arms. Kristin laid hands on Pearl's head as she prayed for them all. As Ian blinked, tears ran down his face. He gave out with one uncontrollable sob. Then Anton prayed. Pearl looked lost. This was the first time Ian felt he had a substantial clue as to why he was here. He thought *Praying for wisdom might be the first thing I must learn.*

The team made three more stops. One was a family whose teenage daughter died seven days ago. Another was Norman, a tall man in his mid-twenties. His arms and legs were the size of twigs. His skull was top heavy due to his weakness. He was in his last stage of AIDS-induced pancreatic cancer.

A family of seven was the team's final stop. Entering through the kitchen, the team passed a dimly lit area with a sofa and a television, then into a room containing four mattresses and numerous blankets on the floor. A thirty something woman lie curled in pain on one of the mattresses. It was covered by flattened cardboard the family lifted from the grocery store dumpster. The smell of urine was pungent. The team stood over the woman. Brent prayed this time. The emotions of the team were slowly hardening since the shock of Pearl a few hours before. Brent's prayer was brief, followed by the strength of Anton's prayer. To him, no one would be cheated out of a good dose of God's love. As he concluded, the team wasted no time moving out of the odiferous bedroom and back to the bus. And as always, Ian trailed. Since he was a child, 'He who goes last goes first in the eyes of God' became subconscious behavior. As he reached the doorway of the bedroom, he heard a soft voice pushing hard to be heard. He turned. The sickly woman raised herself on one elbow. With her wrinkled index finger, she motioned Ian to return. "Sir, come here please." Ian turned. "Come closer, please."

Ian approached her mattress and knelt on one knee. She reached for his hand. He took hers. She pulled him down even closer to her face. "Yes dear, what is it?" Ian asked softly.

Quietly, so no one could hear her secret, she looked into Ian's eyes. "They steal my stuff."

"What, steal what? Who steals what? I don't understand." Ian listened intently. The woman felt safe confiding in him.

"The boxes. They steal the boxes you bring for me. They steal them as soon as you leave." The woman looked scared.

When the HIV team visited a home, they always left supplies: Pap, cereal, powdered milk, fresh water, aspirin, laundry detergent. They also left a few packs of adult diapers. "You mean the supplies in the kitchen?" asked Ian.

"Yes, they steal them. As soon as you leave, the neighbors take it all. They take the whole box. They leave nothing." She was about to cry but she was afraid of retribution.

"So that is why you are on the cardboard. They take the diapers?" Ian squeezed her hand as tightly as he could without breaking one of her fragile bones.

The woman nodded her head and began to whimper. Ian stroked her graying soiled hair and kissed her on her forehead. "I am so sorry. I will talk to Pastor Anton."

"If they ever find out I told you, they will not be nice to me."

"They aren't nice to you now. I will do what I can to keep you safe. Your secret will only be known by me and Pastor Anton. I promise." Ian squeezed her hand once more. She did not let go easily. The depth of his understanding was going even deeper and with it came the constant battle to hold back tears.

All were on the bus and in their seats as Ian climbed the steps. "Where have you been, Ian?" asked Kristin. "We are all ready to go. You might not be, but the rest of us are exhausted."

Ian ignored Kristin and with moist eyes looked at Anton. "We need to talk. They …"

Anton saw Ian's concern and stopped him from saying anything. "I know, be quiet." Ian sat next to Anton this time. Kristin took note.

As the noise of the bus muffled conversations, Ian looked at Anton. "The neighbors steal her supplies." Anton could tell Ian was distraught.

"I know, sir. We do what we can out here. That is another reason we need the Hospice. All this truly bothers you. If you are serious about helping us, it will not be easy. You will cry many more times over many different things and with many different emotions. And those emotions could get the better of you. You will need to be strong in front of my people. I need strong leaders."

Ian stared into Anton's face. "Pastor Anton, I don't know what caused me to be here. I have asked that many times over the last six months. But after today, I do know God has something he needs from me. I have never said that before. Everything I have done, every place I have lived, every place I have visited, everyone I have met seemed to be preparing me for this moment in time. I am not a formally religious man, but I do believe love for each other is mankind's only hope. The philosophy of Jesus Christ is my philosophy. I am being pushed, like there is a hand in my back. Not by these people from Credence, but by something unseen, something unspoken." Anton looked serious. "Pastor Anton, never allow me to forget this day. I must never become numb to what I have experienced in this one, sadly enlightening afternoon."

"Mr. Roberts, you are what I call a vessel. The Lord wants to work through you, and he will, but only if you let him. That is all I will say for now. I will not push you. I will not need to. Someone greater than me has been doing that ever so gently all your life. You are blessed, Mr. Roberts, whether you yourself know it or not." Anton smiled and stroked his goatee. Ian bowed his head with respect.

MR. ROBERTS, WELCOME TO CHURCH

PART 1

Evening approached. It was the team's last full day in the township. They were exhausted from the pace of activities, cold sleeping conditions, and sparse diet. Kristin was especially worn. Sheltered by her father and now her husband, her life had always been comfortable. She was ready to leave. This mission was not what she expected when she joined Credence.

Dinner was served as sunset came early in July. Kristin shared the team's itinerary for the next day. It was simple; church in the morning; airport in the afternoon. She thanked Anton, Esther, and all their people for their hospitality. She led them in prayer. As they returned to their rooms, Anton approached Ian, "Mr. Roberts, may I speak with you? I have a few questions."

"Of course, Pastor Anton."

"I understand you are staying with us for a while."

"Yes, two more weeks. I was told that was cleared with you."

"Yes, it is fine. After they leave, I propose we call each other by our first names.

"I would welcome that, Anton, and call me Ian."

"Tell me briefly what you will be doing for two weeks."

"I want to explore starting a branch of my business here in your township. Will you or one of your staff be available to answer questions on infrastructure and drive me where I might need to go?"

"I can lend you a car or you can rent one, Ian. I have a busy schedule next week; five burials and two church services."

"I am afraid I would place myself and others in grave danger if I tried to drive on the wrong side of the road while shifting gears with my left hand." Ian smiled. Anton agreed with a nod of his head.

"Where will you need to go?"

"I am not sure. I will need to start with your technical capabilities like internet and the skill levels of your people."

"Go with Esther to our prayer meeting in the morning. It starts at 7:00. She is the leader. Between the prayer meeting and service, she will introduce you to our technical man. You can discuss your needs with him." Ian agreed but he knew more than a few minutes would be necessary.

"Perhaps you can give me more information tomorrow night after the Credence people leave."

"I would like that, Anton."

"Goodnight, Ian, you are blessed."

Ian set his alarm. He lay in his bed, staring at the ceiling. He was never an early bird, but nothing he was doing was about his comfort or preference. At home, he was the owner of his company. People worked around his schedule. But here, he must work around theirs. He had no power. He liked it. It was humble.

Ian also confirmed his initial evaluation of Credence. No one could make a move without the consent of the church. Ian's mission must remain independent. Answering to Kristin and Credence would lead to failure. Two levels of management between himself and God would never work. Without permission, Ian joined Esther for her 7:00 A.M. prayer meeting.

The brown desert grass lay thick in the fields, covered by the frozen dew of the morning. The sky was cloudless with the mauve tint of a new day, a new Sabbath Day. Sounds of cars and trucks droned faintly in the distance. The sound reminded Ian of his urban home overlooking

IAN AND ANTON

Charlotte. Ian waited by the car. Esther and her three teenage children, Matthew, Mark, and Joan exited the house carrying a toasted bagel and a hot cup of tea for Ian.

All got in the car. Esther turned the key. The ignition grinded but no success. She tried again. "Is it too cold, Esther?" asked Ian.

Esther did not respond to Ian. Instead, she calmly said "Boys."

Matthew and Mark jumped out of the car. Joan stayed in the backseat. "Me too, Esther" Ian asked.

"Yes please, if you would. But just stand by the car. The boys can handle this."

On the long driveway, the car was already facing the exit gate, a clue to Ian this was not a new event. "Go boys" yelled Esther and the boys pushed. Esther popped the clutch. The car started. Esther gunned the engine. The boys jumped in the backseat, Ian jumped in the front and off they went to the church. Ian didn't say a word, but he was smiling inside.

Esther spoke first, "Anton instructed me to introduce you to Samuel before the main service. He runs our computers at the church, but I'm afraid you will know more than him. You can help us improve in the next two weeks."

I am here to help you in any way I can. First, tell me about the prayer meeting. We pray in our services at home, but either the Pastor prays, or we all pray together. And sometimes a moment of silence for a death or tragedy. I understand you lead the meeting. Is that how it is here?"

Esther giggled like a schoolchild. It was charming. "No, Mr. Roberts, I believe you will learn something new this morning." Ian looked around at the kids in the back seat. They were giggling too. "How do you pray when you are alone, Mr. Roberts?"

"I pray silently. And during the day, I say thank you a lot." Ian thought that made sense. He could not think of another option.

"What do you thank God for, Mr. Roberts?"

"Simple things, like when the light changes to yellow just as I get to the intersection."

"I don't understand?"

"Because I don't have to stop and wait." With that said, Ian was feeling shallow.

"That's it?" said Esther.

"Or when I see a beautiful sunset or a child laughing or just for being alive and healthy." Ian thought that sounded a little better.

Esther did not hesitate. "Would you join us in our prayer meeting, Mr. Roberts? The Lord would love to have you. His arms are always open."

"Esther, I am here to learn from you as well as help you." Ian smiled; butterflies filled his stomach.

"Mr. Roberts, the Lord shares his wisdom with us when we need it. I am glad you will join us in our prayers to him. It is one of many doors you will knock upon, and he will open. He will bless us with your presence, I am sure of it." Chills went up Ian's arms. Esther pulled into her parking place. The kids went one way, Ian followed Esther to pray.

As Esther and Ian entered the room, Ian continued feeling chills from both the winter temperature and Esther's acceptance of his presence. The walls were reddish/brown brick; the floor, gray concrete covered by a thin layer of high desert dust. Two windows protected by iron bars allowed enough sunrise to creep in and assist the lone light bulb dangling from the ceiling.

Elderly women circled the room along with a smattering of elderly men and small children. Conversations filled the air. Ian's attendance did not affect that at all. Like walking into a local bar, he was afraid silence would fall upon the room; it did not. However, he was noticed. Even though he was unable to understand many tribal language conversations, he could notice the subtle glances thrown his way. Curiosity was all around him.

Esther moved to the center of the room. The room went silent. "Good morning, people. This Sunday God has blessed us with Mr. Ian Roberts. He is our guest from America. He is blessed." That is all that needed to be said. Ian was appreciative of the brief introduction, but she did not know much about him. They had spoken only in greetings. She was soft spoken and gentle. She fit the stereotype of a Pastor's wife. That is until she began to pray, and the earth shook.

Her voice was loud. It was strong. It was bold. It was the voice of a Pentecostal preacher. She summoned the Lord with quick lines of scripture. "Let me hear an amen, Brothers and Sisters" invoked an assembly of voices. Bouncing between English and Zulu, she would pray to the Lord.

With hands held high and waving to the heavens, the air was pierced with exhalations of hallelujahs and 'Praise the Lord.'

Then Esther stopped. The room became silent once again. She looked around. 'Dear Lord, hear us pray," and the heavens opened.

Unlike the quiet and controlled services of Ian's protestant upbringing, a flood of emotions filled Ian's soul. It was not fear. He felt engaged with something. He watched these Africans walk around the room, looking to the heavens, some with arms extended upward, some tightly hugging their Bibles. Their voices were loud, and all their prayers were different. Ian attempted to pick out phrases but could only grasp a word of English here and there. But within a few moments it made sense. Although everyone prayed independently, they were all praying on the same topic. The one Esther put forward. They were praying for the sick and dying. He saw tears running down faces. Some dropped to their knees with hands clasped. Then, it reverted to Esther.

"Brothers and Sisters, the Lord has heard us this day. Be loving and be a blessing to each other." Esther's words caused hugs among these children of God. Ian was receiving hugs. As he hugged everyone in return, the phrase 'You are blessed' was always exchanged.

Esther spoke again. This time it was a call to pray for the world to live in love and peace. Like the first time, Ian stayed silent. He folded his hands and closed his eyes. Inside he felt the pleading of souls asking God to bring his love to the leaders of the world. He heard 'Blessed are the peacemakers.' Ian let it soak into him. Chills kept coming. He struggled to hold back his tears.

Then it hit him. *'I told Kristin of the universal God in which I believed. A God that accepts all. Into my head came 'Blessed are the meek, for they shall inherit the earth.' A few days ago, I experienced the sick and dying. I met those who care for them now and in the future. I now stand among those who prayed for the sick and dying and for leaders in the world. This is an indoctrination. I need to be committed or leave this place now. I am being pulled deeper into a purpose. Times will get tough. I am already being criticized by my own church. What shall I do?'*

As the meeting ended, Ian opened his eyes. A warm feeling permeated through his body. Some people were staring, wondering if he was asleep. Esther came to him.

"Are you okay, Mr. Roberts?" she asked.

Ian smiled gracefully. He unfolded his hands and looked to the heavens, "Thank you, Lord." Then he looked at those watching him. "You are blessed."

One by one they approached, grasping his hand in both of theirs and with head bowed to him they whispered, "You are blessed."

Esther led Ian up the back stairs. Samuel was getting the big screen and the PA system ready for the service at 9:00. Samuel knew the Americans were attending the service and he was stressed. After all, they were Americans. Anton informed him they expected perfection and punctuality. African time was not acceptable. As he scrambling to prepare for this special day, he saw Esther and one of the Americans approaching. Samuel was a mess and thought '*Oh my, one of the Americans. He is going to tell me I am doing it all wrong. I know it, I know it.*'

"Samuel, may I introduce Mr. Ian Roberts." Samuel swallowed hard. "He wants to learn about our internet and computers." Samuel looked up and stared into Esther's eyes. He wanted to say not now, but this was Esther, and she was with an American. He could not. "Samuel, say something please."

Samuel finally found the courage. "Please Esther, I can give him all the time he needs after service but…." Samuel was interrupted.

Ian could see the nervous sweat on Samuel's forehead, even in the cold. He knew what he needed from Samuel, but it could wait. "Samuel, it is a pleasure to meet you. I just wanted a quick introduction so we can talk soon. Will breakfast somewhere tomorrow morning work for you?"

"Yes, Mr. Roberts, thank you for not pressing me right now. I must have everything perfect for the Americans. They require it."

Ian patted Samuel on the shoulder. "You have been told correctly. Americans do complain over petty things. All will be fine. If anything is not, I will tell Anton and the Americans it was my fault for distracting you."

"And I will take care of Anton," Esther smiled.

Esther and Ian left Samuel to prepare. They made their way to the sanctuary. Esther stopped. "Mr. Roberts, I am impressed with your acceptance of my people and your understanding of the significance of our prayer meeting. You are the only White man ever to attend one of our meetings. You are doing what you are told, are you not?"

"No Esther, Credence did not tell me to do that or anything else I am doing here."

"I do not mean Credence, Mr. Roberts. I mean the Lord. You must feel what he wants in the silence and say yes to him." Ian bowed his head to Esther's wisdom although he was unsure what she meant. "I insist you sit next to me at service, Mr. Roberts."

"I would be honored." Esther positioned herself in front of the stage with Ian at her side. She welcomed the stream of people coming to worship their Lord and Savior. Sunday was always special. And this Sunday, the people were excited to have Americans attending their service.

She introduced Ian as 'The American who has come to help us.' Ian greeted them all with a handshake and a warm good morning.

"You talk funny, sir," said one sweet little boy.

"Amahle, don't be rude," said his mother.

"No ma'am, please." Ian then smiled, bent over, and gave the boy his hand. "That is how we talk in America. The boy was puzzled. "I am from a long way away."

"Does everybody talk funny there?" he asked.

"Yes, son. We all speak funny. But God knows what we are saying." Ian smiled again and rubbed his cute little head.

"I like it even though it sounds funny. You are blessed, sir." His mother hugged her son and they moved on, both with smiles.

Esther leaned over to Ian. "They like you, Mr. Roberts."

Ian was handed more puzzle pieces to an unrecognizable plan. He now realized he was led to Credence for a reason, but it was not his final destination. In the Bible the word 'church' never refers to a building, it refers to people. Unlike Credence emphasis on their building campaigns, this church is about people, both inside and outside their walls.

PART 2

The team prepared to attend the church service on their last morning in South Africa. They gathered outside in front of the bus. "Everyone ready?" Kristin looked around, "Where is Mr. Roberts? He was at dinner. He knows the plan for today." The team nodded. Has anybody seen him? He is driving me crazy. He is probably still sleeping."

Brent said, "I was half asleep, but I did hear someone in the bathtub, and I also heard a car door. His door was closed when I walked by. I'll check, Kristin."

Kristin knew he was not in his room because she saw him out the window with Esther and the children starting the car. "No, let him be. Worship is not his reason for being here. Let's go everybody, get on the bus." Kristin's disgust for Ian was without limits. She instructed Edward to sit with her in the back so they could talk.

"Edward, Ian isn't asleep. I saw him leave with Esther and the children over an hour ago."

"You said he was sleeping?" Edward was puzzled.

"I said he was probably still sleeping. The question is what was he doing with Esther and the kids without us? Something is going on. He thinks he can come and go as he pleases without letting me know. He is not a team player, Edward." Kristin was upset.

"Maybe Kristin, but…." Edward was interrupted.

"He knows I'm in charge. Jordan will get a report on him and so will my father. I don't trust him, Edward. Why is he going behind my back? And Anton is encouraging him. They sat together on the mission trip. And they met last night after dinner. What is going on?"

"I don't see a problem, Kristin."

"And he is on that rental phone a lot. Doesn't that seem peculiar to you?" Kristin was shaking her head.

"No. He runs a business at home, and he has three children. You talk to your husband and Jordan every day. His mission is different from ours. Joanna will be our main contact with Anton. Bennet is evaluating immediate needs; you are here for political purposes, and I am here to analyze the economic stability of this church."

"Are you blind, Edward. Ian Roberts is here to exploit these people and make money for himself. He is probably going to make Anton a partner in his venture. He is supposed to be here to start a business, create jobs and profits for the Hospice, not for himself and Anton."

"How do you know he is not doing that? Be careful what you accuse him of, Kristin." said Edward. "How much venture capital is Credence giving him to start this business?"

"None, he contacted us first and asked if he could help. We gave him an idea and he said yes." Edward was surprised and more confused.

"So, he is a volunteer, and you are giving him no money. Why do you want to control him? Sounds like he is on his own?"

Kristin was frustrated. She knew Edward was right, but she needed justification to control Ian. "Edward, I have not trusted him since the flight to Atlanta when he told me Jesus was not his Lord and Savior."

"He is a businessperson. What if he succeeds and it cost Credence nothing?"

Kristin ignored Edward again. "We are giving Anton a lot of money to build the Hospice. If Anton and Roberts use that money for their business instead, we will have a scandal on our hands. We have to find a way to control him, Edward."

"Kick him out of the church. Or make him want to leave. What do you have to lose?"

"Jordan tells me three of his business partners are large donors. And he has social contacts."

"Then closely audit the money you send to Anton."

"And the business. How do we track Robert's business?"

"You can't. If you are not an investor, you have no right to audit Robert's business. And Credence is not entitled to any profits. You do understand?"

"Edward, I need you to back me. Tell Jordan and my father neither of us trust Roberts or Anton. If something goes wrong, I don't want to take any blame or disappoint my father."

"Kristin, I have known Charles Wik for a number of years. Tell him your suspicions and let them go. I refuse to discuss this situation with

Jordan or your father. I will only promise you I will not agree or disagree with you. Bellamy was finished.

The team arrived and gathered in the back of the church. Esther arranged for all to receive a woolen blanket for their laps. The room was in the shape of a crescent moon with an elongated stage across the front. The congregation sat in three sections of folding chairs, ten across and twenty rows deep. The aisles allowed people to approach for baptisms, communion, and dancing. The ceiling stood twenty feet high. Bird nests speckled the steel rafters. The walls were standard reddish/brown brick and windows six-foot-high protected by iron bars. And like most structures in the township, no heat.

Kristin looked at Edward. "This place is cold, like a tomb. I have been told the service is three hours long. I can't make it three hours even with this scratchy blanket. My feet are numb already. We could never hold people's attention for three hours back home. This is going to be terrible."

"Suffering is a way of life for these people. The place is already crowded with lots of smiles." Edward was excited.

"You're right. These people have nothing better to do on a Sunday." Kristin stopped. "Edward, look up front. There is Esther." Edward nodded. "And Roberts is with her. They are surrounded by people. They are all shaking hands and smiling.

"It seems he is preparing the way for all of us." Edward smiled.

"He is turning them into his followers." Edward said nothing. The team was escorted to the front of the sanctuary where they were seated in the second row. Their chairs were covered in white linen signifying them as guests of honor.

Ian greeted them all and inquired as to how everyone slept.

"Where were you this morning?" asked Brent.

"Esther arranged for me to meet their IT technician. I had the honor of attending Esther's 7 A.M. prayer meeting. It was inspiring."

Brent smiled. "Tell me about it, Ian. It sounds fantastic."

Kristin interrupted. "You can talk later, Brent." She turned to Edward and whispered. "Why were we not invited?"

"We were. Esther invited us at dinner and you said no." Kristin ignored Edward.

"Come sit next to me, Mr. Roberts. I can answer any questions you may have during service." Ian sat next to Esther in the front row with the Deacons. Kristin and the others sat in the second. Kristin gave Edward a glance of confirmation.

The 8:30 service started promptly at 8:50. After a few squeaks from the microphones, a trio of handsome teens played drums, bass, and keyboard. Eight other teens sang unique South African harmonies. It was beautiful. Then the second song began. It ignited the room. It was what the congregation waited for all week. Anton burst onto the stage. He wore his long-flowered top, his black pants, and his pointed snakeskin shoes. The congregation rose to their feet, clapping, arms in the air and singing. Anton danced athletically across the stage, the teens sang and danced behind him. Ian felt the energy, but he was still too American to go all in. Anton began raising his legs as if running in place. People filled the aisles dancing with their pastor. "What is he doing, Esther? What are they all doing?"

"The Toyi-Toyi. It's a dance we did to protest Apartheid. We were not allowed to speak out against the government, so we danced. They had no idea we were protesting." Esther went back to clapping and singing." The room was filled with the power of God.

Ian watched as the elderly women made their way in front of the stage. Smiling brightly and with Bibles held open in their hands, they spun as if they would launch them onto the stage. Ian leaned over to Esther once again. "What are they doing, Esther?"

"They are throwing the word of God onto Anton and the children." Ian shuddered once more. He began to clap and move. He could not hold back. As he did, an elderly woman approached Esther and her guests of honor, dousing them all with the word of God.

"Open your palms, Mr. Roberts, and accept her love." With that, Ian opened his palms, nodded his head and tears rolled noticeably down his cheeks. "You appear touched, Mr. Roberts." As the celebration was ending, the congregation was smiling, their hands raised to the sky. The team was smiling as well. Kristin had love on her face.

The music lowered to only the sound of a soft keyboard. Anton looked up to the heavens and prayed. He prayed one sentence at a time so the woman next to him could repeat each line in Zulu. It was moving. Ian closed his tearful eyes. The three-hour service was now making sense.

After another song, Anton delivered the first of his three sermons. They were inspiring. After his second, he invited the Americans to join him on the stage. Kristin stood next to Anton. Ian took his place at the far end. A microphone was passed from person to person.

Kristin began. She was talking quickly. The Zulu interpreter gave up. "I am Pastor Kristin from Credence Community Church in America. I am here to meet Pastor Anton and his family and to give all of you my love and support. We are funding your HIV/AIDS Hospice. I bless you and may God's face shine upon you and give you peace. In the name of Jesus Christ our Lord and Savior, Amen." Amens echoed through the sanctuary once again.

Edward introduced himself and said he was here to support Pastor Kristin. Jim Bennet explained how he was here to evaluate immediate needs. Joanna told them she was the liaison between Credence and Anton. Then came Brent.

Brent began waving to everyone and they waved back with smiles. He began. "I am Brent, Joanna's husband." Then he began to tell the congregation how we are all the same. And how God loves us. He seemed to be finished, so Ian was about to take the microphone and finish the introductions. But Brent kept talking and talking. But it was obvious the room was getting bored. Joanna whispered in his ear to wrap it up. He passed the microphone to Ian.

"My name is Ian Roberts. I am here to help all of you start a business, one that will create jobs and help fund your Hospice." Ian hesitated to allow the interpreter to catch up.

But before she finished, Brent pulled the microphone from Ian's hand. "People, Mr. Roberts is going to create a thousand jobs for you." As the interpreter repeated the line, the congregation rose to their feet applauding and yelling halleluiahs. Ian was dumbfounded. He had not even determined the viability of the infrastructure, let alone a long-term business plan. But now, Brent, Joanna's husband, along for the ride, placed Ian in a position to fail. Brent was a middle manager in a Fortune 500 company. He fit in perfectly with the Credence big business mentality. But he had no idea what a small business start-up entailed.

Ian responded. "I am here for two more weeks exploring what possibilities we have. We will work together to achieve our goal in years to come. I will listen and with your help and cooperation, we will do God's work."

The crowd clapped again but with less enthusiasm. Anton and Ian made eye contact. Anton's glance was one of compassion.

The team returned to their seats. Brent leaned forward and whispered into Ian's ear, "Now you know what is important to these people, Ian."

"A thousand jobs, Brent, really? That is called unrealistic expectations. You are giving them false hope."

Brent smiled. "False hope is better than no hope at all. It's called politics. You need to learn to use it and gain power over these people."

Ian was now behind the curtain. Brent was right. As much as Ian disliked it, he would have to play some politics, but not with Anton and his people. It would be with Credence and the big businesspeople of their church.

The service ended at noon. Except for announcements, birthdays, and deaths, and a few mechanical problems, the service was never dull. Many came over to meet and bless the Americans. But people lined up to meet Ian. Brent was smiling. Many asked where they could apply for a job and how soon they could start. Ian felt sick. He was aware how important jobs were in the township; life and death for many. He told people Anton would announce it when the business was set up.

The team left for the airport that afternoon. Anton took them to 'The Apache' for a late lunch. Ian, however, accepted Esther's invitation to visit a small tent service deep in the township. He was introduced to Pastor Gladys, a woman in her mid-thirties. She had an unadorned beauty; peace and love emanated from her soul. Ian sat quietly, absorbing acceptance and kindness from these impoverished people. He was unaware of the respect he gained simply by venturing into their neighborhood. Ian was not planning any of it, he was just saying yes. He was unaware the hand was now firmly on his back.

MORNING HAS BROKEN

When the Credence team left Ian moved to a one room brick hut across from the main house. Wooden rafters supported the high-pitched roof where birds and rats made their homes. An austere bathroom had the necessities: toilet, sink, tub. The water was lukewarm. A small TV sat on a rolling stand, but it did not work. A small kitchen area contained a stove and refrigerator, but those did not work, and a washer and dryer which only served to protect Ian's snacks from a rat attack.

Ian's alarm pierced the pre-dawn chill. He walked barefoot to the bathroom. He sponged his pits and privates, brushed his teeth, and shaved the stubble from his face. Shivering, he dressed quickly, and joined the family for breakfast.

The soft pink sky of sunrise appeared through the window. The sun glistened off the dew of the frozen savannah. It was time to work; the reason he came.

"How did you sleep, Ian?" asked Esther. "I feel awkward not calling you Mr. Roberts."

"I slept fine Esther, but it will take a little time getting used to the jungle in the ceiling."

Esther looked at Anton. The kids looked at the floor. "Is that a problem for you, Ian?"

"No, I have ignored rats before, but if more Americans visit, they will have a problem."

"We know. The married couple were not pleased."

"Esther, it's a simple fix, rat poison. It's not expensive. I will pick some up today."

Esther looked at Anton. "Go ahead Esther, tell him," said Anton.

"We tried that, but the rats ate it, then they died."

"Exactly." Ian was confused.

"They die in the walls or the ceilings. They stink terribly and attract ants and flies, then come the maggots."

"Get some cats, Esther."

"I hate cats worse than I hate rats." Anton smiled and stroked his goatee.

Matthew chimed in, "Mark and I nail them with our shoes." Proud smiles popped on both the boys' faces. Ian smiled as well. It made a lot of sense, but it still would not be acceptable to Americans.

Anton turned to Ian. "Ready?" Anton's voice was hoarse from his prior day preaching.

"Ready," Ian replied. He followed Anton to the van. Esther and the children jump started the car and left for school.

Ian proceeded to the wrong side of the van. Anton followed. Dangling the keys in Ian's face, he grinned, "You want to drive?" Ian smiled and went to the passenger side.

"We are to meet Samuel and a few others at the church to talk about computers, but we need to make one stop on our way."

"You're the boss." Anton smiled. "All the places I have been, I have not seen a car with the steering wheel on that side, and you shift with your left hand. But the clutch is still on your left foot?"

"There will be a lot of things you have not seen before." Anton looked at the road. Traffic was heavy this time of morning.

"Go on." Ian was curious.

"You will see a lot of death, but not a lot of desperation among our people. I perform four or five funerals a week since HIV spread rapidly. I perform two weddings per month. Community and family are important here."

"Why is community important?"

"For centuries we were a tribal culture. We hunted and traded, even fought each other. And we needed to protect each other from the animals. Then the Europeans came, mainly the Dutch, and enslaved us. They honestly believed the Bible told them it was their God given duty. They confiscated our land and our houses. They moved about 3.5 million of us into segregated non-white areas called dormitory towns, now called townships. This centralized the mine and industrial workers. They placed us where they could use us and watch us."

"The townships now make sense."

"After Apartheid, many moved back into the cities. Taking away our tribal culture created a new generation of youth, a generation that disobeyed and rebelled. Johannesburg is known as the rape and murder capital of the world. Out here, it is domestic violence and theft.

"I haven't seen any violence."

"You won't as long as you are with me. It is behind closed doors." Anton knew he must not shelter Ian.

"You say you have strong community?"

"The Christian Church is strong here, predominantly Protestant. It's the strength of God among the parishes that creates our love and respect for each other. The churches are our new tribes." Anton hesitated. "Why did you come here, Ian? Why is a middle-aged White man from America here alone?"

"You mean South Africa?"

"No, I mean in this minivan with me, today, here and now."

"I contacted Credence, said I was an entrepreneur, had time on my hands and was not afraid of third world. They explained to me their idea for a business to be started that would create jobs and produce profits to fund the Hospice. Next thing I know, I am here."

"And whose Hospice is it?" Ian was puzzled by the simplicity of Anton's question. Ian assumed he understood the question.

"The Hospice belongs to you, not Credence, if that is what you are asking. They are only funding it."

"No, it is God's Hospice for God's people; it is not mine; it is not yours; it is not Credence's. And who owns the business you are starting, Credence?"

"Credence will have no ownership or control. All profits go to the Hospice. I will not share in the profits, but I also do not want to lose anything."

"Fair enough. I have no reason to doubt what you say. And you need to know my goals if we are to work together." Ian nodded. "I made it clear to your Pastor West, we welcome his financial support, and he may use us as a marketing tool for his fund raising, but his money does not buy control over me."

"I'm glad we are having this conversation. I suggest you keep detailed financial records. They will audit you."

"Are you saying they distrust me?"

"They are a corporate church, founded and run by high powered executives. They have many lawyers and accountants. I run companies for a living. Audits are routine and necessary."

Anton smiled and stroked his goatee. "I understand. But I will not allow them to own me or control me."

"If all goes well between you and Credence, they will someday offer you money. At that point, they will need to control you. Perhaps that is why I am here, to create cashflow so that is not necessary."

"From the one thousand jobs Brent promised." They both smiled. Things were becoming clearer to both. And both were establishing boundaries.

"There is one more thing." Anton needed to make his last point before this venture proceeded.

"Go on."

"Apartheid ended ten years ago, but the government is still trying to control us."

"I understand."

"They give us meaningless jobs. They thwart our attempts to start businesses of our own. I want you to promise me, whatever you do, Black Empowerment will be the priority."

"Please define."

"My church is growing and becoming strong because we are doing this ourselves. We have no Whites in the church, not because we don't welcome them, but because it was a hard, hateful rebellion. Many White people are scared to come into the township and many still feel God wants us separate."

"I understand."

"When we started, a White church offered to help us monetarily. They told me we were incapable of handling the administration. They are beautiful people and remain good friends, but I graciously refused their help. Looking back, it would have made my life easier."

"Would you rather preach and allow others handle the business side?"

"Preaching is my passion, Ian. I fell in love with preaching the first time I saw my father in the pulpit, pounding his fist and stomping his feet. He inspired me and saved so many."

"Go on, tell me more about you father." Ian was excited hearing Anton speak of him.

"That is for another day. I promise you will meet him." Anton came back to his point. "My long-term vision for this church is to prove to my people we can do this ourselves. They need to have confidence we will succeed."

"You are approaching two thousand members. Looks like it is working."

"It takes a long time to get those inferior thoughts out of their heads. That is why I am starting early."

"The school." Ian grabbed another piece of the puzzle. "Why are you telling me this, Anton?"

"Promise me you will train my people with the goal they take over whatever you start. When they are ready, you will walk away."

"I have no problem with that. However, they will need to be trained and work with my people in the States, and my people are mostly White. Can you accept that?"

"You are sharing your knowledge with us. We need that. Education is our way out. And always remember, this is in the name of the Lord. It is God's work, not ours."

"That is getting clearer every moment, Anton." Ian smiled, "Now I must ask something of you."

"Go on."

"Agree, any venture we have together, you will be open to learning from me, accepting, and respecting my experience as an entrepreneur and a business owner. It seems I have been prepared for this day, but neither of us can be the other's employee. We must be partners, and as partners, we can show your people how a White man and a Black man can work in harmony and equality."

"Before Kristin left, she spoke to me about you."

"That must have been interesting."

"She told me your faith was questionable. She told me you refer to yourself as a 'Christ Follower'."

"Yes, Anton, what I said was…"

"Stop Ian. Nothing wrong with questioning one's faith. It makes it stronger. So, my Christ Follower friend, you build me a business and teach me your skills and I will strengthen your faith and your relationship with the Lord."

They both smiled. It was the birth of a partnership built on trust and mutual respect. No documents, no lawyers, no accountants, and no Credence. Its purpose was to bring peace to the living and peace to the dying. A partnership which would change people on two continents. And like many stories in the Bible, not everything would be pleasant.

MIRIAM

Anton parked on the dirt road in front of a small reddish/brown brick house, encircled by six-foot walls and topped with razor wire. Bars covered the windows. It looked like all the other houses. Security was utmost in the township; impregnable was the goal. Anton glanced at Ian. "I must stop here for a moment. They need my prayers. I will be right back."

Ian sat up straight. "May I come, Anton?"

"Are you afraid out here by yourself?"

"Not at all. I have been in dangerous places in the world, this does not feel like one. But there does seem to be safety concerns by the looks of the houses."

"Safety is not the right word. Other than domestic violence, bodily harm and murders are rare. It's about possessions. Poverty is the norm. Theft is prevalent. People will steal anything, anytime, anywhere."

"For drugs and alcohol?"

"No, for survival. They need food, medication, tools. Don't wear anything you don't want to lose."

Ian was calm. "I learned that lesson years ago, Anton. I carry a few rand in my pocket and carry my driver's license for emergency identification. I never carry my passport. Everybody loves an American passport."

Anton felt comfortable the more he got to know Ian. Ian did not need a babysitter.

"Then I can join you?" Ian felt the hand in his back.

"The neighbors would think you are a police officer. That will make you safer inside than out here by yourself."

Anton smiled. He hopped out of the van and followed Anton to the gate. A strong woman in her early thirties came to greet them. Her faced beamed bright when she saw it was her Pastor Anton. She did not pay much attention to Ian, at least not at first. Then, with a glance, "You are the man at service yesterday who will create a thousand jobs for us. Praise the Lord." She was excited. She gave Anton a respectful hug and Ian a warm handshake.

"Yes Miriam, this is Mr. Ian Roberts. With God's help and our cooperation, he is here to help us." Anton understood the position Brent thrusted upon Ian. No need for an explanation.

"Come in please, both of you. You are blessed." Anton and Ian entered the home. A galley kitchen was situated to the left and two bedrooms were straight ahead behind the small dining area. All floors were covered with worn linoleum. To the right was a cozy living room furnished with a recliner, a love seat, and a small television. Family photos covered the walls. But it was the large crucifixion with the suffering Jesus Christ that, without a doubt, dominated the entire home.

"Pastor Anton, you remember my mother, Magdalene. She is one of our beautiful elderly ladies who throws the word of God on you and our children every Sunday."

Anton smiled and reached for her hand. The endearing woman grabbed it and kissed it. He looked into her worn tired eyes. "Ms. Magdalene, I see you dancing every Sunday. You and your friends fill our hearts with love and joy. You are blessed."

Magdalene smiled with gracious humility. "Thank you for visiting us, Pastor. Your prayers bring us peace and hope."

Anton placed his hand on the side of her face and with his enchanting smile he declared. "God loves you, my dear. You have a beautiful soul." She then sheepishly glanced at Ian. "And this is our new friend from America, Mr. Ian Roberts."

"Yes, I remember him from service. I threw the word of God on him too." She then gave him an excited grin. "You are the man who is going to create a thousand jobs for us. God bless you sir, God bless you."

Anton and Ian gave each other another glance. Anton sat on the love seat, Ian sat on the edge of the recliner and Miriam brought in two chairs from the dining room.

"Momma, get Lerato, please." Magdalene disappeared for a few moments, then returned from the bedroom, pushing Miriam's husband in an antique wheelchair. A conversation between Miriam and Anton ensued in Zulu, then Miriam began to weep. Magdalene patted her daughter's hand. Lerato said nothing. He could not.

After ten minutes of conversation, Anton stood. Placing both hands on Lerato's head, he prayed, again in Zulu. Ian was unaware of what was being said, but he could see heavy tears rolling from the eyes of both Miriam and her mother. Lerato was still. Ian saw a small stream of drool from the side of his mouth. It dripped onto his chest. Anton finished and glanced at Ian. It was time to go. Ian followed him to the door. Miriam grabbed Ian's hand, bowed to him, and kissed it. "We are so blessed the Lord sent you to us, sir. I will pray for you every night. Thank you so much."

Ian followed Anton to the minivan, and as usual, Ian went to the wrong side. Anton jiggled the keys and smiled. The van pulled out and off they went to their meeting at the church.

Ian was not sure what had just happened, but he knew Lerato was a stroke victim. He was emotional, the same feeling he had on the outreach visit a week before. "What just happened?"

"I was hoping you would ask. In fact, I knew you would." Anton wasn't smiling. "Lerato is diabetic. So is their twelve- year- old daughter. She is in school today. They only earn enough money to buy insulin for one. They chose their daughter, Ava. They have tried to treat Lerato with diet, but it didn't work. He had a massive stroke a month ago. Now he can't work. Miriam is trying hard to earn enough to save Ava. And Miriam needs to feed her mother as well."

"Will he get better?"

"No. They give him a month, maybe two."

Ian was visibly upset. He blurted, "Then what? If the mother can't earn enough then what, the daughter has a stroke and dies too?"

"Yes"

"Certainly, there must be programs here, health care plans, government assistance, something. People in the States go to community hospitals for insulin. No one dies from diabetes in the States, not from lack of insulin. There must be something we can do, Medicaid or Medicare or something. This isn't right, Anton. This can't happen in today's world."

"Ian, you know better than that. You've been all over this planet. You've seen it before or perhaps it has been hidden from you."

Ian took a deep breath. "You're right. I have seen it but not this close. I did not know names or been in their homes."

"I told you; things are different here. This isn't America, Ian. We have an 11% diabetes rate. People die every day from things you take for granted. And now HIV has strained our healthcare spending way beyond its limits. 25% of our healthcare costs go to HIV. Lerato will be dead in two months. Nothing we can do. It's too late."

"How do we save the daughter?" Ian was trying to stay calm.

"Miriam needs another job. And even that might not do it. My whole congregation need jobs."

"But what about the rest of the country. What about the Ava's all over your country?" Ian was frustrated.

"Ian, because we cannot help everyone doesn't mean we don't do what we can. We are all attached on the planet. God wants us to do what we can, not complain and be angry over what we cannot."

"I understand, Anton." Ian shed another tear.

THE CHRISTENING

Anton and Ian approached the compound. Ian could not stop his obsession with Miriam and her family. Their next meeting, organized by Esther after the service, would take place in Anton's office next to the schoolyard. Being a technical meeting with Samuel and his staff, Anton looked forward to a break from his emotions. A group of young techies nervously waited, afraid of not meeting the American's expectations. They were unaware of the education they would receive from Ian's staff. It would raise them to a new level of competence, assuring them of future jobs.

It was now 10:30 and the morning chill was receding. The minivan came to a halt. School was in session. "The children attend school in the summer, Anton?"

"They go year-round, but this is winter." Anton smiled. The Southern Hemisphere was confusing. Ian found himself upside down and backwards in many ways, not only with seasons and car doors.

The rooms of the church were now filled with desks, children, and teachers. Anton's school was now through the fourth grade. His goal was a High School level education within the next five years; building funds were the issue. The plan started with the preschoolers. They were the single largest group of students, and the most financially profitable. The working mothers helped keep tuitions down for the upper grades.

IAN AND ANTON

"Ian, we are to meet in my office across the schoolyard. Come, we are running late." Ian followed Anton's hurried pace, but as they passed the preschoolers on the perimeter, he slowed. The little ones were crammed into two small open-faced structures. He took a closer look. He then stopped altogether and smiled. Each child was beautiful. Their clothes were plain and warm, and noticeably clean.

His distraction intensified. Now frozen in his tracks, they noticed him. They began smiling and waving. They began calling something that sounded like 'La cua.' He had no idea what it meant. It was not English. He drifted closer to the teacher, "What are they saying?"

She smiled. "They are calling to you. They are saying "White man.""

Ian smiled at the teacher and asked carefully, "Is that at good thing?"

With an even bigger smile, she answered, "Yes sir, the way they are saying it."

Just then a bell rang. It was recess. Ian was suddenly engulfed in a sea of the most delightful children he had ever known. They tugged with affection at his tall body. Some jumped like puppies wanting Ian to hold them. He dropped to his knees. The children took turns hugging him, touching his hair, rubbing his hands and face. Ian hugged them all, ignoring not one.

Ian looked at the teacher once again. "I don't understand?"

"Sir, our children have never touched a White man."

"Really?"

"White people do not visit here in the township unless they are sent by the government or they are workers, and those types have no interest in our children."

As Ian talked to the teacher, one little cherub took his hand, placed something in it, then closed it. She put her arms around his neck and gave him a hug. Still hanging on, she whispered in his ear, "Sweets for you." Ian looked in his hand. It was a piece of candy. The cherub used the rand her mother gave her to purchase a piece of candy for Ian.

It was overwhelming. Tears ran down his face. His sobs were so strongly subdued he could hardly breathe. He embraced the little angel of God and whispered back, "You have no idea what you just did, little one." He kissed her on top of the head. He thought *I've been given so much because of where, when and to whom I was born. I am wealthy compared to these children. And she spent her rand on me out of love.'*

Anton watched Ian from the doorway. He was amazed at how these children accepted him so quickly. How they gave him hugs and affection as if he was their long-lost uncle. "Ian," Anton finally called from the door of the office, "We need you in the meeting."

Ian stood and held up one finger. He needed a moment. Anton knew what was happening. Ian walked past him and down to the end of the school yard. He stopped at the chain-linked fence surrounding the compound. He stared at the more than modest houses across the dusty road. Tears continued to roll down his face. He remembered Anton's words on the mission trip a week earlier. Ian knew he could not let his emotions get the better of him. Anton needed strong leadership. But Anton also told him he would cry many times for many distinct reasons. These children's lives were in danger from something they knew nothing about. Education was their only hope and Anton was providing it. Jobs and the church would be their way to salvation. It was beautifully holistic.

Ian wiped his face, took a deep breath, and collected himself. He was ready to be the strong American businessman they were here to meet.

Ian received useful information, not encouraging, but not discouraging. He loved a challenge. He loved puzzles even as a kid. The harder the puzzle, the more fun.

The meeting ended, hands were shaken, and help volunteered. Only Anton and Ian remained in the room. "I watched you with our children, Ian. They accepted and loved you immediately. That is unusual for them to take to a stranger, especially a White man. What did you do?"

"They smiled and waved, I smiled and waved back. Then the recess bell rang."

Anton smiled and stroked his goatee. "I was surprised. Their recess is a half-hour late today but go on."

"Next thing I knew I was surrounded by a cloud of innocence. I never felt more loved. It was pure."

"They sensed the love and kindness inside you."

"And they don't know I am supposed to create a thousand jobs." Ian smiled.

"Anton smiled and continued to stroke his goatee. "No Ian, they don't. I believe I have a new name for you. From here on you will be known as 'Uncle Ian'."

"Anton, you are kidding?"

"No, I insist. Those children accepted you into our family, no questions asked. Their love for you is unconditional. This is a sign from God. I have been watching my people give you their respect and the respect you give them in return. From here on, I will introduce you to my people as Uncle Ian." Anton was not one to embrace, but at this moment, he did. Uncle Ian was born into the township; christened by sweet little angels of God.

"Ian, let us grab lunch and I will return you to the house. I must perform a burial this afternoon for one of my congregation's fathers."

"Can I go with you?" Anton smiled at Ian.

"First Miriam, then the children. Are you sure your emotions can handle this?"

"Let's find out." Ian smiled back.

After lunch, Ian and Anton made their way to the cemetery. As they entered the gate, Ian observed it to be the same as any cemetery in the U.S. "This is nice Anton, trees, grass, flowers, nice monuments. I expected it to be larger with the AIDS epidemic."

"We are in the White section. Only Whites are permitted to be buried here."

"A remnant of Apartheid?"

"Yes, but us Blacks do not want to bury our loved ones in here anyway. Could not afford it if we did."

They drove farther. The landscape was now sparse, but there was some patchy grass, the monuments modest. "Is this where the burial will take place?"

"No, this is for the Coloreds."

"The Coloreds?"

"Anyone who is not Black, you know, interracial, a combination of Black, White, Indian, Asian. As long as they are not pure Black." Ian stayed silent.

They crossed into the Black section. No trees, no grass, but some weeds. The landscape was barren, but it was not flat. Two-foot mounds of dirt covered each grave. Artificial flowers lay muddy on the ground.

Anton parked the van. He and Ian approached the gravesite. Anton greeted the family with his kind words of condolence. The air was temperate, but the sun was hot. Other than a few umbrellas, no shade was available. After a brief but moving service, the casket was lowered into the grave. Anton motioned Ian to join him. "Grab a shovel, Ian, you can help."

"What, you want me to shovel the dirt on top of the casket? Is it appropriate I do that? These people don't know me."

"They will when we are finished, Uncle Ian. But no dirt yet, the dirt comes after." Anton led Ian to the grave. "Shovel, Ian."

In front of Ian was a mound of freshly mixed cement. Ian followed Anton's lead along with four other men, throwing cement on top of the casket. Not looking up, Ian whispered to Anton. "Tell me, what are we doing?"

"Grave robbers. If the casket is not sealed with cement, grave robbers will dig it up. They will steal anything on the corpse they can sell like rings, jewelry, watches, glasses."

"What about the security guards?"

Anton didn't say a word. He gave Ian a blank stare. Ian understood. The same people who paid for the landscaping and groundkeepers paid for security – no one.

The grave was now covered with dirt on top of cement. Ian was sweating profusely in the hot sun. People approached him with their gratitude and their blessings. Ian returned with his condolences. Word spread quickly among the congregation of this lone American, now a new friend and house guest of Pastor Anton and his family. He was the only White man staying in the Black township and hard to miss. His name was Uncle Ian.

Anton dropped Ian at the house and continued his day. It was past dinner before Anton returned home. The children were in bed. Esther greeted her husband with the love he deserved. She warmed his dinner and brought it to him in the family dining room. "How was your day? I heard you took Ian to the burial."

"I did. How did you know that?"

"Sheila and two others called me. Sheila asked me if that was the man who is going to create a thousand jobs."

Anton smiled. "I know. That was not fair, but it does not seem to be affecting him. Where is he now?"

"When he came back, he looked drained. He went to his room to answer emails and rest."

"Did he eat?"

"Yes, he had dinner with me and the children. He asked them lots of questions about their school and sports and their interests. I have not seen them open up so quickly. Dinner was delightful."

"Esther, the man has been through much this past week, our AIDS ministry, your prayer meeting, the funeral."

"Don't forget the preschoolers."

"The preschoolers really hit him hard. It was such a coincidence their recess was late today. I thought you planned the meeting for 10:30 so the children would not disturb us, but the bell rang just as we arrived at my office."

"That's odd."

Anton looked up from eating. "Esther, did you?"

"Did I what, Anton?" She had a look Anton was very familiar with.

"You called Sophia and arranged for recess to happen just as we arrived, didn't you?" Anton smiled.

"He needed to meet our little ones. That is where it all starts, Anton. We both feel it. He is different than the others who pass through here just to help some poor people. And he is different because he doesn't realize he is different. He admits it, he doesn't know why he is here."

"I know that look, Esther. I hope you are right. My fear is he will not be able to handle his emotions. He wept on our AIDS mission, he held it inside at Miriam's, he walked off and bawled over the preschoolers, and he was visible touched by the love of our people at the funeral."

"And his eyes were moist at the prayer meeting."

"And on top of all that, Credence gives him no emotional support whatsoever. Instead of trying to strengthen his faith and help him grow, they shun him. I am afraid he will quit before he starts."

"Anton, he is an American. They have their material needs between them and God. We are closer to him. They don't feel the way we feel. Didn't you tell me last week he asked you to never let him forget what he saw in the township?"

"He did as we left to return."

Esther moved to Anton's end of the table and pulled a chair close. She put her hand on his and looked into his eyes. "Do you remember ten years ago when we came here and started the church."

"I do."

"You made your first rounds in the township to learn first-hand the suffering those people with HIV/AIDS and their families were going through; the terrible pain, the grief, the heartbreak. And what did you say to me."

"Go on, Esther, say it."

"You told me to never let you be numb to their suffering. The same thing Ian said to you. Then, you dropped to your knees and wept into my lap. He is here for a reason, Anton. He is here to remind you of what God wants from you, but more specifically, why."

Esther rose from her chair and stood next to her husband. She cradled his head to her breast. Anton sobbed. Then Esther said, "And I also am told, we have a new uncle." Anton looked up. They both smiled.

A SILENT DECLARATION OF LOYALTY

There was a tap on West's door. "Come in." Pastor Kristin entered. "Good afternoon, Kristin, what can I do for you?"

Kristin sat in the comfortable chair in front of West's desk. "Jordan, I must make you aware, two weeks ago on the plane back from South Africa, Jim Bennet informed me of a conversation he had with Anton."

"And that conversation was?"

"Anton told Jim he needed another $80,000 before he could start construction of the Hospice."

"And why does he need an additional $80,000?"

"Jim wasn't sure what Anton was saying, so I didn't think much of it. I assumed he wanted a cushion, or it has to do with Ian Robert's business plan."

"Did he say that?"

"No, so I have waited to see if Anton would say any more about it."

"Has he?"

"Yes, he called Jim yesterday to see if you made a decision."

"I have not since this is the first I have heard of it. What do you think, Kristin?"

"It is a bluff. For some reason, I don't trust Anton. He wants to bleed us a little at a time forever."

"Go on"

"If we say no, that will be the end of it. He will start construction and we honor our commitment of $200,000."

"You oversee this project, Kristin. Tell him no."

"Thank you, Jordan, I will have Jim call him tomorrow with your answer."

Seven days remained in Ian's initial exploration of the South African business landscape. As frustrating as the creative process can be, Ian stayed positive. Some ideas were keepers, some were not. The puzzle pieces gathered were simply clues at this point. Ian remained patient. He pulled from Einstein's quote on problem solving. "If I had an hour to solve a problem, I'd spend fifty-five minutes thinking about the problem and five minutes thinking about the solution." The solution to profits and job creation needed to be more than technology and infrastructure; it needed to be holistic. The last two weeks were emotional and frustrating. He felt love, he felt resentment, he experienced grief, and he sensed a presence he could not explain. When he returned, he was anxious to share his findings with Credence. He expected their support and cooperation. He would be surprised.

Another long day was ending. The family sat around the dinner table, Anton, Esther, Matthew, Mark and Joan, and their newest member, Uncle Ian. Ox tail was served once again. It was Ian's favorite African dish. The children rarely spoke at the table, but this night, Anton and Esther were quiet as well. Ian sensed a touch of fear permeating through their silence.

Worried it may be something he did, Ian wondered whether to break the silence. That afternoon he met with the telephone company about a new internet line. He was stern with the agent as they were clearly trying to take advantage of Anton. He was concerned he had been too forceful, making Anton upset.

"When do you break ground on the Hospice, Anton? And what is your estimated completion date?" Anton looked at Esther. The kids kept eating.

"I don't know, Ian." Anton's response was short.

"What do you mean you don't know? You have the blueprints, and you have bids from most of the contractors. You must have some idea." Anton did not look up. He kept eating. Esther was silent.

Finally, Anton spoke, "Children, take your plates to the kitchen and finish there please. I need to speak with Uncle Ian." Confidential conversations were nothing new. But they detected something different. Esther rose from her chair. "Esther, I want you to stay, please." She sat back down.

Ian spoke first, "Anton, something is wrong. Was it my actions with the phone company? I told you sometimes one must come over the desk at someone. I wasn't angry. It was a negotiating tactic."

Anton shook his head, "No Ian, we both know the phone company is in partnership with the devil. You were great. I wish I could do that, but in my profession, no. That is why I have you." They both gave a quick smile.

"Then, what is it?"

"I have been trying to find the right time to tell you. Since I only have you here for another week, I need your help."

"You know I will if I can." Anton was noticeably distraught.

"You are familiar with my architect Jack?" Ian nodded. "Jack met with me before you and the Credence team arrived."

"Okay, go on."

"He told me I needed to talk to Credence about the Hospice. The construction cost of $200,000 US dollars is $80,000 short in the present day."

"Jack made a mistake. Was it in materials, labor, furniture?"

"No, the $200,000 was correct when we gave it to the Credence accountants in 2002. We double checked all the numbers."

"You have me confused."

"It's our economy. Our exchange rate has gone from eight to six and we had a 10% inflation rate in 2002 and 8% percent last year in 2003."

"Anton, I'm not a big finance guy. Make me understand?"

"As Jack explains it, the original budget at the beginning of 2002 was $200,000."

"Right."

"But between the exchange rate and the inflation rates, today I need an additional $80,000 U.S. to cover the current cost. I refuse to start if I cannot finish. A half-built Hospice sitting vacant in the township would look like failure. And it would be failure. I will not disappoint my people with that."

"Have you told anybody before now?"

"Jack and I sat with Jim Bennet. Jack explained it to him just like I have you, only in more detail. It appeared he understood. The team was to go back and tell Jordan West of the situation."

"What did Jordan say?"

"It's been two weeks since our meeting with Jim, so I called yesterday to inquire as to a decision."

"Did he make a decision?"

"Yes, Jim called me this afternoon. He met with Pastor Kristin. She said the additional funds were not approved and I either make the Hospice smaller or find ways to cut construction costs." Anton stared into space. "We would need all new drawings, pushing the construction out as much as a year."

"And by that time, exchange rates and inflation rates may cause the same problem we have now."

"Exactly." said Anton. "I'm afraid you have come all this way for nothing, Ian."

"Hold on Anton, usually I am the doubter."

Anton gave a small grin. "Okay Ian, go on."

"As part of Credence fund-raising campaign, Jordan West, from the pulpit, told the congregation they were partnering with a church in South Africa to build an AIDS hospice. The thought of building an AIDS hospice in Africa was exciting. Credence had pledges of $23 million, 15% over its goal of $20 million. They raised $3 million more than expected.

"$23 million dollars, that is a lot."

"Yes, but with all the hype about your hospice, they are giving you less than 1%." Their key word is 'Partnering,' not helping, not funding, 'Partnering.' They would not be naïve enough to bust this deal over $80,000. Let me talk to Jim tonight before he goes to lunch. There is something wrong. And Anton, do what you do best."

"And that is?"

"Pray loudly."

Esther and the children were in for a sleepless night.

With a nine-hour time difference, Ian's call at 7:00 P.M. might catch Jim before lunch and early enough for him to start working on the problem. Ian made the call.

"Credence, Jim Bennet."

"Hello Jim Bennet, Ian Roberts here."

"Ian, how are you, my friend? I've been thinking about you. Making any progress. Ian, hello, I'm having trouble hearing you, but I can hear you well enough, I suppose."

Ian left the folding chair in his room and went outside. It was dark and chilly. "Is that better, Jim?"

"Oh yes, much better, what's up?" Ian knew Jim was being coy. He was the one who called Anton with the unwelcome news.

"As you are aware, we have a problem with the Hospice construction costs. Anton and his architect spoke with you and explained the exchange rate and inflation situation."

"We talked before I left, but I didn't fully understand."

"Anton tells me Jordan said no to the additional $80,000?"

"Uh, yes, he and Kristin talked and decided a deal was a deal. We suggested he cut the project down."

"That's not practical Jim, as long as exchange rates and inflation continue upward. We will always be playing catchup."

"We? You sound like you are one of them." Jim chuckled. Ian did not.

"What about Edward Bellamy, the man Kristin brought with her. He is a big business guy. Has anyone run this passed him?"

"Kristin told me she would talk to him about it."

"Did she?"

"I assume she did on the plane. We had plenty of time."

"Would you please give me Edward's email? I want to be sure he has the correct facts from Kristin."

"Sure Ian, but don't tell Kristin I gave it to you. She is protective of Edward's privacy."

Ian immediately sent an email:

Dear Edward,

We are having a problem in South Africa. We need an additional $80,000 to begin construction and Credence has refused. Can you see if the additional funds are warranted with the following facts? I have copied Kristin, Jordan West, and Jim Bennet. Please share your findings with them as well.

$200,000 original estimate in 2002

Exchange rate from eight to six on 2005

10% inflation in 2003

8% inflation in 2004.

Ian Roberts

Within two hours, Bellamy returned a spreadsheet to all showing the new number to be $287,000. And within minutes, a 5:00 P.M. meeting was set by Jordan with a mandatory attendance flag including himself, Kristin, Bennet, and Bellamy.

The small conference room was furnished with coffee, bottles of water and tiny chicken salad sandwiches. All were present. Small talk ended as West entered the room. He began talking even before he reached his chair at the head of the table. "What is going on people? I thought you had this hospice thing under control. We send you over there and you come back telling me Anton is trying to rip us off for $80,000. I hold the line. Kristin, you oversee this project. And you too, Jim. Talk to me."

Kristin spoke first. "Jordan, I told you when we returned that Edward and I did not trust Anton or Roberts. They seemed too chummy for just meeting. They had private conversations. Roberts snuck off early to the church service the morning we left. He and Anton's wife went to a tent revival without inviting any of us. It all has to do with Robert's business venture."

"How so, Kristin? Do you think this $80,000 is about the business and not the Hospice? Were you aware of these economic factors before now?"

"Jim told me something about it, but I assumed Roberts and Anton were attempting to get seed money for their business. I still say it is a bluff."

"What proof do you have, Kristin?"

Not solid proof, but Anton and Roberts spend five days together and now Anton needs $80,000."

Jim began to speak but Kristin cut him off.

"I've had a feeling about Roberts from the beginning. Call it a warning from God. Roberts is not a team player. He is in this for himself. He will use cheap labor to build profits for himself and Anton. The man is not even a Christian." West was listening. He had his own misgivings about Ian from the beginning.

Finally, Jim Bennet was given a chance. "Jordan, I personally have not seen anything unusual about Roberts. He knows, without a doubt, we're not giving him a penny. He knows this is his own private venture to make or break."

Kristin jumped in again, "Exactly Jim, he knows we're not going to fund him. But Edward doesn't trust Roberts and Anton either. It makes perfect sense, Jim. Since they cannot get money directly from us, they scam us out of it. Open your eyes folks."

West looked at Bellamy. "Is that your take, Edward?"

Bellamy hesitated. "Kristin has her suspicions. Anton and Roberts did become friends quickly. But as I told Kristin, Robert's mission on that trip was different than ours. I can't agree or disagree." Kristin was getting angry. She thought Bellamy promised to agree with her, but he promised not to disagree with her in public.

West looked at Kristin, then back at Bellamy. "You have run numbers for us, please share."

Bellamy handed each a copy of his spreadsheet. "I researched the inflation rates and exchange rates between 2002 and 2005. I used the South African Government financial statistics. Inflation has been averaging 9% in the last two years and the exchange rate has dropped from eight to six. We were given accurate data."

"Fine Edward, but what does that have to do with Anton and Roberts needing more money?" asked Kristin.

The room became silent. West had a copy of Bellamy's report earlier. He began. "Edward has prepared a very simple report, even one of us clergy can understand." All chuckled except Kristin. "It shows, through no fault of Anton's, he will need $285,000 of today's dollars to build the Hospice." He looked back at Bellamy. "Edward, do you think this is a legitimate request?"

"I do Jordan."

Kristin broke in once more. "God is still telling me something. How do we track what they are doing with that extra money?"

Edward spoke up again. "Kristin, that's easy. Receipts, pictures of the construction site, routine audit procedures. We have been over this."

"Do you know how easy it would be for them to falsify receipts." West stopped Kristin.

"I do have one question for Jim. Why didn't we get all this information about the shortfall before now? I mean before I decided not to fund the $80,000?"

Jim was afraid that question was going to be asked. "I knew about this the day we left South Africa. Anton and his architect met with me."

"So why keep something that important to yourself, Jim?"

"I didn't. I told Kristin about it on the plane. She said she would handle it as soon as we got back. The next time I heard anything was two days ago when Kristin told me to call Anton with your decision. I did. That's when Roberts called to talk."

"And you, Edward?"

"Today 's email from Roberts was the first I heard of it."

West took a breath. He now knew everything he needed to know. "Okay, people, I have a problem. At some point we must show trust in Anton. I told the congregation we have a partnership with a church in South African to build an AIDS hospice. We must do that. Regarding Roberts, I don't particularly like or trust the man, but that is irrelevant. He is an independent contractor. He is not one of us. Unless we fund his business, we have no control over him. That is true with Anton as well. Anton is the boss. He will make all decisions for his people. He told me the first time we met; Black Empowerment is one of his top priorities. He wants to teach his people they can succeed without a White church as their boss."

Jim looked at West and spoke. "Anton made that clear to us as well. He is dedicated to God and to his congregation."

Jordan thought for a moment. "I do have some faith in Robert's judgement. I have checked him out. He has a nice business here in town. He and his partners are good sized donors. The last thing he wants is a scandal, especially one that rips off a church. And he knows a lot of people. That gives him power."

Bellamy spoke. "Jordan, approval of the funds is a wise decision. Anton and Roberts have us over a barrel. He knows how much we raised. To bust this deal over a small amount would be petty. They are being reasonable. The $80,000 is legitimate. Actually, a bit low."

"Jim, call Anton. Tell him we ran our own numbers and think we need to give him $97,000. Let us pray. Thank you, Lord, for the wisdom you have given us to make this decision. We pray for the poor and the sick who we help in your name. We pray that together our congregations will become united in the brotherhood of Jesus Christ. And we pray all decisions we make will be out of our love and caring for each other. In his Name. Amen."

All left the room. Kristin would report the decision directly to her father, Charles Wik, Chairman of the Board.

The sunset was serene. The temperature was dropping quickly. The boys built a fire in the stone fireplace to take the chill off the living room. Esther and her friend Sheila were preparing dinner. Anton was writing a sermon for an upcoming funeral.

Ian was lying on his bed reading a novel. His cell phone rang. "Hello, Ian Roberts."

"Hello Ian, Jim Bennet. How was your day over there?"

"Not sure until we finish this conversation. Have you made a decision?"

"We have. Is Anton around? I would like to have him on speaker if that is possible."

"Give me a moment. I need to go to the house."

Ian's heart began to pound. He had been preparing for the worst. His trust in Credence management was questionable. He rehearsed his arguments in his head over and over if the answer was no. Ian entered the living room. "Anton, Jim Bennet is on the phone. He wants to talk to us."

Esther came from the kitchen. She stood quietly behind the couch.

Anton began. "Hello Jim, hope you are well."

"Thank you, Anton." Jim continued, "Anton, the team met yesterday and had a lengthy discussion about your problem. From the information Ian gave us, Edward Bellamy researched it and presented his findings to Jordan West."

Ian interrupted. "Jim, was that the first time West new of those circumstances? I thought Anton revealed that to you before you left. Are you saying a decision to reject was made without that information?" Anton grabbed Ian's arm and put his finger to his lips. He needed Ian to be silent.

Anton jumped in "Jim, let's get to the point. Where are we now," Bennet was happy to move on.

"Okay, after reviewing the facts, we came to the conclusion, because of the economic changes in South Africa, you are indeed short of funds." Esther took a deep breath.

"Go on."

"Since it may be a year of construction time, we think a better number would be $97,000. That way, we will not have need to revisit this again. How does that sound?"

Esther raised her arms in the air and mouthed a smiling halleluiah. Ian and Anton exchanged smiles.

Anton spoke," Jim, that is wonderful news. You have done well for my people here in the township. God has put us together for a holy and benevolent purpose."

"Yes, he has, Anton." The smile on Jim's face could be heard through the phone.

"Tell Jordan, and all of you, we love you and you are blessed. Esther is crying. My staff will pray for all of you at service. Thank you, Jim." The phone call ended.

The last few days were taxing for Anton and Esther. They went to bed early. Holding each other between soft sheets and a heavy comforter, Anton broke the silence.

"He saved our Hospice and our relationship with Credence tonight, not just with his presentation and business knowledge, but his friends at Credence. He has shown us his loyalty to our mission. You did well Esther taking Ian to the prayer meeting and introducing him to the children."

"And you with Miriam, Anton."

"But the funeral was all Ian. He asked if he could go with me."

"Esther, none of this has been our idea. We did not find him, he found us. The Lord needed to test him, he is testing his faith, and testing his commitment. Now we must teach him to recognize when the Lord speaks to him."

"He hears it, Anton. You told me he calls it 'The hand in his back.' I saw it in his eyes and the silence in his heart at the prayer meeting. And you saw how our children accepted him immediately. He is a blessing. Thank you, Lord. Good night, my Love."

"Good night."

THE DEDICATION OF THE HOSPICE

PART 1: THE RETURN OF JORDAN

If it is possible for perception to be reality, then it is possible for reality to be flawed. To those who have not experienced adversity, the beauty of controlled chaos has not been enjoyed. The rotunda of this South African airport was such a place, a copious gathering where each person possessed their own unique agenda.

Inside, the climate was one of a late spring freshness mixed with the humid odors of human existence. Three weary travelers huddled together, their wrenching hands and roaming eyes scanning for a glimpse of their rescuer, but their innocent anxiety heightened by the lack of faith in the rescuer himself. Approaching thirty minutes, their leader's patience was growing thin. "Jordan," cried a voice in the crowd. Ian and Ezekiel appeared through the multitudes. But before Ian had a chance to say anything more, West lashed out. "Where have you been, Roberts? We have been waiting for more than thirty minutes. You were to be here at 1:30."

"I tried calling you, Jordan, but a strange voice answered. They did not speak English. Joanna gave me your number, but I must have written it down wrong."

"No, you wrote it down correctly. My phone was stolen. Even before I set foot on this continent, they stole my phone."

"Who Jordan, who stole your phone?"

"They did. C'mon Roberts, you know what I mean. They stole my phone on the plane."

"Someone pickpocketed you? That is common in the rotunda, but not on the plane. Or do you mean it happened in customs?"

"No Roberts, I was on the plane."

"You were sleeping?" Ian was trying to understand.

"No, I was awake. It needed to charge before we landed. There was an outlet in the bathroom."

Ian hoped Jordan was not going to say what came next. "I still don't understand."

West slowed down and proceeded as if talking to a child, "I plugged my charger, into the outlet, in the bathroom, on the plane. I returned to my seat. I only left it for twenty minutes, just enough charge to get through the airport and to the church." Ian stayed quiet with no expression. It was hard.

West shook his head, then gazed out over the masses. "Somebody out there has my phone. Some scum bag took my phone right out of the bathroom and took my charger too. This is a scary place, Roberts. I don't understand it. These people are all liars, cheats, and thieves." Ian still showed no expression. Laughter would have been appropriate, but not well received.

"Roberts, I have an idea. Call my number. Maybe we will hear it ring and catch the guy. Go ahead, Roberts, call it?"

Ian said nothing for a moment. A call would be futile, but he did as he was instructed. No ring was heard, but a voice answered in what sounded like an Eastern European accent. "Someone has answered, Jordan."

West swiftly snatched the phone from Ian's hand, "Look, I don't know who you are, but you stole my phone, hello, hello, I know you can hear me. Answer me, I want it back right now." Click. "Why that son-of-a-bitch hung up on me. We need to report this to security." Ian retrieved his phone quickly before it was smashed on the marble floor.

Ian took control. "Let's solve the problem, Jordan. There's a phone rental right over there. You can all get rental phones before we go any farther." Ian motioned for the entourage to follow him.

"No, that won't be necessary for us, Mr. Roberts. James and I still have our phones," said the young camera operator.

"I suggest you rent a phone here with an international sim card. Your calls will be a lot cheaper. Then you can pack your phones away and keep them safe."

West pouted all the way to the booth. "This place is such a hassle. The rental phone won't have my contacts. What good is a rental phone without my contacts? How will people call me? How will I call them?"

Ian smiled. "Jordan, when we get to the church, make a list of all the people you need to contact, then one of my young ladies will email Joanna. She can get the numbers and send them back."

"What do you mean, your young ladies?" West had a secondary agenda on this trip and Ian knew what it was.

"My employees, my transcriptionists. They are on the bus waiting for us. Jordan, take a deep breath. Have faith, all will be fine."

West didn't want a lecture from Ian on faith nor did he want to be reliant on him in any way. He found it abhorrent Ian was even present. He would make it clear to Anton; Ian had no position of authority in the Credence administration. But in the next few days, West would need him more than he imagined.

Everybody got a simple flip phone to complain about. Ian sent Ezekiel to retrieve the bus.

"Follow me, gentlemen." Ian led the group out of the rotunda to Curbside. The four stood shoulder to shoulder, engulfed by the throng of arriving passengers. Bedlam outside was the same as bedlam inside, only add honking horns and thick fumes. Ten minutes passed. Blasts of exhaust whooshed across their faces. Ezekiel arrived and double parked. He sprung from the driver's seat and scurried to the curb. He grabbed the camera bags along with Jordan's solo piece of luggage.

"Off, off, get off." Jordan began to tug.

"Jordan, that is Ezekiel. He is our driver. You just met him inside. He is putting your bag on the bus."

Just then a stocky security guard charged the bus, his whistle pulsated over and over. "No, no, let's go people. No stopping here. It is illegal. Move on." Ian paid no attention, neither did Ezekiel. The camera operator grabbed the rest of the bags. He and Ezekiel loaded them onto the bus. Jordan and James followed.

Ezekiel hit the gas. Horns continued as they did all day, every day. The security guards continued to bark orders as they did all day, every day. And Ezekiel joined in the symphony of horns as he snaked his way through the mess. And now, the bus was not only in the traffic, it was the traffic.

Jordan was visibly nervous about Ezekiel's driving. He came close to other cars, he cut people off, he honked continually. Ezekiel learned from the best. "Welcome to South Africa, Jordan. Anton taught me that traffic laws are only suggestions here. The first time I questioned him on his driving, he quoted Jesus Christ."

"Sure, he did, Roberts. Go ahead, what did Jesus Christ say about traffic laws two thousand years ago?"

"After he drove on the shoulder past thirty cars backed-up at a stop sign, then forced his way in at the front. I looked at him and said, 'Really, Anton?'"

Without even looking at me he said, "You know what Jesus Christ said to his apostles, Ian?"

I said, "No Anton, what did Jesus Christ say to his apostles?"

"He said, 'I am here for a greater purpose than to follow the rules.'"

"It does sounds like something Jesus would say. Where is that in the Bible, Roberts?"

"I have no idea, Jordan. I didn't ask. But that is how Anton thinks, and it works for him. It is fun to watch and learn." Ian gave West a big grin. The smile was not reciprocated, but the camera operator chuckled.

Out of the airport, West finally looked to the back of the bus. "Are those the young ladies you spoke of?" Six South Africans in their twenties waved at West with big smiles. They were so happy their emotions simulated popcorn popping.

"They are the reason we were late but be aware, South African time is plus or minus an hour. Punctuality only happens by accident. That will help your stress level once you accept it." This was the first time Ian felt West might have listened, but probably not.

"Hold that thought, Roberts." West instructed the camera operator to get the hand-held video camera from its case. He did, and within a minute he was ready to film. West instructed him to shoot traffic out the window. He then told the story of his long trip, and he told the camera an abridged version of the phone theft. He introduced his friend James. He made no mention of Ian. When finished, Ian assumed West forgot about the reason they were late. He did not.

"Okay Roberts, now what is the story with these young ladies of yours?" West had a suspicious look on his face.

"We were held up at the U.S. Embassy."

"The U.S. Embassy. Why were you at the U.S. Embassy? Did you get these young ladies or yourself in trouble? But that still doesn't explain why you were late. You were told the exact time? You should have planned better. You should have been waiting for us."

"I'll explain more at the restaurant." Ian needed to watch Ezekiel. He could get lost.

"Roberts, we don't have time for lunch. Joanna's itinerary says I am to meet with Anton as soon as I arrive. We need to shoot footage, edit it, and send it back to Credence for tomorrow night's service. That is our top priority. We have no time for lunch."

"Jordan, Anton told me he could not meet with you until 17:00. He told me to take you to lunch, then show you around the compound."

"Joanna has my itinerary planned down to the minute. The congregation back home is excited to see this Hospice Dedication. And use American time, Roberts, not that seventeen hundred thing."

"Okay, five o'clock, and all will be fine, Jordan. He must meet with the women who are cooking, the musicians, and he must supervise the tent construction."

"No, Roberts, I need the footage today, in the sunlight. You are not listening to me, are you Roberts?"

"I hear you. You will get your footage. We will be back at the church by 4:00, I promise you. That gives you three full hours of good light. And there is no place for you to eat in the township; no place where you would feel safe."

"Roberts, why are you and Anton fighting me?" Jordan was now impatient with both Ian and Anton's attitude. West saw himself as the sponsor, the financial supporter of this Hospice. He needed to be the priority. "We are on a tight schedule. We must get the footage back to Credence by 5:00 P.M. so they can prepare it for Saturday night. That will give us one hour. Now do you understand?"

"That means you must transfer by 11:00 P.M tonight."

West shook his head. "Roberts, I just said 5:00 P.M." Jordan glanced at the camera operator who was staying out of whatever was going on between Jordan and Ian, however, he was shaking his head in the affirmative. Jordan went quiet. It finally sunk in; the time difference.

Jordan did not take orders from anyone except the Chairman of the Board; certainly not a non-Christian as Kristin described him. Jordan accepted that, but only if Ian knew his place.

The bus arrived at the restaurant. All got comfortable. "I still want to know what the U.S. Embassy has to do with you being late. But before we order, I must make you aware, I am not authorized to pay for their lunches nor for yours. I can pay for the bus driver since he is Anton's employee."

Ian decided to give an abridged version of the Embassy. He told Jordan he started a medical transcription business, how the ladies from Anton's congregation needed professional training, and Visas needed to be obtained so they could return to Charlotte with him. But as he spoke, he could tell, West was not interested.

PART 2: THE TOUR

It was November 4th. The year was 2006. The sky flaunted a faint blue hue and a peaceful breeze whispered gently over the compound. As promised, the bus carrying Ian, his shipment of young ladies, and guests arrived sharply at 4:00, not an African minute or hour late. The grounds swarmed with a horde of Anton's congregational volunteers. They resembled an ant hill in full construction. A canvas circus tent stood tall in front of the newly finished Hospice. Titanic poles, twenty feet in height, lifted the construct allowing an elongated stage at one end and six hundred folding chairs to be strategically arranged beneath it. Everyone proudly awaited the arrival of dignitaries, renown pastors, bishops, and honored guests in less than twenty-four hours.

The congregation meticulously raked the barren soil as others followed behind arranging folding chairs in well-ordered rows. The stage was ready for the triumphant singing and dancing of Anton and his teens. Large speakers were positioned on each side of the stage; smaller ones positioned in the back of the tent. Beautiful arrays of flowers were arranged flawlessly by the elderly women in appreciation of their Lord's blessing. And finally, the beautiful carved wooden cross was moved from the sanctuary and placed behind Anton's pulpit so it may cast its loving light upon this sea of grateful followers. All of this to honor a Hospice, a Taj Mahal dedicated to a poor Black township ravaged by a terrible virus. Anton's vision, inspired by God's love and his mercy, now stood amid the suffering. At this moment in time, Jesus seemed touchable.

Ian escorted West around the compound as the camera operator shot his footage. As they walked, Ian explained to West the history of the school buildings, the expansion of the church, the additions of Anton's office and the office building for the medical transcription business. In turn, West briefly relayed the history of the school and the church to the camera. As they passed by the preschoolers, the children prepared their backpacks for the weekend. They waved to their Uncle Ian. They called out his name. Ian waved back with a smile. "Would you like to meet them, Jordan. They are precious. They are angels. They are waving to you."

IAN AND ANTON

"They are waving to you, Roberts, not me. I told you we do not have time for that. I must get footage to Credence by what time?"

"By 11:00 o'clock our time. That will make it 4:00 o'clock their time," said Ian. "All will be fine."

"But what if something goes wrong?"

"Nothing will go wrong, Jordan. Let's move on."

"Why are you always so sure everything will be fine, Roberts?"

"Because I've been around Anton and this place since 2004. It always is." West rolled his eyes. He perceived Ian's confidence as arrogance.

As they walked on, the little cherubs kept waving. Ian veered over for a moment and gave as many hugs as possible. "Let's go, Roberts," called West. "You can play with the kids some other time. We need to get footage of the Hospice before it gets dark."

They crossed the barren field. Ian was stopped once again. West gave out with a sigh of frustration. It was Miriam. Ian extended his hand. "Miriam, how are you, dear? How is Ava and how is your mother?"

Miriam took his hand and with a half kneel, she kissed it. Ian placed his other hand gently onto Miriam's cheek and looked caringly into her eyes. "They are all well, Uncle Ian. Mother is doing laundry work. Her back hurts most of the time. And Ava is doing so well in school. Thank you so much, Uncle Ian. You are blessed."

"Miriam, this is Pastor West from Credence in America. He has come to celebrate the Dedication of our Hospice. Pastor West, this is Miriam."

"Hello, nice to meet you." He turned to Ian. "Robert's we must get this shoot done before the shadows appear."

"Yes, Jordan." He turned to Miriam, "Take loving care of your girls and give them a hug for me. You are blessed, Miriam."

"You as well, Uncle Ian. I will see you tomorrow." She bowed and walked on.

They continued to the Hospice. West leaned towards James. "What was that all about? Who does he think he is, the Pope?"

James shrugged his shoulders. "He does seem popular with the people, doesn't he?"

"That's why he is dangerous. People follow him. He is not clergy, he has no title, he holds no office. It is a hero worship I cannot figure out. But I have some ideas I need to explore."

"Have you talked to Anton about him?"

"I will before I leave. I want your opinion before I do. That's one of the reasons you are here."

Sunlight streamed into the lobby of the Hospice as the day approached dusk. Shadows majestically highlighted the floor. The first floor was furnished with the bare necessities, just enough to exemplify its purpose. The reception offices contained desks, but no office equipment. The camera operator constantly rolled as Jordan performed a guided tour. Only one of the patient's wards was ready to be occupied.

"Do you have office and medical equipment to show yet? And what about supplies?"

"They're in the vault at the school. We pull them out as needed."

"The vault? I don't understand?"

"Theft, Jordan. If it's known we have medical supplies, PC's, copiers, and such in here, they're gone."

"You mean stolen? You don't have locks on the doors and windows?"

"We do, but we also have a roof. They cut through our tile roof last year and stole a copier and two PC's. Lifted them right through the ceiling. That's why we have a vault. Let me take you to the second floor." The group climbed the stairs and into a large open space. The room was vacant, the walls patched with concrete, the floors unsealed.

"This is what cost us both one hundred thousand dollars? Still feel good about it, Roberts?" James looked at West with a wrinkled forehead. He was not following, and he was not supposed to hear that.

"I do Jordan. The second floor needed to be done now. It will serve a great purpose someday."

"Like what, you said more patients?"

"No, I never gave you a specific. Anton and I felt it was the right thing to do for the patient's below, and we are sure it will have a purpose."

"What might that be then?"

"That will be revealed to us in time." West rolled his eyes.

IAN AND ANTON

"Will this second floor be called 'The Roberts Wing'?" Jordan starred at Ian. "And what's with the patched walls? Why isn't it complete? It looks like somebody screwed up. Did you run out of money again?" Ian could tell West was insinuating something. Ian needed to be careful.

"The problem, Jordan, was all about good intentions. As we are all aware, one of Anton's foremost priorities, besides bringing people to Jesus Christ, is his Black Empowerment doctrine, creating work for his people in the township."

"Yes, Ian, I've been reminded many times. I do support him on that. But what about all these concrete patches on the walls?"

"After we obtained the funding for the second floor...."

West interrupted, "You mean, you and Anton. Go on."

"Yes, after Anton and I obtained the funding, Anton approached me. He wanted to discuss the roof. He needed my opinion."

"Something was different from the budget, I assume. Not exchange rate this time?"

"No, after the initial bid from a quality roofer, there came a second bid from a Black start-up company. Now Anton had two bids, one from a Black-owned company and one from a White-owned company."

Jordan interrupted, "The problem was the Black company was more expensive and he had to make a financial decision against his doctrine."

"No, it was the opposite. The Black company came in significantly lower."

"I don't get it. What was the problem?"

"Anton struggled with it. He knew the quality of the White company was superior, which challenged his Black Empowerment. He told me the roof was the most critical part of the entire construction project."

"So where do the patches come in?"

"Anton hired the Black company. Remember, this opening was scheduled four months ago, and it was pushed back until now."

"I do. I assumed you were behind on your timeline."

"No, we were on schedule. I was here four months ago. When I met with Anton, he had a look on his face that was chilling. I only saw it once before. He brought me up here to show me this room."

"Go on."

"While he was visiting his former church in Namibia, the roofers ripped all the copper wiring out of the walls. Copper has a good street price on the scrap market. I mean, they pulled it right out of the walls with their bare hands, like a rope in a tug of war."

"Like how they brazenly stole my phone." Ian and James made eye contact. Ian continued.

"That is why we were delayed. The electricians had to rewire, and the White roofing company finished the job."

"But the company reimbursed you for the theft?"

"No, they said it wasn't their workers who stole the copper, but it was. The neighbors saw them do it but were afraid to speak up."

"How about the police?"

"Right, the police." Ian smirked. "In the end we had to rewire the whole second floor, fix the walls and finish the roof. It cost an additional $50,000."

"And the money came from where?"

"Anton felt it was a problem caused by his decision, so he borrowed $50,000 on his own home."

"I guess he found out Black Empowerment doesn't always work."

"In this environment, Jordan, things rarely workout the way we plan. But they do workout according to God's plan. Anton has taught me to have faith and that faith has taught me to trust. God watches over this place. This cannot be a series of coincidences."

"That's enough, Roberts. Can we get this footage sent back to Credence? And I must meet with Anton. I have no idea the schedule for tomorrow other than the Dedication starts at 2:00 P.M."

Ian led the group to the transcription office to transmit their footage.

PART 3: THE BATTLEGROUND

Dusk advanced on the compound. The soft breeze of the afternoon was slowly picking up in intensity. Miniature dust devils danced their way across the grounds. Volunteers placed their finishing touches on the stage, some straightened renegade chairs into perfect alignment, some raked those last phantom footprints out of existence. Anton's congregation felt such pride in themselves and in their devotion to their God.

Ian set the camera operator in front of a PC, one that traded voice and document files between South Africa and the States. The software was rudimentary. It took the camera operator only a few minutes to figure it out. He said, "Mr. Roberts, have you ever transferred video files on this PC? What is your bandwidth?"

"I don't know exactly. I know we transmit at an acceptable rate for our own purposes. But those are voice and data only."

The camera operator began the transmission. Ian left the room to call Anton. While he was out, the camera operator looked at West. "Jordan, we may have a problem."

West went into panic mode. "What now? What are you going to tell me, we can't get this footage back to Credence? Don't say it. I knew it. Roberts is worthless. He is incompetent."

"No Jordan, not at all. But you need to know it will take longer than if we were back home."

"How much longer?"

"Back home it would take fifteen to twenty minutes."

"And here?"

"Hour and a half, two hours."

"But it can be done by eleven o'clock?"

"Yes, we have plenty of time. We will need to hang out here for a bit longer than we expected."

"Good, keep going."

After a few minutes, Ian reentered the room." Jordan, I just spoke with Anton. He apologizes. He is still busy and will be for the rest of the night. He said he will meet with you tomorrow morning over breakfast at his house."

"Tomorrow morning? Credence is funding this whole thing and I'm not feeling I'm a priority. We need some recognition, some appreciation, some notoriety. Who are you, Roberts? You sound like Anton's assistant? Is that all you are, his secretary?"

"I do what I am asked to do, Jordan. All will be fine. Like I said, things follow a strange plan over here."

"What about the rain, Roberts? What will that do to this strange plan you speak of? I thought this was high desert?" West was now being smug. He was getting tired of Ian's attitude, even more than before today.

Ian went to the window. A solid wall of black sky was approaching from the West. A strong wind was picking up, leading the way for the darkness. Dust kicked up and filled the air. Ian did not recall rain in the forecast for at least a week. He turned back towards Jordan. "All will be fine, Jordan. It's just a pop-up thunderstorm. They happen from time to time. This could be a good thing. It will keep the dust down for tomorrow." West shook his head again at Ian's optimism.

Suddenly the sky lit up like a flash from a camera. A crack of thunder rolled over the compound. The windows shook. A sheet of rain was now visible. Huge raindrops scattered across the groomed landscape like tiny meteorites attacking the earth. The bolts and claps were coming closer and closer together. Then a big one hit. Intense wind gusts slapped against the sides of the buildings. Rain pelted hard against the walls and windows. People ran for the shelter of Anton's offices and the church. Others ran for the safety of the tent. Then it happened. Looking out the window over the assaulted landscape, Ian witnessed the entire tent collapse like an imploded smokestack. He heard the horrific clanking of the huge steel poles crashing onto the helpless workers. Ian bounced down the steps and into the storm. Lightning was cracking, the wind pushing Ian and the other rescuers sideways. One by one, those under the tent were found and pulled into the tempest, frightened but unharmed. Some showed small cuts and bruises on their face and hands; some, their faces caked with mud from the small rivers flowing under the canvas. Then, just as quickly as the storm came, it went. The sky cleared and the wind returned to a soft fresh breeze. It lasted less than fifteen minutes. And, in those remaining minutes of daylight, the sky was transformed into a magnificent orange sunset cast in peace. Nighttime was upon them.

Ian, soaked like a river otter, his shoes covered with mud, made his way to find Anton and Esther. He found them in the sanctuary where they comforted those traumatized by the brutal strike.

"You all okay?" asked Ian.

"We're good. You okay? How about West and his friends? Are they safe?"

"They're upstairs transmitting their video. I need to check on them. I'll talk to you later. We should be back at the house in a couple of hours. Wait." Ian looked around.

"What is it, Ian."

"The power is out, not good; no power; no transmission. They are intent on getting that footage to Credence tonight. They must be flipping out. Will we have the electricity back any time soon?"

"I would not count on it." Then Anton hesitated. "Wait, follow me. Let's look." Ian and Anton climbed to the second floor of the sanctuary. "Look out there." Anton pointed.

"What, where?"

"Way over there. That distant glow on the horizon. That's the mall. Their electricity is on. The storm must have missed them."

"What are you thinking?"

"We went to a cybercafe over a year ago to test your transmissions, remember? I am sure that place is still in business. Get West and his friends together and I'll have Ezekiel drive you over. You can grab dinner while you're there."

"Right, and it's probably a much broader bandwidth than here. Sounds perfect. The mall closes at 10:00 on Friday, right?"

"Yes, go. We have things under control here. I'm glad you're here this weekend to take care of them. I have no one else that could have done it. Now go."

"See you back at the house. Get some rest. You too, Esther."

"Ian, I always remember what my father, Pastor Nkosi, would say when things seemed dark and hopeless."

"What's that?"

He'd look me in the eye and say, "Remember son, it looks bad now, but 'Sunday's Comin,' Yes, it is, my boy, 'Sunday's Comin'."

Ian gave Anton a puzzled look. "I have no idea what you are talking about. What does that mean?"

"You'll understand someday, Ian, because I'll make sure you understand. Just remember those words." Anton gave him a sly smile. Esther did as well.

PART 4: THE VICTORY LAP

Ian called the mall. It was confirmed. They had electricity and the ability to complete the transmission before ten o'clock was possible. Once West was talked off the ledge, Ian explained his options. He could surrender to the misfortunes of the day and get a good night's rest or pack up and head to the mall. Without hesitation, and with their luggage still on the bus, the camera operator grabbed his equipment. They headed out.

Silence normally reigned over the compound this time of night, but it did not. As they loaded onto the bus, Ian heard the muffled sound of voices emanating mysteriously from somewhere. The bus trudged over the muddy grounds and as it did, Ian noticed candlelight flickering in the window of Anton's office. He rose from his seat and placed his hand on Ezekiel's shoulder. "Stop, Ezekiel, stop the bus." Ezekiel slid to a stop. Ian looked back at West, "Jordan, I'll be right back. I want to make sure everyone is okay in there."

"No, come on Roberts. Anton can handle that. We are running out of time. We need to get to the mall right now. Roberts, let's go, now."

Ignoring West, Ian hopped down the steps of the bus. Approaching the building, the muffled voices were getting louder and more distinct. They were not cries for help. They were numinous, almost transcendent. Opening the door, Ian entered a room filled with flickering candlelight. The odor of wet clothing and damp hair permeated. It was packed with those of Anton's flock. Portia, Anton's assistant, stood amid all of them, her arms raised to the heavens, her voice crying out in prayer. "This is our day, Satan, not yours. It will never be your day here. See us, hear us. This is our day. You will not kill our joy. You can try, but you will fail today, and you will fail every day. You will lose again. Just as God's Archangel Michael defeated you in the heavens. God and his army will continue to defeat you." The room came forth with powerful amens and halleluiahs. "We are the children of God. We are the followers of your son, Jesus Christ. We are powerful and undaunting in our faith. You will never defeat us. We have built this monument for our Lord's poor and his sick. You will not defeat us with your virus or with your diseases. You will not defeat us with your suffering. You will not defeat his son, Jesus Christ, our Lord and

Savior. Your storm has failed you once more." The amens burst forward and louder than ever. One after another, Anton's flock took turns rebuking their enemy.

Ian prayed with them. He gave Portia a hug and whispered in her ear, "I will be right back. I need you to repeat what you said when I return with Pastor West." Ian ran back to the bus.

"Jordan, you must come with me for a moment. You need to see this. You need to hear this. You must give them your blessing."

"Roberts, we do not have time for this. We have just over three hours to get this film back to Credence. Why do you not do as I say? Why do you always have to be difficult?"

"Jordan, it will only take five minutes. They need you. I pray you come with me for just this moment. What's going on in there is why we are here. Why you are here. Why Credence is here? It will reveal to you your mission. For your sake, I plead with you, just this one time, don't fight me."

"Okay Roberts, five minutes, then we go." West was frustrated. He got up from his seat.

West followed Ian into the building. As they entered, West was taken back. Silhouetted by candlelight, shadows dancing on the ceiling, people raised their voices against the enemy of their Lord. They had cast him out from their grounds. Portia turned to Ian, then placed her hand on West's forehead. "Satan, you have challenged the wrong people. The Lord has brought us Pastor West from America. He and his people have built this haven from suffering so our people can die with dignity and respect. He and his people have joined us as God's warriors against you." The amens abounded. "You will not kill our joy, Satan. This is our day." Cheering filled the room.

Jordan was stunned. He raised his hand over the people. He began to speak. Silence dominated. All listened intently to what God's preacher from America was to say. "Blessing to all of our Lord's believers. I am here with you all. My people from America are here with you all. We are all one person in the name of our Lord, Jesus Christ. And just as Jesus rebuked the great storm and calmed the Sea of Galilee centuries ago, he has done it once again. Today he has strengthened our faith in him even more. He loves us. He will always love us. As he said in Corinthians, 'So now faith, hope and love abide; but the greatest of these is love.' This is our day, a day of faith and hope and love for those in pain. Our faith in the Lord has once again been victorious. Bless you all and peace be with you." Hands and amens were once again raised to the heavens.

West turned and left the building. With chill bumps on his skin, Ian lifted his hand to all as he exited. Tears were in his eyes. He hugged Portia. As they approached the bus, Ian looked at West. "That was moving, Jordan. I am glad you followed me?"

"First off, I will never follow you Roberts, but I can understand how these people have tainted your loyalties. They may be simple people, but they are dedicated to their faith. Okay, that's enough of this. Let's get to the mall."

PART 5: THE DEDICATION

Morning broke on this blessed day. God's seed planted inside Anton decades prior survived its long and difficult gestation and now it had come to fruition. Anton and Esther managed to grab a few hours of sleep, but as the early morning light peaked over the horizon, Anton's phone was assaulted. Damage to the tent was beyond repair and the grounds far too muddy to insult six hundred pairs of courtly shoes. As the storm subsided, Anton made an instantaneous decision to move the Dedication inside to the sanctuary. Unable to seat as many inside as out, the windows would be opened, and speakers placed outside allowing all to hear. This Dedication would not and could not be stopped.

Anton entered the kitchen. It was bustling. Without saying good morning to anyone, he headed straight for Ian. "Where are West and his friends? They're out of bed, I hope. He wanted a brief interview with me this morning and I can squeeze him in right now. Get him down here but tell him it must be brief."

"That's not going to happen, Anton."

"Why not? Don't tell me he is still asleep?"

"Doesn't matter if he is. After we successfully transmitted his footage back to Credence, he insisted he needed a good night's sleep in a comfortable bed, and he needed a nice breakfast."

"He changed the plans on me? He was supposed to sleep here last night. This is the only time I have for his interview and he's not here. That storm has...."

Ian interrupted, "Anton, I know, the storm complicated things, but there is plenty of time for an interview. They were travelling thirty hours, then they were on the run all day yesterday. Certainly, you understand. All will be fine."

Anton sighed. "I understand, it's West that does not understand. He needs to realize things are never easy here, and certainly not comfortable. He is not on vacation; this is not America. He can rest on his plane ride home."

Ian smiled and pretended to stroke a nonexistent goatee. "Anton, I've never seen you this stressed before and you do have reason to be stressed.

But what do you always tell me? Everything works out according to God's plan. You know, the faith thing."

Anton took a deep breath and looked back with raised eyebrows, "Okay, Uncle Ian, I get it." Anton smiled. "Where is he now?"

"Ezekiel and I checked him into The Safari Hotel. It was the only place close, and Ezekiel told me you house guests there often."

"Okay, that works. Thank you, Ian. Sorry if I snapped at you." He squeezed Ian's arm. "I need you and Ezekiel to get him to the church by 12:30. I might be able to squeeze the interview in then. What you do with him between now and then, I don't care."

"I will tell him, but he will not be happy."

"Well, if he complains tell him, if he had been here for breakfast, the interview would be finished."

"I'll tell him he can have an interview at 12:30."

"No wait, 12:30 won't work either. Promise him before the reception. That will give him plenty of time to send back footage. Have him at the church by 1:00."

"I'll tell him."

"No wait, tell him it will be after the reception."

"I'll take care of it, Anton."

"And did I tell you I moved the Dedication into the sanctuary? That tent is in a heap and the tent people cannot come back until Monday."

"I heard. Glad the storm was last night. Can you imagine?"

Anton looked at Ian. "He would not have dared to attack us today." Ian smiled. "Ian, tell West I would like to have a one-on-one after service tomorrow at my house. I want to get his take on all this before he leaves on Monday."

"One-on-one, Anton? Sure, I'll tell him." Ian gave Anton a smirk.

"Yes, one-on-one. What's that look all about, Ian?"

"Nothing Anton, I'll tell him."

Ian separated Ezekiel from his breakfast. "Let's go, kid. We need to give the boys the new plan. Grab some toast and juice." Ian grabbed an apple. "We are taking the minivan today. Do you remember how to get to the hotel? I don't."

"I have been there many times, Uncle Ian. I know it was dark when we were there, but did you see the lions?"

"Lions, they have lions? No, I didn't, but I will make sure I do this morning. They have lions, really?"

"Yes sir, Uncle Ian, they have lions, big ones, a lion, and a lioness. And a tall fence, thank the Lord." They both laughed.

Ezekiel drove to the hotel. They parked. They sauntered into the lobby. West, James, and the camera operator were seated at a table in front of a powerful two-story stone fireplace adorned with the head of a water buffalo. The breakfast buffet was copious. "Good morning, gentlemen. You look well-rested and well-fed."

"Good morning, Roberts." West greeted him with a grin. "Yesterday was one of those never-ending days. And after that fine dinner last night and a few drinks from the scotch bottle, I fell asleep with my clothes on. This place is great Roberts, good idea."

"Thank you, Jordan. Glad you like it. It was Ezekiel's idea. You need to thank him." Ian placed his arm around Ezekiel's shoulder and smiled. Ezekiel grinned with pride.

"We need to leave soon. Anton said he would meet with me this morning. Have you seen him? We need to do this interview and talk about the service."

Ian knew he was about to get another taste of 'The Wrath of Jordan.' "Yes, Jordan, I saw him. In fact, I just left him. He was headed to the church."

"Alright, we can leave here in what, thirty minutes?"

"At this point, Jordan, there is no hurry. Due to the storm last night, Anton moved the Dedication inside. He's been on the phone non-stop since sunrise. The Dedication is only five hours away and he has a lot to do."

"Wait, are you saying he doesn't have time for me, again? He promised me interview footage this morning. And I need to know what he wants in my message."

"I know, and he knows. He was disappointed, but he did have half an hour set aside this morning at breakfast for you, but you changed your plans. He couldn't wait."

"It just keeps going, doesn't it? I need some cooperation here. My people will be terribly upset if we do not get some gratitude on film. They deserve it. They have given Anton a lot of money from their pockets." Ian let him vent.

"Anton wants you there at 1:00, so I will pick you up here at 12:30."

"What are we supposed to do for the next three hours, nothing?"

"We could drive you through the township and you could see the hustle and bustle of the marketplace. That would kill a couple of hours."

"No, we have been on the go for days. We will just stay here until 12:30. What a mess you have over here."

"Jordan, all will be fine. Rest for a while. I assume you already know what you are going to say today. And you will get footage of the Dedication, of your preaching, and of the guests at the reception. All that will be left is your interview with Anton. He told me to promise you, it will be following the reception."

West sat at the table shaking his head in disbelief. "I am so tired of you telling me everything will be fine. It's not, Roberts. It's not fine. How do you people ever get anything done over here? You have no discipline. You have no punctuality. This whole thing has been chaos since the moment we landed. Somebody needs to grab the controls. I'll see how we can get him some professional help over here."

"I am sure Anton will be appreciative of any help Credence can give him. In the meantime, we have no choice but to have faith God will take care of these people."

"Really Roberts, that coming from you? You're not even a Christian from what Kristin tells me. Come on, you know what I mean; a businessman over here preaching to me about faith?"

"Jordan, I am a businessman at home. Over here, I am a social entrepreneur. There is a difference." West rolled his eyes.

With a few hours to kill, Ian and Ezekiel left for the church to help in any way they could. At noon they returned to pick up West and his friends. The morning dew was in the past. The sky was deep blue. The air was cleansed following the strike on the compound. As they waited, the two walked the grounds enjoying the zebras, giraffes, wart hogs and, as Ezekiel promised, the lion and his mate. They found their way to a bench across from the majestic cats. It was a pleasant morning.

West appeared through the lobby door. "Okay boys, get me to the church on time, as they say. We can get a few interviews with some dignitaries before the big show."

James interjected, "Jordan, do you want to interview Mr. Roberts while we have him here?"

"No," said Jordan. Ian smiled.

They walked briskly down the path to the van. Out of nowhere, the male lion charged the fence. It went right for West. A cloud of dust exploded into the air. It was chilling. It was violent. West fell into a bush. "What the hell was that?" West shouted. He was shaking.

Ezekiel leaned over and whispered, "Uncle Ian, I have never seen that lion do that before, not to anyone, ever. Usually, he just sleeps all day and swats flies."

It was now only one hour before the Dedication. The sanctuary was filling with dignitaries, distinguished visitors, bishops, archbishops, and politicians from all over South Africa. The congregation, including the beloved Momma Mary, watched with delight as news crews scanned the room.

The Dedication was resurrected in one morning like the Phoenix, like Lazarus, like Jesus Christ from the dead. The flowers were rescued from under the tent, repotted and rearranged with a special kind of love. Mud was washed from the folding chairs. They were repositioned inside the sanctuary. As guests arrived, Esther greeted them as the event's official host. No one was more suited for the job. But Anton, he was last seen walking into the township with his father, two hours prior.

Noticing Ian had arrived with West and his friends, Esther approached them. "Pastor West, we are so glad you are here. When it is time to be seated, we need you and your friends to take those three seats on the aisle in the second row. That will allow you clear access to the stage when Anton introduces you." Jordan nodded his head. "And Ian, I want you to sit next to me in the first row." Ian nodded.

West imparted a curious glance towards James. Esther took Ian by the arm, and they made their way to the front. On the way, Ian whispered to Esther "Of all the dignitaries and truly important people in attendance today, why do you have me sitting in such a prestigious place next to you?"

"Because, Ian, you are the only person here that doesn't scare me." Ian was surprised at her charming response. It was so meek. "Ian, look around. So many of these people are blessed with riches and power beyond my comprehension, but you." Esther hesitated.

Ian smiled once more. "I know, I'm a nobody and I'm fine with that, Esther."

"No, Ian, let me finish." She squeezed his forearm. "I'm saying, many people are blessed. You are blessed. But you are different. Not only are you blessed, but you are a blessing as well. Few are both."

Another variety of moisture entered Ian's eyes. In this surrounding, however, a tear was inappropriate. He patted her hand. "I love all of you. You have been so kind to me. I have learned so much. There is nothing more God could give me."

Esther jumped on that. "Yes, there is Ian. You need a wife. You need to be married." Ian grinned sheepishly.

"Esther, not this again." He stared into her eyes with a smile. "Jesus Christ wasn't married."

With no hesitation, she smiled and said softly, "Ian Roberts, he is Jesus Christ. You are Ian. Let us sit."

People began to take their seats. As soon as Ian sat, like a spring on the chair, he bounced back to his feet. A dignified woman approached him wearing a long slender blue and orange kente print dress, along with a matching Doek head wrap. She was stunning, yet unpretentious. She was South African. "I have been instructed to sit here with you and Mrs. Nkosi. Is that correct?" Ian extended his hand. She did not take it.

Esther overheard and intervened. "Yes, that is correct. Please, join us, and please call me Esther. This is our good friend, Mr. Ian Roberts. He and Anton work closely together here in the township."

Ian was reluctant to extend his hand a second time. It felt unfitting to do so. "Good afternoon, I am Ian Roberts. It is a pleasure to meet you."

"You as well, Mr. Roberts. You don't sound South African. You have an American accent; I would say Mid-Western?"

"You are correct. I live in the United States and travel here a few times a year."

"And where do you stay when you are here, Mr. Roberts?"

"I stay with Pastor Anton, Esther, and their family. It is wonderful, a little chilly in the wintertime, but I would not stay anywhere else."

"Here in the township? You mean you stay here in the township, Mr. Roberts?"

"I do, but I am sorry, I do not understand your question."

"I am asking if you feel safe in our township?"

Esther leaned in, "Deputy Speaker, we consider Mr. Roberts one of our family. Our people call him Uncle Ian. I assure you, he is quite safe."

"Did you say Deputy Speaker, Esther?" This time he did extend his hand. "I'm so sorry, but we have not been formally introduced." This time she embraced his hand firmly and gave Ian a subtle, but intriguing smile.

"Anton and I are friends from the Apartheid days. I am Michele Ntombela-kaMandela. And yes, I am the Deputy Speaker of Parliament."

"It is a pleasure. Would you like to sit, Madame Speaker?"

The woman sat down, leaned closer to Ian, and whispered, "I appreciate the official address, but when we are out of the spotlight, I insist you call me Michele. That is pronounced 'Me and jelly only with a ch'."

"I would be honored. And call me Ian, but please, not Uncle Ian."

She smiled. "Of course, but tell me more about why you are here in our country, especially why you stay here in one of our townships with no fear. We do have a lot of crime."

They sat. No one interrupted their conversation; no reporters, no dignitaries. The conversation flowed as if they were the only two in the room. Ian noticed two men in black suits and sunglasses stationed at each end of their row. Those men were undoubtedly the reason she and Ian were left alone.

The droning of the crowd receded as the teenagers took the stage. Dressed festively, they grabbed their instruments. They plugged them into their amplifiers. The time had come. The presence of the Lord was upon this born-again Christian church, a church in the middle of a poor Black township stricken by the worst AIDS epidemic on earth. The singing and dancing began. The crowd rose to their feet. Voices were raised to the heavens. With knees high, Anton and his teenagers danced the Toyi-Toyi. The people outside danced as well. The dignitaries, although not dancing, joined with their smiles and their hearts. All hands were clapping.

Next, Momma Mary and her beloved AIDS workers were honored with loud cheers and applause for their bravery and devotion. Revered clergymen gave short messages of appreciation and respect. Jordan West received a robust round of applause as Anton introduced him, letting all know Credence was their source of funding.

Now, the time had arrived. It was time for Anton. But, as West left the stage and Anton approached the pulpit, Esther unexpectedly rose from her chair, and ascended to the stage. The congregation cheered for their beloved matron. Anton was puzzled. He gave her a curious nod.

As only Esther could, she graciously welcomed everyone. She then proceeded. "We have a special birthday in our house today. A man who most of you surrounding our sanctuary outside know and respect. And I am blessed to know him more every day."

Ian began to quiver. 'Oh no, she isn't going to do this. Please God let it be someone else.'

"He has shown our youth a White man can love them and respect them. He has shown our adults a White man and a Black man can stand side by side as equals. He works with us as a teammate, not as a boss. He is a mentor to both young and old. He is creating jobs for many of you. And he has become a close friend to Anton, my children and myself. He has been blessed by God in so many ways. And he does it all with humility. He has been sent to us by God and he doesn't know it yet. Let us sing Happy Birthday to our Uncle Ian." She motioned for Ian to rise. A respectful wave of applause entered the sanctuary from the surrounding windows, "Let us sing."

Harmonies filled the air as only South Africans can sing. Ian was overcome. It was one more on his list. He raised his hand to those in the back of the church and to those watching from outside. He turned to the stage. He bowed respectfully to Esther and to Anton with hands folded. Anton gave Ian a huge smile, along with the classic stroking of his goatee.

The song ended. The room clapped one more time. Ian sat. Modesty filled his soul. Michele put her hand on top of Ian's hand. She could see he was unable to speak. "It seems they love you around here, Uncle Ian." Her smile was genuine. Ian regrouped, staring without sound at the floor.

THE DEDICATION OF THE HOSPICE

Silence embraced the sanctuary like a parent hugging its child. It was time for this resolute man of God to show his appreciation to the Lord who planted the seed of hope within him and delivered all those necessary to open his doors. He began with his four favorite words, "Let us pray together." It was the 23rd Psalm. Nothing could have been more appropriate for the Dedication of this Hospice devoted to the sick and the dying, and blessings to the caregivers.

The Lord is my shepherd; I shall not want.

He maketh me to lie down in green pastures: he leadeth me beside the still waters.

He restoreth my soul: he leadeth me in the paths of righteousness for his name's sake.

Yea, though I walk through the valley of the shadow of death, I will fear no evil: for thou art with me; thy rod and thy staff they comfort me.

Thou preparest a table before me in the presence of mine enemies: thou anointest my head with oil; my cup runneth over.

Surely goodness and mercy shall follow me all the days of my life: and I will dwell in the house of the Lord forever.

The room filled with soft joy as they all came together like a flock dating back to the days of David. The room finished the words of their Lord with a tender 'Amen.'

Anton began by relaying the history of the vision, a vision coming to him before HIV/AIDS existed. He shared how God and his father, Pastor Nkosi Sr., groomed him for this day. He gave a brief recap of how the vision was shared between Pastor West and himself in Chicago. He thanked his architect and enthusiastically thanked Esther and his children. But now it was time for Anton to do what he loved most, preach.

"I want you all to know God's presence lives within all of us here today. He is in this room. He is deep in our souls. Feel it. The Lord is here. He is resting on your very shoulders. He is deep in hearts. He is the love we so wonderfully give to our people who suffer from this terrible disease, a disease that is greatly misunderstood. A disease that, by the end of this year, will have infected eight million of us here in South Africa, and is still infecting two thousand of us each and every day. A disease that has killed over one and a half million of our brothers and sisters. A disease that has created nearly two million orphans and that number continues to rise. A disease that tears apart families and moral structures for so many of our brethren living without Jesus Christ in their lives." Scattered amens came forth.

Anton paused. Silence ruled the sanctuary. He moved from behind his pulpit and slipped off his shoes. His naked feet were revealed to the world. He raised his arms and spread them. He was an angel from the heavens. "Children of God, followers of our Lord and Savior Jesus Christ, at this time I ask you all to remove your shoes and stand together with me. Let the bareness of your feet feel the ground on which you stand." Without reading from his Bible, but reading from his heart, he began reciting Exodus 3:4.

"So, Moses thought, 'I must go over and see this marvelous sight. Why is the bush not burning up?' When the LORD saw that he had gone over to look, God called out to him from within the bush, 'Moses, Moses! Here I am,' he answered. 'Do not come any closer,' God said. 'Take off your sandals, for this place where you are standing is Holy Ground.'"

With that, organ music began to flow softly through the sanctuary and into the spirits of the multitude.

"To all who come here today, the Lord has commanded us to take off our shoes, to take off our sandals, and to pray together with me, for at this moment, in this barren field, we are all standing on Holy Ground. This ground does not belong to Africa. This ground does not belong to our government. This ground does not belong to you or to me. This belongs to our Almighty God. He has reclaimed it. He has brought his miracle upon it. His miracle has come forth on this very ground. The Lord has built us a beautiful church. He has built us a beautiful school. And now he has built us a beautiful Hospice from where we can love and give our people a place to die in his arms. A place where they can be raised high and die with peace and dignity. A place from which we can spread his word. A place where all his people can reserve their everlasting life with him in heaven. Feel the souls of your naked feet on this Holy Ground, God's Holy Ground. Knead your toes into it. Feel it through your bodies. He is with us here and now. Let us pray together a prayer of thanks and a prayer of humility to our King. You are all blessed. Remember this day for like Moses you are standing on Holy Ground." Anton led the Dedication in 'The Lord's Prayer.'

Weeping could be heard. Tears filled every eye.

As the prayer ended, the choir bestowed one last hymn upon this blessed' gathering with sacred veneration. The room was still.

'We are standing on Holy Ground and I know there are angels all around
Let us praise Jesus now We are standing in His presence on Holy Ground
In His presence there is joy beyond all measure
We are standing in his presence on our Lord's Holy Ground.'

As the hymn came to its soft conclusion, divine silence reigned once again. Anton moved to the front of the stage; his arms spread like the wings of a dove casting its love over this sacred assembly. With eyes closed, he spoke.

"May the Lord bless you and keep you.
May the Lord make his face shine upon you and be gracious unto you.
May the Lord lift up his countenance upon you and give you peace.
In the name of the Father, and of the Son, and of the Holy Spirit.
In Christ's name, Amen."

Music from the organ rose in volume. Gentle amens droned in reverence. Everywhere tears flowed, hugs and handshakes were exchanged along with the emotional 'You are blessed.' As with Jesus, Anton disappeared off the back of the stage to pray in the depth of his own silence.

Of course, like so many other times, Ian's eyes were filled with gentle tears. Michele's were as well. She hugged Ian. Ian hugged her back as well as Esther, Mamma Mary and so many others. They were truly in the presence of the Lord and standing on his Holy Ground.

The reception was delightful. Ian and Michele stayed close to each other, introducing one another to their unique and diverse circles of friends. They enjoyed each other's company. By the end of the day, Michele and Ian had formed an unexpected friendship. Although unspoken, there was a mutual desire to see each other sometime soon. And they would.

PART 6: THE FINALE – THE AWAKENING

Sunday morning came quickly. Ian left early with Esther to join her in her prayer meeting. Ezekiel was to fetch West and his friends for the main service at nine o'clock. Everything was routine other than the hoarseness in Anton's voice. He was visibly exhausted in the aftermath of the previous day's events, but once the service started, he was filled with the spirit and as inspirational as ever. He repeated his 'Holy Ground' message for those unable to attend on Saturday, but for those who would hear it again, it was still powerful.

By mid-afternoon Anton's yard was filled with honored clergy and special guests. The archbishop and his entourage arrived in black Mercedes Town cars. The men wore black suits, white shirts, and yellow silken ties. The wives dressed in colorful print dresses with matching head wraps and adorned in exquisite jewelry. Unlike Anton and Esther, these were big city pastors. Unfortunately, Michele had a Sunday luncheon and returned to her mansion in Cape Town's Presidential compound.

As Esther and her staff prepared a delectable backyard luncheon for the guests, Anton approached West. "Jordan, the time has arrived for us to speak privately. Please follow me inside and thank you so much. You have the patience of Job."

"Anton, I understand. This time has been special as well as fascinating in so many ways."

The pastors closed themselves off to the world in the small dining room used for the family.

"Is Roberts joining us? I have a few questions for the two of you."

"No, Jordan, he goes into the informal settlement on Sunday afternoon to worship at Pastor Gladys's tent revival. She and her people hold a special fondness for Ian's visits. And he loves spending time out there with them."

"Does he preach?"

"Sometimes. I would enjoy your impression of what you have experienced these last three days. Do you have any suggestions for us? And you may ask me anything you wish. This is your time."

West gave Anton suggestions about his PA system. He warned him of the dissatisfaction of future visitors as it pertains to the rats. He relayed

Kristin's complaint of no heat at night. He suggested space heaters. Anton listened. They spoke of bringing three hundred people over from Credence with a mission to plant gardens and build three houses. They agreed on a group baptism to bond the two churches together even more. Anton was about to shake hands with West and return to the lawn, but West continued.

"Anton, this has been an intense and constructive trip, but you did say I could ask you anything."

"Yes Jordan, go ahead."

There is one subject I must breach before I leave. It is of importance to my superiors."

"I will help if I can."

"It is about Roberts. Do you trust him?"

Anton was surprised. "I'm sorry Jordan, I don't understand your question?"

"Do you trust him? One of my pastors and some of my superiors question his motives. They feel he is not part of our team though it appears to our congregation that he is."

"I am still unclear as to your question. He did come over with your initial team and he is a member of your church, correct?"

"That is true, but..."

Anton continued talking. "What do you mean, do I trust him? He has done nothing but good things since he has been with us. And I know there is more to come. This is just the beginning; I can feel it."

"Frankly Anton, we are afraid of his power, the influence he is obtaining over parts of our congregation."

"I'm still not following. He wields no power I have experienced. Give me examples."

"When he picked me up at the airport, he was thirty minutes late. He told me a brief story about the young ladies on the bus; something having to do with the U.S. Embassy. Are they in some sort of trouble? Why would the U.S. Embassy want to meet with them? Do you feel they are safe around him?"

"Be more specific. Safe in what way?"

"You know. Kristin constantly points out he is divorced, and he has money. And he is here surrounded by poverty."

Anton sighed. "If you are insinuating Ian would somehow take advantage of one of our girls, you can stop right there. You could not be further from the truth. He obtained visas for them so he could take them to the States. He is going to train them in medical something."

"Medical transcriptionist?"

"Yes, that's it. He tells me it will give them skills they cannot receive here. He didn't explain that to you?"

"He was telling me something like that at lunch, but we had just arrived, and I was worried about getting footage back to Credence and…"

Anton stopped him "You are saying you were not paying attention to him." West nodded.

"Jordan, the community loves him for what he does for us. He tells me you are not involved financially or in any other way with his business. Is that correct?"

"Yes, that is correct. We have purposely not involved ourselves."

"Do you mean you don't support what he is doing? I understood from Jim Bennet that you approved his offer to help us because you needed a person with his skills. Is that true?"

"Yes, that is true. But since his first trip over here, he strong-armed us twice for funds."

"I am confused. He never mentioned anything like that to me. How much and in what way, Jordan? That does not sound like him, and he does not keep things from me."

"First, he pushed us to give you an additional $80,000 at the beginning."

Anton leaned forward. "I explained to Jim Bennet about the inflation and exchange rate when he was here. You told us no. Ian sensed something was wrong. Your refusal did not make sense for several reasons. Then he called Jim. Next thing I knew, Jim called me to tell me you were giving us more than we asked. What did Ian not tell me? How did he strong-arm you?"

West thought back at the situation. He realized that was exactly what happened. It was Kristin that blocked the additional funding. "That is true, Anton. I lacked the facts, and I made an unwise decision initially."

"Good, Jordan, I am glad we cleared that up."

West continued. "Then, earlier this year, he forced us to give you another one hundred thousand to put a second floor on the Hospice."

"That second floor looks great, does it not?"

"I have to give you that, Anton. It is simple, but impressive."

"Imagine the Hospice with only one floor, Jordan. The second floor makes it powerful. And if we waited, think how it would be for the patients? They would need to endure the construction overhead, the noise, dust falling onto their beds. It was for the patients."

"That is exactly how Roberts explained it to me in my office. But isn't the second floor the reason he is so loved over here?"

"Why would that be, Jordan? I don't see the connection."

"Because he funded half of it. He must be a real hero to your people."

"He what? Say that again, Jordan. He funded half of what?"

"The second floor, he matched the hundred thousand we put in. He gave me first shot at funding the whole two hundred thousand. I had no intention of funding any of it. So, he said he would raise it himself. That is when I tried to bluff him."

"How did you try to bluff him?"

"I thought he wanted to be a hero to my congregation and yours, so I told him if he wrote me a check for one hundred thousand dollars out of his own pocket, I would match it."

Anton grinned ear to ear. "And he did it?"

"He went straight to the parking lot, got his checkbook, and wrote a check right there on the spot. He wrote it on my desk with my pen."

Anton began to laugh, "I had no idea. So, you matched his check."

"Of course, I did. I had no choice. He was going to raise the money elsewhere if I said no, probably from our members. It would have made us look cheap. And he would look like a saint. He is clever, Anton. That is why we don't trust him. We can't control what he does or says."

"Sounds like someone else in the past the Pharisees could not control. Ian was helping me, Jordan. I assure you; his motive was honorable, not selfish."

"Perhaps but look at the power that funding will give him if he ever decides to reveal it."

"Now it is making sense. Ian asked me to keep quiet on a few things he has done around here. He quoted Matthew 6:3, 'Don't let the left hand know what the right hand is doing.' Ian is funny that way."

"Really, Roberts can recite scripture?"

"He is quite well-versed in scripture, Jordan. You didn't know that did you?"

"Anton, all this time you thought Credence gave you the entire two hundred thousand?"

"The whole two hundred thousand was wired from the Credence bank account."

"Roberts and I agreed to say nothing to anyone in the States. But we assumed, no, I assumed, he would spread the word of his generosity here."

"Let me understand. One of the reasons you don't trust him is exactly one of the reasons I do. He is dedicated to our project and my people, not himself. I saw it on our first mission trip together. He genuinely cares." Anton sat back in his chair and stroked his goatee.

Jordan thought back to the beginning. "Anton, this started when Kristin came back and told me Roberts wasn't a Christian and we needed to be careful. But she told us to watch out for you as well. She insisted both of you were in cahoots and the business was in both your self-interest, not the Hospice."

Anton smiled again and continued to groom his goatee. "Sounds like you have some suspicious people giving you consult. What else Jordan?"

"I am still concerned with what appears to be some sort of power he has over your people, especially your women."

Anton opened his eyes wide and shook his head in confusion. "Tell me more."

"Friday afternoon when I arrived in the compound, we were heading to the Hospice when a thirty something woman approached us. She came up to Roberts, stopped him, then bowed, and kissed his hand."

"Miriam" Anton said immediately.

"Yes, that was her name. He asked about her daughter and her mother. And he placed his hand on her cheek. It seemed as if something was inappropriate. The kissing of his hand was a bit much."

Anton proceeded to relay the story of Miriam's husband's diabetes, his stroke, and his death. Then about her daughter Ava's need for insulin.

"Okay, but why the kissing of his hand like he is the Pope?"

"She may see him that way. Ian sends money to me, $300 per month, to pay for her daughter's insulin. That is what keeps her daughter alive."

"But what about Matthew 6:3. Why did he let her know?"

"He didn't, I did. I refused to let Ian go unrewarded though he insisted he remain anonymous. Miriam promised to remain silent to protect Ian from being overwhelmed with requests. That is not Ian's fault, it is mine." Anton nodded his head.

"Okay."

"Let me tell you one more story. A tall skinny man named Daniel liked Ian's long black overcoat. After service one Sunday, he told Ian, 'If I had a coat like that, I could get a wife.' So, Ian gave him his coat right there." Anton chuckled. "And the next time Ian returned, the man was engaged. He also bows to Ian, but with a huge grin on his face, but no hand kissing." West finally smiled.

"Okay, Anton, I have one more."

"Go on"

"We are concerned about a scandal. We say he is not part of our team, but he is perceived as one. Many outside our church are jealous of our success. They call us a cult. They would love to defame us."

"I understand, Jordan. I still go through that when I preached condom use from the pulpit. What scandal could you fear?"

"As I said, Roberts is unmarried, he is healthy, and he is successful. What was going on between Roberts and the politician woman yesterday? They looked very friendly at the reception. That could not be the first time they met. They were inseparable."

"Michele is a good friend of mine, and they did meet yesterday for the first time." Anton laughed aloud. "My wife tells me, continually, Ian needs to be married."

"Why is that?"

"Marriage is big in our culture. We believe marriage is necessary for happiness in front of the Lord."

"Do you see why we are afraid of him becoming involved with someone in your congregation?"

"Esther and Ian agree, that is a bad idea. Ian for moral reasons and Esther because she would never lose one of our flock to America."

"But the politician is okay? Are you saying Esther is okay with the politician?"

Anton sat smiling and nodding his head. "That is exactly what I am saying. I am not a matchmaker, but she is. I reluctantly agreed to it. Ian was blind-sided. So was Michele. She is a powerful woman. She is the Deputy Speaker of Parliament, and a direct descendant of Nelson Mandela. She has a lot of connections. They are both single and the same age. Perhaps God has a reason for them to meet. Jordan, I have learned to never question God. And I have learned to never question Esther. She has a direct line to him." West laughed.

"Do you think there is any chance of scandal. Is interracial marriage accepted here?"

"Is it in your country? How about in your church? Jordan, seems like a personal issue, not ours. We cannot consider that a scandal. We must preach acceptance. But, if that relationship did happen, Michele has a lot more to lose in her position than you and your church."

"Fair enough."

"Are you finished? Have you come to understand more of what goes on here? This is not America. As far as Ian Roberts goes, I have not shunned him or been suspicious of him like your church. I embraced him. We spend a lot of time together. We have many discussions. He is my closest confidant and mentor. I learn many things just by watching him. Although he is still a doubter as Thomas was with Jesus, he now considers himself a Christ Follower. From his extensive travels, he accepts all people and their religions, not just one. That makes him one of the most Christ-like people I have ever met."

"Anton, that is quite a compliment coming from the most Christ-like person I have ever met. Thank you, I have learned much in three days. Thank you for enlightening me on many topics. You and Roberts make a good team. Stay with him and bring him closer to the Lord. Perhaps we should have tried harder. But you realize my superiors still will not allow me to acknowledge him as part of our team."

"Jordan, he does not want to be part of your team. You two will have a relationship like the Pharisee Nicodemus and Jesus Christ. Does that sound about right?"

"Let's not push it, Anton." West smiled.

The two shook hands and moved to the lawn to join the luncheon. As they did, Ian and Pastor Gladys arrived from the tent revival, a bit dusty but both with joy in their eyes. Ian introduced Pastor Gladys to Jordan. "Wonderful to meet you, Pastor West. I enjoyed your message yesterday and I want to thank you and your church for all the support you have given us. The Hospice would not have been possible without you. You are blessed, sir." Gladys and Ian started for the food line.

West called to Ian, "Roberts, wait a moment."

"Yes Jordan?" Glady's went on ahead.

"I learned a few things about you today."

"All good, I hope? So, what's up?"

West looked away then back into Ian's eyes. "I must have seemed pretty silly these last few days."

"To be honest, Jordan, yes you were." Ian gave West a kind smile. "This is a hard place to understand. There is a lot of death and a lot of love. There is a God thing going on here. I would say one must view everything through a pair of Jesus Christ glasses. Reflection is constant and it makes one cry a lot, but in such a good way."

"You do that, Roberts, you look through Jesus Christ glasses? I've been told you are not a Christian. Are you, or aren't you?"

"Well, probably not in the same definition and doctrine you and your staff follow."

"Go on."

"I used to understand only bits and pieces of this place. Most of the time I was just following the path in front of me. Then Anton gave me a unique perspective. It is the same one Jesus' apostles needed to understand. On my first visit, I was agnostic, what you call a seeker. I shared my doubts about Christianity with Anton. I'm an empirical kind of guy. He then quoted a verse from the Gospel of Thomas."

Jordan interjected, "But that Gospel is not in the Bible. I only know it is part of the Gnostic Society."

"Correct, his gospel is strictly the quotes and parables of Jesus. The verse reads, *'Know what is in front of your face, and what is hidden from you will be disclosed to you. For there is nothing hidden that won't be revealed.'*"

"So how did that change you?"

"I no longer need to figure things out all the time. I am on some path, and I don't know where it is going. But I have faith it is going in the right direction, and that is all I need to know for now. Someday it will be revealed."

West did not know what to say, so he went with no response. "Well, Roberts, I just want to say thank you and I am sorry."

"Thank you, Jordan, you are welcome." Ian began walking. "Come on Jordan, wait until you taste Esther's oxtail."

CAPE TOWN DINING

PART 1: 'CONFESS YOUR WEARINESS TO THE LORD, AND HE WILL SEND YOU COMFORT'

Daytime progressed rapidly, overtaken by the pink and purple clouds of dusk. Sunlight grew dim on the runways of Cape Town's International Airport. People from around the world arrived for business, pleasure, and asylum. But even though the season was summer in February, an Antarctic chill swept through the unheated concourses like an invisible serpent. A small band of unseasoned diplomats awaited their last-minute and uninvited puzzle piece to join them. Impatience invaded Anton as the flight delivering this lone and unknown pilgrim from Arkansas had been delayed by weather out of Atlanta. The hour of the distinguished dinner party was dangerously near.

Inside the fuselage of the South African jetliner, the panic of one inexperienced senior gnawed like a rodent on his insides. He never traveled outside the United States, or even his state of Arkansas, or even his hometown. His odyssey, beginning on his pig farm to his destination in South Africa, gobbled up thirty-five hours of his life. As the plane landed, he was ill from fatigue, but more from the unknown encounters that lie outside the hatch.

His hands began to quiver, his body in the clutches of dismay. Like a lemming, he followed other passengers deplaning, unsure of where he was headed. He gave thanks to his Lord for the signs in English, without which he would have lost all self-control. He wanted to cry.

"Dear Lord," he prayed silently, "I am so tired. My body is in terrible pain. How can I go on?" He questioned his reason for embarking on this holy mission, but he knew it was requested by his deceased wife. It was the only motivation giving him the strength to put one foot in front of the other, gently, and persistently.

He turned the corner of the passageway. He stopped; his heart pounded harder. He saw an immense room packed with people of every race and color, daunting both plain clothing and colorful fashions. He had never been in a place where his Whiteness was the minority.

Like the black snakes on his farm, rows of people slithered back and forth, like the license bureau on a Saturday afternoon. He froze. People rushed past him like his pigs to the feeding trough. His Lord gave him a clue, a sign reading 'Immigration.' On each side were two signs, one reading 'Citizen' and one reading 'Alien.' He saw a large Black woman in a tight unwrinkled uniform; her badge pointing towards the ceiling. As he approached, she looked at him, "Citizens to the left, Aliens to the right."

"'Scuse me?" asked the old man.

"Your passport, is it South African or are you an alien?"

"I ain't no alien, I'm American," he retorted with a U.S. accent of which she was unfamiliar. Her brow wrinkled.

"To the right, next." There he saw the epicenter of endless rows of people. His legs were exhausted. He shuffled across the concrete floor and took his place at the end of the line.

As he secured his position, he heard someone calling, "Sir, sir, over here." A man was waving from halfway forward. The old man was confused. He looked behind him to see who this man might be hailing. *'It couldn't be me,'* he thought, but he answered anyway.

"Y'all callin' me?" asked the old man, his voice cracking from a mixture of anxiety and fatigue.

Huddled together was a family, one he had only seen on TV news or in a documentary. The men wore colorful turbans and stylish kaftans, the women in beautiful long black abayas. The children wore Western attire like he would find back home, only cleaner. Their skin was brown, but not like them colored people back in Arkansas. This was the first time he encountered anyone of the Islamic faith. His fear level rose. He assumed the man hailing him recognized him as an American and wished him harm. *'They all hate us and want us dead,'* he thought. *I saw it on the TV.* But he was confused by their joyful and patient nature. The children were smiling and well-behaved. The man waving to him had a loving demeanor and a smile displaying an aura of benevolence.

The man in the blue turban then addressed the rows behind him. "Excuse me, will you let our friend through so he may join us?" The man spoke impeccable English with an Indian accent. His request was kind and confident. The old man was confused. The man motioned him forward. People moved aside.

He limped to join the family. When he arrived, the man in the blue turban gazed into the old man's blood-shot eyes. "Sir, you look dreadfully tired. I want you to go in front of us, please. It will take a while for them to process my entire family and we still have twenty minutes left in line."

"Sir, you are so kind, my mind and body are bushed. I feel like I just finished workin' in my field all day, cleanin' my pens, and sloppin' my pigs. Y'all are most kind. May God bless you and your family, sir." But before he made his move in front, something compelled him to converse with the man. "Where y'all from, sir?"

"We are from India, my friend. We come here to celebrate our Islamic holiday Eid al-Adha in Cape Town with my wife's parents. We spend one year here and the next back in Bengaluru." The man smiled proudly.

"What's that thing you just said? Did you say it's a holiday? I reckon it's havin' somethin' to do with Mohammed, right?" The old man was trying to be kind by taking a stab with the only thing he knew of Islam. He knew little of religions other than his own. In his town, there were only two religions: Baptist and Catholic.

The man in the blue turban unleashed a compassionate chuckle. "No sir, this holiday celebrates something that happened way before Mohammed. It is to honor the profit Abraham who was faithful to Allah as he was about to sacrifice his son Isaac as Allah commanded. But Allah was testing Abraham's dedication and at the last moment an angel of the Lord stopped him, assuring Abraham his sacrifice had already been made."

"Wait sir, Abraham's from the Christian Bible. You're Islam. Why in the blue blazes would you honor Abraham?" The old man was confused once more.

The man in the turban did not challenge. He knew the difference between the Old and New Testaments and there were no Christians in the days of Abraham. He assumed there was another reason for his statement. "Sir, you are not well versed in religion, I assume," asked the Muslim.

"With all due respect sir, I have read the Bible cover to cover many times. I am a Christian preacher and true man of God. That's why I am confused." The old man did not understand why he was being insulted. This man seemed nice at first. *Maybe I am here because God wants me to educate this confused soul,* he thought.

Continuing his kind demeanor, the man responded, "Your God has sent you here for a reason, perhaps many reasons, but I can see you have not travelled much by the uncomfortable shoes on your feet. I will start by telling you our religions possess many commonalities. We have many prophets, parables, and stories common to both your Old Testament and our Quran."

The old man decided to open his mind just a pinch, though it was not part of his culture to do so. *This man appears to be too educated and sophisticated to lie to me.* "How do y'all celebrate that holiday, sir."

"You mean Eid al-Adha. We sacrifice an animal, just as Abraham sacrificed a ram, then we cut it into three pieces. One third stays with my family, one third goes to other friends and relatives, and one third is given to the poor. Sir, are you O.K?" The man was sensing something was wrong and it was not emotional. The old man was fainting, or worse. Sweat was breaking on his brow; his face turning pale.

"I'm really tuckered and feelin' pretty weak, sir." He dropped to one knee.

The Muslim raised him under the armpit and circumvented the rows of people. He took the old man to the front of the line. "Officer, this man is weak from his long journey and close to exhaustion. I believe he will collapse. Let us pray it is nothing more than fatigue."

"Is he your friend?"

"Yes, he is. Can you help him through the line please? I'm afraid he will not be able to stand much longer." The officer buzzed someone on her intercom and a wheelchair quickly arrived. The man sat. "Is that better, sir? These people will help you. It was a blessing our God brought us together."

"Thank you, sir. I needed help and the Lord sent you to me, the God of Abraham." The old man strained to see the man. He began to slump in the chair. His eyes blurred.

"Do you have any chest pains or dizziness before I leave you?" asked the man.

"No, just feels like I was lookin' through a tunnel. I needed to sit. Thank you for your kindness and may the presence of God be with you and your family." The old man reached out to touch the young man's hand.

"And may Allah bless you and keep you safe." They squeezed each other's hands. The man returned to his family. A young South African girl wheeled the old man to the next immigration desk. He pulled himself to his feet. His stiff clean passport lost its virginity with the loud thud of a rubber stamp and off he went to baggage claim with his new precious seraph.

"Thank you for your help, young lady. I'm feelin' strong enough to continue on my own. Where might I find my friends, who are waitin' for me somewhere?"

"See the line over there. Once you retrieve your bag, go through customs then through the exit doors to the main terminal." The young girl hesitated for a moment with an obligatory smile, then turned and left with the wheelchair, and without the tip she expected. The old man was appreciative, but the only person he ever tipped was Pearl at the coffee shop in town.

The old man's ragged piece of luggage arrived. From a distance, it reminded him of a swollen, well-fed hog at slaughter time. Grunting, he pulled his bag from the carousel, he made his way through customs, and out the exit to the main terminal as instructed.

Like immigration, the terminal was bustling with people of all races, nationalities, sizes, and shapes, mostly an abundance of bright robes and flowered moo moos. The place was buzzing like a beehive. Solders roamed the crowd in camouflage uniforms toting intimidating Uzis, some with

German Shepherd's strapped tightly to their wrists. His brain in a whirl of confusion, the old man walked slowly down the aisle hedged by steel barricades. The barricades were lined with people pushing and crowding, bubbling with excitement as they waited for a glimpse of friends and relatives. Approaching the end, the next wave of fear caused his throat to tighten. *'What if no one shows up to gather me? What if they don't recognize me? What if they left since my flight was delayed?'* Like stepping off the bow of a ship, he was immersed in a sea of people. He found himself unable to emotionally tread water. His mind was drowning. And even if he could swim, where was the shoreline? His eyes darted throughout the terminal for a Black man of medium stature, sporting a goatee. Aggressive cab drivers infringed upon his concentration. Desperation was upon him since most men in the rotunda were Black and of medium stature. His legs weakened once again. But what he was not comprehending, unlike his small town in Arkansas, he was one of a few elderly White Americans in the crowd. He was the black sheep in his pasture, the rooster in his hen house. He stood out like a reverend in a pulpit.

Unable to get close to the barricades, Anton and his party stood in the middle of the rotunda. They scanned the people in all directions. Anton received an indistinct copy of the old man's passport. From what he ascertained, the man was near sixty, messy gray hair receding like an ocean tide. He was White and unhealthy. Ian made Anton aware the man would have a distinct accent; one he may find hard to understand.

The chaos caused the old man's heart to pulsate. He gritted firmly on his molars to prevent an ugly accident on the floor. *'Oh Jesus, why have you put me in harm's way? Give me a sign like when your father turned Moses's staff into a snake. Give me something.'* No sooner did he ask, he heard a voice call, 'Mr. Hendricks.' He waived his arm over his head and like angels from heaven, Anton and his team approached with smiles. Introductions were made, then Anton spoke briskly.

"Sir, we are running behind for our dinner engagement. Due to your flight's delay, you must join us. I will clear it with the host when we arrive at her mansion. If we hurry, we can still be on time." Anton was now fixated on the huge clock on the wall.

"Pastor, her mansion? Am I dressed properly? I've never been in a mansion sir, I….." Anton quickly interrupted.

"No, you are not dressed properly, but we are having dinner at the Deputy Speaker of Parliament's mansion in the Presidential compound."

"Holy firecrackers." The old man's heart began to pound once again. He thought he was only coming to work with the poor and plant gardens, not this. *'Oh, my gracious Lord, have you brought me all this way to have my heart explode?'*

We do not have time for you to change or clean up. I assume the clothing in your bag is of the same caliber as what you are wearing, only more wrinkled, if that is possible." Anton expressed himself calmly and with understanding, but not with acceptance.

"Yes, Pastor Anton. These clothes I'm wearin' are the best I can give ya.' And I must use the bathroom before we leave the airport?" The man was surrounded by a dense cloud of body odor, almost visible. The smell reminded Anton of his construction workers at the end of a long day in the savannah heat, or a musky gorilla at the zoo!

"I suppose, but please sir, hurry. We must leave right away," responded Anton. Ian was concerned as well. He had seen Anton drive in heavy traffic when he was in a hurry. He remembered Anton's rule; 'Don't hit anybody and don't let anybody hit you.'

The man carried his bag into the restroom, then into a stall. The stalls were disgusting; human feces and urine coated the floor. The clogged toilet brimmed and only the turgor pressure held back a tsunami of waste. He shut the door and stood crammed inside the narrow partitions of rusted metal. Wedging his suitcase between his chest and the door, he proceeded to open it. Right on top lay a gilded hunting knife sheathed in a leather leg strap. He pulled his pant leg to his knee, strapped the knife to his calf, and lowered his pant leg, concealing his primitive weapon. He used the near over-flowing toilet and, out of utter habit, flushed it. With that, the squalid cascade of filth drenched his shoes and soaked his cuffs, some splattering onto the bottom of his bag. He retreated from the stall and washed his hands. Finding nothing to dry them, he ran his hands through his thin and oily hair. He finished on his thighs. He burst from the bathroom about to vomit and rejoined the group impatiently waiting for him. The group's nostrils were hit hard with the smell of his shoes and cuffs, adding to the foulness of his initial pong.

The four large men crammed into their economy rental car. The old man's aroma and unshaven appearance bordered on putrid. In no way would he be fondly accepted by their distinguished host inside her stately mansion. The thought did cross all their minds to leave him in the car like a dirty hunting dog, but Anton, as a pastor of the poor, felt it hypocritical; now anyway.

After an hour of Anton's lawless driving through Cape Town in what resembled a circus clown car, they approached the compound's guardhouse. Two soldiers in powerfully hued military uniforms and spotless white gloves stood inside. Before exiting the guardhouse, eight other soldiers suddenly appeared, dressed in camouflage fatigues. Four positioned themselves around the perimeter of the defenseless vehicle with Uzis pointed skyward. In front of the swinging steel gate stood two more guards. And finally, two soldiers firmly held warlike German Shepherds with leather leashes hooked to their spiked-chain collars. The dogs were led around the car; no one was smiling, no tails wagging.

"Passports please," commanded the guard as he bent over, studying each of the visitors. A stench poured from the half-opened windows. "You are here for what purpose, gentlemen?"

"We are the invited dinner guests of your Deputy Speaker, Ms. Michele Ntombela-kaMandela," Anton responded, cool and confident, as always. The three Americans found their breathing shallow.

The guard scanned his clipboard then glanced at the driver, "I am assuming you are Pastor Anton Nkosi? And you are Dr. Tyler Joseph? And you are Ian Roberts? Do you have a title, Mr. Roberts?"

"I do not, sir. Is that a problem?" The guard ignored Ian's question. Anton smiled.

He studied each passport as he matched them to the list on his clipboard. "And who is this old man with the stink on his body? He is not on my clipboard, but this remaining passport makes me assume he is Dallas Hendricks."

Anton stayed arrogantly calm. His behavior seemed as if he were in charge, not the guard. "He is an American here to teach my people to farm. I apologize for his odor. He just came off the South African Air flight from the US. The flight was delayed out of Atlanta. He did not have a chance to bathe, nor change his attire. I will be happy to explain this to the Deputy Speaker on your phone and have him cleared for entry." The guard felt compelled to honor Anton's request for they all may be pastors. And even though he was trained to be skeptical of anyone passing through his gate, he also was raised by his parents and his culture to respect the cloth.

Anton was given the guard's phone. He spoke briefly in Zulu to someone on the other end. Within seconds, Anton handed the phone back to the guard. With simplicity, Anton cleared the stinky man to enter.

The guard handed Anton a map with a pronounced line drawn in blue marker. He did not want this motley crew to get lost and roam the compound. "The map will assure you find your way out when the time comes. Follow the guard on the motorcycle." He pointed to the other side of the gate. "He will escort you to the Deputy Speaker's mansion." The gate opened and Anton put his Bozo-mobile into gear.

A flash struck Anton's eyes from his rear-view mirror. It was an armed jeep with a machine gun mounted on the back. A gunner rode ready to fire. They weaved their way through the compound, then up a gradual incline lined with perfectly trimmed hedges and flowers lit by colored spotlights. All silently stared at the eminence of the exquisitely adorned landscape leading to their destination.

The car approached a driveway which formed a semi-circle to the main entrance. It was paved with cobblestones. But before they drove into the semi-circle, their car was stopped once more. Again, four well-armed guards surrounded the car. The guard in charge stepped to Anton's window. Anton's window was halfway down, making the odor a bit tolerable. But with no movement, the stench was unbearable.

"Please, Pastor, will you and your friends be so kind as to exit your vehicle and place your hands on top of your heads? I'm sorry, if it were only you, this would not be necessary. But they are foreigners so we must. They could be terrorists." Anton smiled, and looked calmly at the guard with his peaceful, bucolic smile on his face.

IAN AND ANTON

"I understand," said Anton. With that, he leaned over and whispered in the guard's ear. "I suggest you check the man with the odor more closely. I do not know much about him. I just met him an hour ago. The other two are co-workers of mine. I trust them completely."

His entourage stepped out of the car and placed their hands on their heads. The old man was scared. As the guard studied the papers given to him by the soldier on the motorcycle, the others frisked the group for weapons, which included the removal of shoes. The waft of the old man's feet was the final coup de grace to the olfactory lobes. The guards covered their noses with their sleeves. The main guard fanned his clipboard at the source of the problem.

Then, without warning, the old man was thrown face first to the ground. His hands were cuffed behind his back and an Uzi pointed into the back of his neck.

"What do we have here?" asked the guard. "Why, man of stench, do you have a knife strapped to your calf as you are about to enter the residence of our Deputy Speaker?" The guards turned their Uzi's toward all of them.

With his face held to the driveway, he spoke loudly so he could be heard by all. "Pastor Anton, I didn't mean no harm. I had no idea I'd have soldiers searching me like this."

Anton was puzzled. *Was the knife meant to kill me? He knew nothing about this dinner. When did we tell him about it? What was the knife for?* "Explain the knife please," responded Anton firmly. Ian and Dr. Joseph were in a state of panic as to what would happen next.

"I was told when I left the States by my brother Will, how dangerous it is here in Africa with all of them snakes and lions and rats, but especially the crime and so many of them African Americans," blurted the stinky man in a quivering voice.

The guard answered, "Pastor Hendricks, we have few African Americans in this country. We are Africans, not Americans." Anton smiled and shook his head at the man's innocence. It was starting to make sense.

"The airline didn't allow me to carry no knife on the plane, but they allowed me to pack it in my bag. I strapped it on my leg in the bathroom. I was scared to take it off at the first guard house. I had no idea they'd frisk us, Pastor Anton. I swear, I meant no harm. I was just protecting myself like my brother Will told me to."

"You're a pastor in the US?" Anton asked with curiosity and surprise.

"Yes sir, a Baptist preacher for near on thirty years now. I'm wearing a collar in my picture. Didn't you see it?"

"I could barely see your face. You told me you were coming here to teach our people to grow gardens. I will never stop any of you, but you know the vegetables die from lack of water, or the neighbors steal them, but what is left, the rats eat. But you Americans mean well. Most come here to make themselves feel better. And the things you are worried about; the snakes will bite you before you know it and the lions, really, a knife? And criminals you are worried about, they will shoot you before you pull that toothpick off your leg." The guard was holding back his laughter.

"Pastor Anton, I doubt I could hurt anything or anybody even if I wanted to, exceptin' maybe a lion." Anton rolled his eyes and asked to speak to the guard in private. The old man's head was still pressed tightly to the ground.

Anton began "Sir, Michele is a friend of mine and Mr. Roberts. We have done excellent work together in the township. I must admit, I know nothing about the old man except he is another naïve American preacher. In his email, he told me he has never been away from his small town in the US. He told me, after his wife died a year ago, he wanted to do something in her memory. His email said he wanted her to be proud of him as she watched him from heaven. That is all I know. I had to give him that opportunity."

"He does not look dangerous. He looks and talks stupid but," replied the guard.

"You are right. I agree. Allow me to go into the mansion and explain to Michele what has happened. We will let her decide. Frankly, if he had to wait out here, that would be best. If he does, I suggest you keep him in the car and park it a distance away. I doubt even the dogs want to sniff him." Anton smiled as he stroked his goatee.

"Go ahead Pastor, and believe me, I know what you mean. That boy smells like he needs a diaper change!" They both smiled.

IAN AND ANTON

Anton entered the imposing doorway to the vestibule, greeted by an elegant and stunning Indian woman. Anton, turning on his charm, requested a moment with Michele who was entertaining a raft of pastors in the sitting room. Anton waited. The greeter found Michele and whispered into her ear. "I am so sorry, but there is something urgent I must attend to." All her conversation circles gracefully excepted her need to excuse herself.

Michele went to Anton and gently pulled him aside. They were now at a distance where they could not be overheard. "Pastor Anton, it is wonderful you could attend, but I was hoping Mr. Roberts would attend as well. I was looking forward to seeing him, I mean, getting the insight of a White American as to what he has experienced with you in the township."

"Michele, thank you so much for the invitation." He gave her a dignified and gentle hug, along with this captivating grin. "Ian is outside along with Dr. Joseph, the optometrist Ian brought with him to perform eye exams on our children and our elderly congregation."

"That is magnificent. Have them come in, please!" Michele responded in her ceremonious tone.

"Michele, I first must talk to you briefly about a problem we have." Anton proceeded to explain the flight delay and the misunderstanding caused by the old man. When he finished, Michele gave Anton one of her sweet but strong smiles.

"Anton, if you trust him, I trust him. We both work for all of those who mean well, and I would not embarrass you or him by refusing our hospitality. He may join us. We will set another plate at the table."

Unlike Anton's unconditional acceptance of everyone, he leaned closer to Michele and spoke in a whisper. "Please allow me to challenge you on this predicament. Perhaps you misunderstood." Anton was correct. Michele was confused. "I was to drop him off at the hotel and join him later. We had no choice but to come directly here."

"Go on, Anton," Michele motioned with her hand.

"Michele, I believe he has a good and simple soul. He is a pastor in a rural part of America. But he has a problem."

"Oh my, is he ill?"

"No, he is fine, but he smells bad, I mean really bad!" Michele began to chuckle at Anton's candor. "I have never smelled a person as whiff as he is now. I am afraid your dining will be tainted. People will be unable to enjoy their meals, and I am sure he would be equally embarrassed for himself. I believe he will completely understand my position and welcome it."

"If you are sure, Anton? I would gladly give him a chance to bathe, but I have no clean clothing for him. As you know, I have been a widower these past two years. I live here with my dearest friend, Makeda." Michele was gracious politically whenever she found the opportunity, and that was most of the time.

"He will understand, especially after the weapon incident."

"Weapon?" Anton interrupted Michele.

"It was a tiny hunting knife he thought would protect him from our big cats." Anton smiled. So did Michele. "And I may be prejudging this poor man, but I'm not sure what he can add to our conversations."

"It is not what he can give to us, it is what we can give to him. But if you are sure, Anton. I do not want it to be said I refused to feed a weary traveler, especially an American." Michele always protected her reputation.

"The reason we are here is for Ian and his observations, correct?"

"I respect your judgement, Anton. I will make sure the man is fed well outside."

Michele returned to her guests. Anton went to gather his entourage.

Anton explained his conversation with Michele and told the old man why he was excluded from dinner inside. Ian and Dr. Joseph silently breathed a guilt-free sigh of relief, especially for their nostrils!

"Pastor Anton, I understand. I can hardly stand the smell of myself, not to mention the appearance of these here clothes of mine. I'm just a simple farmer back home and the pastor of a bunch of elderly folks. I never experienced people of this caliber, nor have I been around many African Amer…., I mean, Black people. I'd be uncomfortable and feel inferior there. Maybe this here stink is a blessing from God." The Pastor looked relieved, so relieved he was about to cry.

"Pastor Hendricks, God is close to us here. Do not consider yourself inferior. Many of my people feel that way. You will learn much during your stay with us. God has much to teach you. Talk to Ian. He expressed to me he came here to help us and found God gave back to him many times over. Remember, Jesus Christ was the son of a carpenter and his apostles common. They were fishermen, one a zealot and Matthew was a hated tax collector. And I'm sure his apostles did not smell fresh. You are blessed, my dear man. I would hug you but…."

With a smile on his face, the odoriferous clergyman responded, "I understand, Pastor Anton. I doubt even one of them lions would eat me right now. Perhaps this was Daniel's secret in the den." Anton smiled.

The trio of honored guests left their newly emerging man of the world. They entered the mansion for a night of superb dining, wonderful conversation, and something Ian would find completely unexpected.

PART 2: 'HE WHO HAS EARS TO HEAR, LET HIM HEAR'

The entourage was escorted to the door by the two guards accessorized by sleek German Shepherds. The dogs stared at the trio hoping they would be given just one chance of snarling fun with the boys. The door opened and a distinguished Black man, high in stature, donning a classic tuxedo. It fit him like something out of a 1940s Cary Grant movie.

"Welcome to Cape Town, gentlemen. Quite an ordeal getting in here, is it not? I must endure that degrading routine every morning and I have worked in this complex for over twenty years. It started after the Soweto Uprising in 1976. Nobody trusted anybody after that, especially the Whites and Blacks." The man's English was impeccable, unique with its South African lilt and coupled with a beautifully sonorous voice. Ian was mesmerized. "Anyway, it is a pleasure to have you as our honored guests. The Deputy Speaker and the others are in the sitting room. Follow me, please."

As the three entered the room, their attitudes were intrepid on the exterior, but internally, only Anton had his emotions harmonized with his outside. The other two were Americans; Ian Roberts and Dr. Tyler Joseph, a second-generation Indian immigrant; both had swarms of butterflies fluttering about. The sitting room went silent, conversations stopped in mid-sentence. All eyes turned to this interesting mix of men being given such welcoming hospitality from their Deputy Speaker. Breaking from her conversation circle, and with a heartfelt smile, she came to greet the trio. She was followed closely by a server with a tray of wooden grails; some with wine, but mostly with water. This Black Christian clergy had sworn a vow of abstinence to alcohol. And that included Anton.

As at the Dedication, Michele was impressive. She was a handsome Black South African woman with a strong, almost athletic physique. She sported a dignified suit of navy, with a white laced V-necked blouse. It exposed an appropriate touch of femininity. She was a distant relative of the politician and freedom fighter, Nelson Mandela, who became president in 1994 following his exile on Robben Island from 1964 to 1982. President Mandela brought the nation together in an historical act of forgiveness and unity called the 'Truth and Reconciliation Commission,' an act never attempted by any politician after a civil war. The act brought peace to most of Southern Africa. In less than ten years, the economy rose to an unprecedented point of prosperity. Michele's enchanting pride and her political capital stemmed from this family history. Being in her mid-fifties, she was well-educated and effortlessly charismatic. The combination of all those features, along with her title, caused her to not only be respected by Ian, but his masculinity found her to be powerfully attractive.

"Pastor Anton, I cannot say it enough. It is such a pleasure to have you and your guests joining us this evening." Her fascinating South African accent seemed reminiscent of a cultured Southern Belle from America's past. This time, in public, she gave Anton a respectful hug. Anton responded with a smile. He began his introductions.

"This is Dr. Tyler Joseph of whom I spoke. I do not believe you two have met. He is an optometrist from the US. He is truly a blessing to all of us." They shook hands, all with political gentleness.

"Michele, you remember Mr. Ian Roberts?" Michele knew who Ian was for sure, but stayed silent as Anton went further into his introduction. "My congregation has adopted him over the last few years. He is known as 'Uncle Ian' to both our adults and our children. They love him because he is the first White man our young children ever touched. And he shows them his love in return. When he walks through the schoolyard, he always takes a moment to kneel among them and exchange hugs." Anton placed his hand gently on Ian's shoulder.

Michele interjected with a smile, "Anton, truly you jest. Of course, I remember Mr. Roberts. We sat together and had wonderful conversations at the Dedication of your Hospice last November. And if I am correct, it was your birthday, Mr. Roberts. Pastor Anton's wife surprised you by having us all sing 'Happy Birthday.'" Michele gave Ian a warm embrace and a soft, enchanting kiss on both his cheeks. Ian had made an impression. A mysterious thought entered his head as they caught each other's eyes.

"You have a good memory, Deputy Speaker. That was such a surprise and such an honor," Ian replied with a slight bow of his head.

"Mr. Roberts, I insist you all call me Michele. Once inside this house, we are all friends, all equals, no formalities. Leave that to the soldiers outside. She bowed her head as well. "And if you don't mind, I would prefer to call you 'Mr. Roberts.' It's more cultured and fits your demeanor and charm more than 'Uncle Ian'." He and Michele gazed at each other once again with attempted subtlety. "And calling you Uncle Ian makes me sound, well, a bit too young, like a schoolgirl perhaps." The room snickered, showing respect for the Deputy's attempt at humor. "But after being with you in the township and the stories shared with me by Pastor Anton, I completely understand why they call you Uncle Ian. In our culture, it is a great honor to be called 'Uncle' when not of a blood connection. It means they hold you in the highest esteem for the love and respect you have shown them. And Anton told me you arranged for Dr. Joseph to come to the township. For that, I again must insist I call you Mr. Roberts, out of even a higher respect."

"I am honored, Deputy---, I mean, Michele." Ian, with his eyes only, took a quick glimpse in the direction of Anton. He was smiling and stroking his goatee. He knew what was happening and so did Ian. And neither knew what was appropriate and what was not. This arduous social exchange was becoming awkward. It was beyond protocol and moving beyond social norms. But Anton knew Ian and Michele were both unmarried and both graced with social decorum.

"Good, now allow me to introduce you to the others. I have told them a little about the work you and Anton are doing." She took Ian by the arm, as if he was her date. Anton gave a restrained grin as the introductions began.

Men in black tuxedos and white gloves served aperitifs. Ian was questioned on a variety of subjects; his family, his occupation, township projects, and by one astute clergyman, his relationship status. Ian's answers were purposefully short and succinct. He wanted no misunderstandings or controversy due to language or cultural barriers. And even though all conversations with him were respectfully in English, that did not guarantee they understood his meanings. Ian knew South Africa recognized eleven official languages, the most of any nation in the world, and members of the Black population spoke at least five fluently. He found it fascinating, the enjoyable mixture of vernacular and dialect floating through the room.

The guests consisted of four Black pastors, including Anton. Eighty percent of the South African population was Christian; mostly varying sects of non-denominational Protestant. As in the case of Anton's church, most denominations were of South African origin. Anton was considered the most aggressive and influential pastor in the country. He was humble but powerful, a pastor of the people, and a true working-class hero. He dressed plainly, no collar, no black suit, no yellow tie, and no fancy car. Many of them had seen Anton preach and knew his power and wisdom. And they heard he was an incredible dancer. Still his power did not come from his stage presence; it came from his vision and relentless work ethic. He believed true Christians practiced their faith outside the church, not only inside. His visions, or as he said God's visions, were never-ending. Michele was a huge proponent of her friend since their adolescent days.

Also, in attendance was Michele's top advocate and mentor, Makeda, a Jamaican woman in her mid-fifties with a strong Rastafarian persona. She was to Michele what Ian was to Anton. As the night's conversations progressed, it was obvious Makeda was dedicated to Michele. She focused on Michele's philosophical needs and contemplations more than her political decisions.

After thirty minutes of both light and meaningful conversation, one of the servers came to the entrance of the sitting room and tapped a chime. "Dinner is served, Deputy Speaker," he announced.

As the nine moved to the elegant dining room, Ian hesitated in the anteroom waiting for his seat to be assigned. He remembered Jesus's parable from the Book of Luke, 'When you are invited by someone to a wedding feast, do not sit down to eat at the place of honor since a more distinguished guest than you may have been invited.' But as he hesitated, Michele, in full stride, reached her arm through his. "Mr. Roberts, would you be so kind as to sit next to me on my right as our honored guest?" She looked up and smiled.

"Thank you, I consider it my duty and a privilege," Ian replied, even though he thought the seat of honor should belong to Anton. All stood behind their chairs. Anton thanked the Lord for all his blessings. When finished, Ian stepped quickly in front of one of the servants and pulled out Michele's chair. It was a chivalrous gesture.

"Why Mr. Roberts, I usually leave that to our help. That was truly kind of you." The room, especially Makeda, noticed what was transpiring. When Michele sat, everyone sat.

As dinner progressed, multiple conversations intertwined like a symphony in a mixture of languages and dialects. Every so often, Michele would pat Ian on the knee under the table and ask him if he was enjoying the food. She would then educate him on the history of each dish.

"Mr. Roberts," she inquired. "What is the timeline of your current trip? When will you be returning to the United States and how often do you visit?" The conversation was between the two of them as the others were engrossed in their own topics.

"It depends on what requires my attention and when Anton needs me. I would say once a quarter is the pattern we have entered," replied Ian.

"And do you always stay with Anton in the township, or would you enjoy becoming more familiar with Cape Town? It is a fascinating city. When I am not in session, I could introduce you to our city and people who can help you with your work."

"That sounds wonderful. I suspect I will be back in mid-June."

"Perfect, my schedule is light in June. I will plan for your stay before you join Anton."

The salad and main courses were served, and the plates and utensils cleared from the table. Dessert was presented with one's choice of tea or coffee. Conversations around the table reached saturation which brought a moment of silence to the room, as if it were strategically planned before Anton's arrival. Michele sat up straight, folded her hands on the table, glanced down at Makeda, then directly at Ian with a dominating stare. Ian could feel the change, like the cool breeze before a thunderstorm.

"Mr. Roberts," Her tone changed to formal. "Rarely, if ever, do I have an opportunity to speak candidly with a non-politician or someone who wants nothing from me other than my company. Therefore, I must ask you a serious question?" The table chuckled.

"Not at all, and you are correct. I have the utmost respect for you and your family's accomplishments, guiding this country peacefully out of Apartheid. It is the same respect I have for Anton and his family. You are also correct in saying there is nothing I want from you other than your friendship and your respect, providing, I earn it." Everyone stared at Ian as he answered.

"Thank you, and I assure you, from my discussions with Pastor Anton, you already have my complete respect. You are a unique American, Mr. Roberts, having learned much from your visits to many countries with different religions, races, and cultures. You have spent much time with Pastor Anton in one of our poorest and most overpopulated townships. You have observed more poverty, death, and disease than any other place you have visited in the world, at least at this level of intimacy. So, my question is, 'What do you think, Mr. Roberts, is our biggest problem in South Africa?'"

Immediately a ball of thought exploded through Ian's brain. The thunderbolt clapped. *I am a simple, White, middle-aged American. One grandfather was a factory worker, the other an auto mechanic. My parents were small-town politicians. Since Vietnam, I have avoided political conversations and controversy. Now I sit as the guest-of-honor of the Deputy Speaker of Parliament, the 25th largest nation in the world and asked a question worthy of deep reflection and with far-reaching ramifications, depending on my answer.*

An abstract feeling entered him. *'We've been here before, Ian, just say it. I've got you.'*

Looking directly into Michele's eyes with sincerity and compassion he blurted "Parenting." He glanced across the table at Anton. Anton stared back into Ian's eyes, but this time no emotion, no smile, no stroke of his goatee.

"Parenting, Mr. Roberts? That is certainly not an answer I expected, but I find it most intriguing and one I could consider an insult to my people." Tension filled the room. Michele and Makeda glared at each other, impatiently awaiting an explanation that may destroy Ian's virtue in South Africa; a virtue which came to him so naturally. "Are you saying we treat our children improperly? Are you saying we are incompetent parents, not giving our children the love, respect, and the education, they deserve?" Ian took a deep breath. Anton held his. Ian began.

"I do not mean that at all, Michele. I heard a saying shortly after I arrived in your country, one of which your people are immensely proud. And I have found it to be, without a doubt, true. As it goes, 'South Africa's greatest resource is not its mines, nor its vineyards, nor its game preserves. It is its people.'"

"Yes, we are all familiar with that, go on."

"Your people are kind and gentle and have been respectful to me. They have made me cry more than anywhere else in the world. But not only from their losses and sadness, but their caring and appreciation towards each other. The meaning of my statement "Parenting" is due to your health crisis. I have spent a lot of time with Anton and his AIDS workers, teachers, and his wife; not to mention the AIDS and diabetic patients themselves. Many have spoken to me in confidence, entrusting me with individual experiences. I find it an honor."

Michele and Makeda glanced again at each other but now with far less anticipation. "Go on, Mr. Roberts."

"Your census reveals a 21% HIV/AIDS rate in many of your townships, particularly the northern region around Johannesburg. Of the 21%, 17% are women between 16 and 24 years of age. And unlike the United States, where HIV infection is spread and dominates mostly in male homosexuals, it is spread heterosexually. In confidence, woman have shared with me, it is spread by male promiscuity and the violent forcing of men upon your women. I am told extramarital affairs are common, thus bringing the infection home to their spouses. The females are aware of their husband's mistresses, referred to scientifically as 'relationship undesirables.' Frankly, I do not know what that means."

Michelle looked at Makeda, but Makeda was still fixated on Ian as was the rest of the table. "Mr. Roberts, I am aware of the term and its definition, but not one I wish to expose in this setting. Please continue," said Michele, still not sure where Ian was heading with this argument. Ian continued.

"The wives tell me, if they confront their husband, asking him to wear a condom, the husband twists the request and accuses his wife of cheating on him, insinuating the condom is to protect him. Then, many times violently, he insists she surrender to his demands and that is why such a high female rate. It's a wicked game of danger and deception. The wives stay quiet to keep their breadwinner. The family is held for ransom, as if the social pain endured by these women caused by their husband's infidelity is not destructive enough."

Many thoughts were going through those at the table, and many wanted to challenge Ian, but they knew he had done his homework, both reading and first-hand accounts. Ian continued unchallenged for the moment.

"However, the critical and far-reaching consequence of this game within your society is if, or when, the wife and mother become infected, her husband proclaims her to have been unfaithful. He says her infection is an embarrassment and disgrace to both their families and their children. He leaves them to live with his mistress, continuing to spread the disease to others. The concluding chapter of this disastrous cycle comes when the wife dies and her children are left parentless, to be taken into the crowded homes of other family members, neighbors, or orphanages. These people try their best but are unable to give these children the needed love and attention necessary during their early grief-stricken years."

"This is from your observations and conversations with women in our township, Mr. Roberts? This is not hearsay or fabricated by an angry wife? Do you agree with this observation, Pastor Anton?"

"I do, Michele. Ian has been by my side on many personal visits to both homes and funerals. He has become close with Momma Mary, the head nurse of our HIV/AIDS ministry. She educated him as to our problem and introduced him to many of our patients and workers. He has helped me tremendously by being a good listener for my people. They share with him things they will not share with me because of my position as their pastor."

"Mr. Roberts, I have heard rumors of this problem, but like Pastor Anton, people will not share these stories with me because of my position. And I am unable to visit the townships for security reasons. Do you have suggestions as to solutions?"

"First, AIDS awareness and education are key. Anton was the first pastor to mention the word HIV/AIDS in the pulpit and suggest the use of condoms among his community. It was not well received by the clergy or the government, but he continued." Some of the pastors smiled and nodded their heads, some did not. Anton stayed silent.

"We find education crucial as well," said Michele. "Your term is AIDS Awareness?"

"Yes. Anton has built his school through the eighth grade at present, but the secondary grades are the most important."

"And why is that Mr. Roberts?"

"In adolescents, these are the grades they become sexually active. And that is where the education must begin. Once he finds the funding for the high school, it will be built, and AIDS Awareness will be mandatory as part of the curriculum. They must know the consequences of their newly found sexuality."

Michele looked at Anton, "Pastor Anton, that is a brilliant idea. Slow the spread of the virus beginning with our youth." Anton smiled. Ian continued.

"Secondly, and this may upset you, but the medical and scientific world are calling for the silencing of your Minister of Health, Ms. Tshabalala-Msimang. She officially stated HIV/AIDS can be cured with a mixture of easily accessible vegetables such as African potato, garlic, and beetroot. Michele, that has no pharmaceutical foundation whatsoever and an unofficial census states the position has cost over three hundred thousand South African lives." Ian paused for a response. This was dangerous ground, and he knew it.

"Mr. Roberts, I am afraid you may be right, but as Deputy Speaker, I cannot comment on your statement, however, I will take a serious look into the situation." Michele knew better than to argue the point. She was aware of Ian's allegation and equally impressed with his knowledge of South African politics.

"Michele, allow me to be frank and say something of which I have no proof whatsoever," Anton breathed deeply.

"Please do, Mr. Roberts."

"The use of antiretroviral therapy works, however, the rumor in the US press is Africa is being used as the testing ground for the development of these drugs. In other words, your people may be like 'lab rats' for these big pharmaceutical companies. But I assure you, African potato, garlic, and beetroot are not the answer." Ian stopped.

"Thank you for your theory, Mr. Roberts. I have heard those concerns as well. But please continue with your former direction about our parenting." Michele was again impressed with Ian's research of their situation.

"Parenting is a matter of love and respect, giving children the confidence and ethical training to care for themselves and treat woman, mothers, and daughters with moral respect as they grow. It starts with teaching children right from wrong and the consequences of their actions. I don't know the rules of your constitution. In the United States there is significant importance placed on the separation between church and state. But in the end, everywhere, God is the ultimate parent. These pastors around your table are the key to nurturing these orphaned children, else the cycle continues. If it were me, I would continue to give your educational systems ample support, and in addition, give your pastors support to strengthen your country's future generations." As Ian looked across the table, Anton finally had a subtle look of agreement on his face. He was both satisfied and proud of Ian's resolution of the question.

"Well, Mr. Roberts," Michele spoke with eyebrows raised. "You have observed and grasped a lot in a short time. You are blessed to have a wonderful friend and mentor in Pastor Anton. With your submergence into our culture, you have experienced more than our White South African population."

"Thank you, and I thought I was called to South Africa to teach. I have been the student." Ian glanced at Anton with a grin on his face; Anton reciprocated with a nod.

Michele looked around the table. "It is getting late. I thank you all for attending and sharing your thoughts and kindness with each other. It has been a beautiful night of beautiful people." Michele finished her closing address and rose from her chair. When she rose, all rose. She shook Ian's hand sweetly with both of hers, then asked him if she could speak to him in private. They went into the sitting room." Anton and Tyler looked at each other with ever so slight grins on their faces.

"Now that we are alone and out of the formal setting, I can now call you Ian?"

"Please, Michele."

"I would so enjoy your company in a more relaxed setting. Your conversation is charming and between you and me, I find you attractive, and I say that to a gentleman very seldom."

Ian felt that was coming, between the looks Michele gave him and the pats on his knee. "Michele, I would enjoy that. And without insulting a woman of your statue, I find you beautiful and intriguing as well. I would enjoy seeing you again."

"This must be private, Ian. We can see each other in June when you return. But no one, especially Anton, must know. I do not know if he would approve. And a relationship with a White American may not be accepted by some. My private email is 'mimdlyd@lantic.net.' I look forward to your company."

Ian and Michele gave each other a gentle hug and a kiss on the cheek; nothing more, since in the world of politics no one knows who is watching. They returned to the vestibule where Anton and Joseph waited.

"Pastor Anton, what a pleasure to have you and your friends join me. I find your secondary education brilliant. Let me give that some thought. I understand why you have such a friendship with Ian."

"Yes, Michele, God has put us together. Thank you for your gracious hospitality," responded Anton.

Two cars awaited. The pastors climbed into their beautiful black Mercedes Benz. They drove off quickly. Anton's car was brought forward. Pastor Hendricks was still in the back seat with the windows down. Anton could see pieces of the Pastor's dinner still on the hood of the car.

Ian, once again trying to enter the wrong side of the car, stood face to face with Anton. "Be careful, Ian. I will not be able to help you if you get in trouble. Politics can be a rough game, understand?"

"I do, Anton." Anton jiggled his keys and Ian went around to the passenger side. By the time he got there, Tyler was in the front seat. The car still wreaked. Ian gave Tyler a smirk and climbed into the back seat next to the prevailing odiferous force.

As they pulled away, Anton spoke, "You did well, Uncle Ian," looking in his rearview mirror. "That was an intense question. I did not see that coming! I was scared, especially with the other pastors and the Jamaican woman at the table. But only for a moment. You have not let me down yet!"

"Anton, a feeling came through me, and I spoke. I knew I would be fine."

Anton smiled, "You keep telling me you are not a preacher. You have learned to let the word of God flow straight from your heart and through your lips. That is a preacher."

Anton drove down the road, unescorted this time. Reading the map, Tyler told Anton to take a left and then a right to leave the compound.

Suddenly, a bright light shone directly into Anton's eyes. It was blinding. Anton slammed the brakes. Two soldiers stood on each side of the car, only this time their Uzis were aimed straight at them. The soldier with the spotlight approached the car. Anton rolled down his window completely. He gazed up at the soldier. Somehow, he remained calm.

"Place your hands on the steering wheel, sir. The rest of you put your hands on the ceiling." They did what they were told and quickly. "What are you doing here?" he barked in a cold and threatening tone.

"We are leaving to go back to our hotel. We were at the Deputy Speaker's house for dinner. Is there something wrong?" Anton spoke. The others stayed silent.

"Yes sir, I would say something is wrong. You are lucky we did not open fire when we first saw you. You are on the driveway approaching the Presidential Palace. Do you have a reason to be here?" The soldier was humorless.

"Sir, we were just following the map given to us by your guardhouse." With that, Anton took the map from Tyler's lap and gave it to the officer.

"Sir, your friend is reading this map upside down." The soldier looked at Anton over his glasses and shook his head.

Anton chuckled, but just a bit. Ian sensed fear and embarrassment coming from Anton. "We have no reason whatsoever to be here. We want to return to our hotel." (Anton never called anyone "sir," although this was a suitable time to start.) "If you can help us find our way out, we would be most appreciative. I am deeply sorry for our mistake."

The soldier pointed his spotlight behind the car onto the road from which they had erroneously turned. "Put the car in reverse and back it down the driveway. Do not damage any of the landscaping. Then go downhill, not up, about one quarter of a kilometer. Then take a left." The soldier walked to Tyler's door and pounded on it. "This way, sir – this is left. That will lead you to the exit gate. You sure you understand?"

"We will find our way out eventually," Anton responded as he regained his arrogant tone. "You and your soldiers are blessed."

"Have a safe night, gentlemen. Let us not go through this again. And hey, what is that horrific odor?" As Anton pulled away, the soldier shook his head, finding their stupidity to be trying.

That night, staring at the ceiling of his hotel room with a clean Pastor Hendricks snoring in the bed next to him, Ian traced his life backwards to connect the dots. Five years earlier this night was unfathomable. And what else was unfathomable, his newly established friendship with Michele. So, with that thought, Ian fell asleep.

THE U.S. ARMY

It was a quiet afternoon in the compound, the weather was pleasantly cool for February. The lack of breeze allowed high wispy clouds to lie stagnant overhead. It was hard for everyone, especially the students, to stay awake. Ian was teaching Samuel to install dual screens for the new data entry business. Pastor Hendricks returned with Ian and Anton from Cape Town and was at Anton's home, teaching a few families how to plant a vegetable garden. He was at peace fulfilling his deceased wife's last wish. Interrupting the tranquility, Anton burst into the office. "Let's go Ian. Consider your Whiteness on duty."

"Anton, I need to test this software while Samuel is still here. My people are awaiting the transmission in the States."

"I need you now, Ian." Samuel and Ian stared at each other. "We can swing by the house so you can comb your hair and shave. And grab the sport coat you wear to service. Let's go, Ian."

Ian followed Anton to the minivan. Anton's hands were trembling on the steering wheel. "You are shaking, Anton. Is somebody sick? Are you sick? Why do I need to clean-up?"

"I'm not sick, but I could be. This is big, Ian. This is a blessing and the person who called me said I must bring you. I don't understand how they know you or how they know you are here, but they do."

"Spill it, Anton. What can be so big it makes you talk faster than Esther praying?"

THE U.S. ARMY

"You remember the first day you walked through the sea of preschoolers?"

"I do. Like it was yesterday."

"Since then, I have only been able to fund the school through the eighth grade. At that point, our children must leave and go to the public school, which is not good."

"I am aware."

Anton took a deep breath and, on the exhale, "We have an appointment with the U.S. Army."

Ian smiled with a curious wrinkle on his forehead. "Why the U.S. Army? We are invading Zimbabwe?"

"Ian, this is serious. I have heard the U.S. Army gives money to non-profits for AIDS Awareness. I have tried many times to contact them but with no success."

"How much are they offering and what would you do with the money?"

"I would build the High School."

"How much do you need?"

"$100,000 would do it."

"You can build a High School for $100,000?"

"Ian, it's bricks and mortar. I have the land next to the church. Jobs are scarce, so labor is cheap. The Hospice was way more complicated."

"Will the Army give you that much?"

"'Ask and it shall be given unto you.' For two years I have prayed for this funding. I had faith God would help when the time was right."

"And the time is right, but where do I come in?"

"I don't know, but they insisted you come."

The minivan came to an abrupt stop in the driveway. "Get cleaned up and meet me back here in fifteen. Remember, the sports coat, but no tie. We do not want to scare them. They want us there at 15:00."

Ian called to Anton as he hurried to the house, "Dress like you, Anton, nothing more. They will love it."

Anton returned. Ian was waiting. Ian looked casual but professional. Anton wore his long African-print shirt, black pants and his cool dress boots, the ones he dances in at service. Anton shifted gears and they were off to meet the U.S Army. Ian propped his right foot on the dashboard as Anton drove crazier than ever.

They arrived at the gate of the U.S Embassy and the Army Headquarters. The guardhouse was standard, like one you would see in a movie. The MPs were well-groomed and intimidating as they should be. A uniformed guard looked past Anton and across to Ian.

"State your business, sir."

"We have an appointment with Colonel Courtney at 15:00 hours. My name is Ian Roberts and…." Ian was interrupted.

"Hold on, sir." The guard scanned his clipboard and confirmed the appointment. "Your driver can drop you off at the front door and wait for you in the parking lot to your right."

Ian glanced at Anton sporting his classic grins. He loved it when this happened. "No sir, the driver is Pastor Anton Nkosi."

"Then who are you?" The guard was confused.

"I work for Pastor Nkosi. He is my boss." Ian looked at Anton with a look that said, *'You love when this happens, don't you?'*

"Okay, I see his name on my list as well. Proceed to the right. You will see a visitor's parking lot. No weapons or firearms are allowed inside the Embassy. Leave them in your car or they will be confiscated."

"Yes sir," said Ian. He thought it would be fun to give the officer a salute, but wisely, he did not.

Anton put the car in gear and as he did, he glanced at Ian. "Uncle Ian, the Lord and I love your 'Whiteness.'"

Ian smiled. He looked at the daunting structure in front of him and responded, "I am glad the two of you know when and how to use it."

They entered the building and showed their passports. Their information was recorded. They went through metal detectors; no weapons were found. They were escorted to the second floor, down a long hallway to a door which read:

U.S. Army Headquarters
Office of Colonel P. Courtney

After checking in, the desk clerk instructed them to take a seat on a small, extremely uncomfortable wooden bench. The walls displayed pictures of historic land battles. On the dominant wall behind the clerk was a picture of President George W. Bush. For Anton and Ian, their wait was close to an hour. Little was said between them. Ian assumed the military to be unfriendly and unreasonable, but he knew few active-duty soldiers in his lifetime. His impression came from movies or the news. He would begin the meeting by being a good listener.

A call came to the desk clerk. "The Colonel will see you now. Follow me please."

As they entered the office, a strong woman in uniform sat behind an equally strong mahogany desk. She was in her mid-fifties with dark cropped hair. She rose and came around her desk to greet her visitors. "Gentlemen, I am Colonel Patricia Courtney. I understand from the Deputy Speaker of Parliament, Michele Ntombela-kaMandela, and excuse me if I pronounced the name incorrectly, you gentlemen could use some money. I understand you have built an HIV/AIDS Hospice in the township. Is that correct?"

Anton began to speak, but before he could, the Colonel turned to Ian. "I assume you are Mr. Roberts?" She looked at Ian and offered a handshake.

"That is correct, Colonel."

"And you must be Pastor Anton Nkosi who built the Hospice." She offered a handshake to Anton, then turned back to Ian. "Mr. Roberts, I spoke with the Deputy Speaker. She seemed quite impressed with you. She told me you understand much about the HIV/AIDS problem in South Africa. She tells me you and she have spoken twice, once at the Dedication of the Hospice and the other at a dinner party at her home in Cape Town." Ian glanced at Anton. Anton nodded for Ian to take the lead.

"Yes Colonel, I have gained first-hand knowledge by working closely with Pastor Anton over the last two years."

"Impressive. And you are an American?"

"Yes, Colonel, I live in Charlotte, North Carolina and I have travelled extensively."

"She tells me you stay in the township. I would suspect there are few White Americans there."

"Yes, maybe none."

"Why are you here in a South African township, Mr. Roberts?"

"Without over detailing, Colonel, I came to start a business that would help fund the operations of the Hospice and create jobs."

"You are a businessman."

"Yes. I have a thriving business in the States as well. But something happened here I did not foresee. I became a student rather than a teacher. I am being enlightened by these people's love and their compassion for one another."

"Who sent you on this mission?"

"Not really a who, Colonel. Something pushed me here, and it felt right. I have seen events and opportunities arise from nowhere. I can no longer cast them off as coincidence."

Anton looked towards the ceiling and gave out with a silent 'Amen.'

"I am not a believer in divine intervention, Mr. Roberts, but according to the Deputy Speaker, your mission does have merit. This money you seek, what will be its purpose?"

"We heard rumors you have money earmarked for AIDS Awareness."

"That is correct. We have grants for that purpose, but if you are seeking money for your Hospice, I consider that too late for awareness. Give me some other way we can help you." That is what Ian wanted to hear. *Knock and the door shall be open unto to you*, he thought.

"Colonel, this is not about helping us. It is about helping the children."

"Go on, Mr. Roberts."

"We need $100,000 to educate our children about the danger of HIV/AIDS."

"That is getting closer to AIDS Awareness. How would you educate them?"

Anton looked at Ian. He was about to speak, but Ian continued. "We need $100,000 to build a High School. We all agree, Colonel, awareness is the first step towards prevention. Our needs coincide."

"I am not following, Mr. Roberts."

"Over the last few years, Pastor Anton has slowly built a private grade school. It is currently through the eighth grade. The quality of teachers and the curriculum are impressive."

"I applaud you, Pastor Anton. Education is the key to everything, especially this country's Black Empowerment doctrine."

Anton nodded and smiled, "Yes Colonel, it is the foundation."

Ian continued. "Now Pastor Anton wants to finish with grades nine through twelve."

"Keep going, Mr. Roberts."

"What better way to exemplify AIDS Awareness than to have a school building, especially at the High School level, overlooking an AIDS Hospice. The students come to school every day and see a two-story AIDS Hospice fifty yards away. They will be aware, firsthand, of the consequences of AIDS."

The Colonel was nodding her head. "Build a High School, you say?"

"Yes, Colonel. Since High School is the age these children become sexually active, the curriculum will include mandatory classes on the transmission, effects, and treatment of the disease."

"Do you have the land? That alone would use much of the $100,000, would it not?"

The stage was set for Anton to close the deal with his charm and enthusiasm. He told her he already had the land and the blueprints. He shared details of the project. He pointed out the jobs it would create, construction, teachers, and office workers. Then in summary, he emphasized the children would receive a quality education and exposure to God.

The Colonel was impressed by Anton's holistic approach. For herself, she had an American and an African working together and both seemed trustworthy. She had the backing of the Deputy Speaker of Parliament. And politically, it would gain notoriety and please both governments. For the Colonel, it was perfect.

"Gentlemen, I find your proposal workable, however, I will require one final condition before I approve of the grant."

"What might that be?" asked Anton.

"After performing my due diligence, I am required to make a site visit to your compound. I have not been in a township, and this is an opportunity for me to do so."

"We would be honored, Colonel. Let us set a time very soon," said Anton. Hands were shaken and smiles exchanged. The meeting ended.

As Ian and Anton were escorted out of the Embassy, Ian leaned over to Anton and whispered, "Nice finish." Anton exhaled heavily and stroked his goatee.

"And where, Ian, did you come up with your AIDS Awareness proposal? Sounded rehearsed."

"It just came out, Anton."

Anton smiled.

One call to the Speaker and the due diligence was over. Plans were made for the Colonel and her entourage to visit the compound. When they arrived, Ian and Anton both greeted them. They toured the church, the school buildings, as well as the site of the new High School. They took a tour of the Hospice. Then to seal the deal, Ian took them to visit the preschoolers, the place where God sealed the deal with him years before. Ian insisted the Colonel inspect the troop of little cherubs up close. The excitement of the children was overwhelming. They were touching real American soldiers and giving them hugs. Deal sealed.

Colonel Patricia Courtney was shown God's reason for her presence in South Africa, the same as he did for Ian. She experienced the beauty of the South African people and the resiliency of a people who lived through oppression. A people needing education for their children so they may rise from poverty and become empowered. Through faith in God, Anton and those God sent to help him, would build a High School, saving countless young lives from a terrible fate.

THE CAPE OF GOOD HOPE

The long flight was nearing its end. The ding dinged, tray tables lifted, and seat backs returned to their upright positions. All seat belts were fastened. Touchdown in twenty minutes. Ian loved this eighteen-hour non-stop from Atlanta. For him, it was a well-deserved mini vacation. While in the air, his cell phone was not functional. He had no access to email nor did it to him. In his snug seat he was brought drinks, three miniature meals, and multiple movies were at his discretion. Rarely did he speak to passengers, not out of rudeness, but his quiet time was seldom and therefore precious. However, this trip was different. He made friends with a fifty-something French Canadian named Peter Dubois traveling from Quebec on business. Peter was to negotiate a mining contract. He was handsome and educated. Ian found the conversation not only easy between them, but he learned much about the South African mining industry.

Winter was approaching in South Africa the middle of June. The setting sun caused a chill to drift into the airport. As the two deplaned, they headed for immigration. This early evening arrival was busy. Ian had arrived at this time before. He found it taxing but unavoidable. As they headed to the end of numerous lines, they passed two men in dark suits and sunglasses. As Ian glanced at them, he noticed they held a professionally printed sign reading, 'Ian Roberts.' He nudged Peter, "Follow me."

"Follow you where, Ian? We need to go through immigration, and it is over there."

"Follow me, Peter." Ian walked toward the men. Peter then noticed the sign, but he also noticed both men were wearing shoulder holsters.

"Are you Ian Roberts, sir?" asked the man with the sign.

"Yes, I am Ian Roberts."

"I need to verify you are who you say you are so please show me your passport." Peter was concerned. "And is this your friend, Mr. Roberts? What is his name, please?"

"His name is Peter Dubois. He is my travelling companion."

"I must see his passport as well, sir. And I will need your baggage claims."

"Hold on, Ian," Peter's voice was cracking. "What is going on. I am not giving anybody my passport or my baggage claim. Who are you, Ian?"

Ian chuckled, "These men work for the person I am visiting here in Cape Town."

"Ian, you told me you were working in one of the townships with a pastor. Pastors need bodyguards over here?"

Ian chuckled again. The men waited patiently. "No Peter, pastors do not need bodyguards. I am going to the township after I visit a friend for a few days."

"So, the person you are visiting needs bodyguards." Peter still gripped his passport tightly in his hand. "Ian, I will just go through the line like everyone else. It's okay."

In a deep voice, the other man with the shoulder holster looked at Peter. "Mr. Roberts, how well do you know this man. Can he be trusted? You do realize we can only take him around these lines, but once we get outside, he must leave us."

"I understand, sir." Ian looked at Peter. Do you understand, Peter? I can save you an hour in this mess, but once we get curbside, we must part. All will be fine, Peter. You are in good hands."

"I do not know what is going on, but if you say it is all good, then, I will trust you. But tell me, who are you?" Ian said nothing.

One man took their baggage claims and left to retrieve their luggage. Ian and Peter followed the other to an immigration counter that read,

'Clergy and Dignitaries.' With no waiting, their passports were stamped. Ian and Peter were escorted to a private lounge and offered food and drinks. It was not long before they had their luggage.

Peter and Ian were escorted to the curbside where a long black limousine awaited. The windows were blackened. Two more men in black suits stood by the back doors. "Peter, this is where I must say goodbye for now. I'm sorry if I scared you. This whole thing is strange for me as well. I have your email. Someday I will tell you what is going on. You have been a pleasure, and you are blessed, my friend." They shook hands.

The door was opened for Ian. "Come on Ian, it's killing me. Who are you?" Ian climbed in and as he did, Peter caught a glimpse inside. It was a woman. The door was shut.

Ian smiled as he sat on the plush leather seat. The woman slid across, put her arm through his and kissed him on the cheek. "Mr. Ian Roberts, I have been looking forward to seeing you again ever since my dinner party. Your flight was good, I pray?"

Ian patted her hand that was wrapped around his bicep. "My flight was wonderful. I met a French Canadian. His conversation helped pass the time."

"Did you tell him who you were meeting?"

"I did not, and he was confused." Ian chuckled. "Thank you for getting us both through immigration and customs. That saved a lot of time, Michele."

Michele smiled, "I certainly would not let you endure that madness? And I would have grown terribly impatient if I had to wait any longer to see you."

Ian smiled. "Thank you, that is sweet."

The limo left the airport. Ian and Michele enjoyed a glass of wine on the way to wherever they were going. "I usually have a motorcycle escort, but that would draw attention. I hope you have not mentioned our meeting to Anton."

"I have not. No one knows. That works well for both of us. And frankly, it makes it more exciting." Ian smiled. So did Michele.

"Then you are comfortable with this? Anton told me your church expressed an uneasiness as it pertained to us at the Dedication."

"Michele, their concerns are only political and pertain to their own public image. I am here in South Africa to help Anton and his people. I am dedicated to what is happening with them. Their uneasiness is none of my concern. You are not married, nor am I. That is all that matters to me. But you, are you comfortable? We are in a darkened limousine surrounded by Secret Service."

"First, I agree Ian, if either of us were married, I would not be here. But we are not. Secondly, I am political. This is a way of life for me. I need protection as well as I need to stay out of the tabloids. I don't have a problem with this, but my campaign manager might. Let us enjoy each other for the next few days and stay out of the limelight."

"Sounds perfect, Michele. And before we speak any further, I must thank you so much for connecting us with the U.S. Army. Anton could not be more grateful. He has started construction and will finish by the end of August."

"You are welcome. I was impressed with Anton's plan to educate our teens in regard to HIV/AIDS. It is so needed. Government funds are not permitted to finance a private school, so I made a few calls. The Colonel was quite impressed by you, especially when you sealed the deal by having all the little cherubs, as you call them, give her hugs. You are a crafty politician, Mr. Roberts."

The limo made left turns and right turns. Ian had no idea where he was other than Cape Town. Then he sensed the limo going down a steep grade. The city lights disappeared. He remained silent. The limousine stopped.

The door was opened by one of the men from the airport. Ian was excited and looked around. They were underground in a dimly lit parking garage. The man spoke, "We are here, Deputy Speaker. I will take your guest's luggage to your suite. I have arranged for room service to have wine and aperitifs available before you dine, unless there is something other than wine your guest would prefer?"

Ian looked at Michele. "Actually, a scotch whiskey blend would be nice. Chevais Regal if it is available, but any kind of scotch will be fine."

I'm sorry sir, I do not understand. Chevais, did you say? How do you spell that?" Ian spelled it out for the man. "Oh, you are speaking of

'Cheevass.' I will have it brought to your room right away." The man gave Ian a warm smile.

"What is your name, sir."

"My name is Ryker. And thank you for asking."

"You are welcome, Ryker."

The two were escorted to an elevator situated in a remote corner of the garage. Ian saw four other limos parked against the walls, but no cars. The elevator went straight from the basement to open directly into a two-bedroom suite. One entire wall was glass revealing a faint view of Robbin Island. Michele pointed. "That is where my uncle, Nelson Mandela, was held in exile for eighteen years for plotting to overthrow South Africa's Apartheid system. He was released in 1990 at age seventy-one, then became our first Black President in 1994."

"I am familiar with his history. He and Mahatma Gandhi are two of my most respected men in history, along with Jesus Christ. They were all non-violent revolutionaries."

"You have studied these men?"

I have and it was a long time before I learned Gandhi got his start as a lawyer protesting Indian rights here in South Africa. He took beatings and fought the courts on many occasions. Your uncle held Gandhi in the highest esteem. They were great men."

"I met my uncle once, but that one time changed my life. I never spoke with him, but his mere presence was breathtaking. I want to be just like him." Then Michele paused and said with both humility and a smile. "Before we continue, Ian, I must ask if you would like to take a shower and clean up. I do not believe your thirty hours of travel have been kind to your aroma."

Ian laughed. "I would think not. I would love to clean up, but I am afraid my clothes will be wrinkled coming out of my suitcase."

"I foresaw that, so I have taken liberties. I measured one of my servants back at the mansion. He was close to your size as I remembered. I purchased clothes for you to wear in the next few days. They are in the guest room. I hope you like them." She gave Ian a fleeting glance.

Ian gave Michele a grandma hug, leaning over but not coming too close. He could smell himself, so he knew he must smell bad. "Michele, you are being too kind to me. I appreciate it."

"You are welcome. Now, get cleaned up so we can have drinks, dinner, and conversation. The way Anton talks about you, I believe we have so much to learn from each other." Ian went off to make himself civilized.

After a hot shower and a shave, Ian came from his room. "The clothes fit you perfectly, Ian. And that color looks good on you."

"You did well, Michele. I feel much better."

The two had a perfect evening. Just like the Dedication of the Hospice, it was as if they knew each other all their lives. After a night of cocktails, stimulating conversation and a delectable lobster dinner, Ian and Michele hugged and retired to their rooms.

Sunrise came quickly for Ian. As he awoke, he looked around. He had no idea where he might be. He lay in his bed staring at the ceiling as his memory brought the last couple of days into focus, piece by piece. He decided to shower once again. When he exited the bathroom, he found his bed was made and new clothing laid neatly on the comforter. The outfit was simple. Khaki pants, a blue button-down shirt and a baseball cap that read 'Cape Town Spurs.' It was obvious Michele had something planned and Ian loved new adventures. He dressed and entered the suite's main room.

Michele was busy at her PC in the corner. 'Good morning, Mr. Roberts. You slept well, I pray?"

"I cannot tell you how good it felt to lie down after that long flight." Ian stretched. A breakfast of tea, fruit, and bagels were on an elegant China platter located on a table overlooking the bay and Robben Island. Ian thought how different things look in the daylight. It was majestic. And he also thought, so was Michele.

"Ready for a road trip, Mr. Roberts?"

"You are in charge, Deputy Speaker. I will go anywhere you want to take me." She gave Ian a mischievous grin.

"Have you been to the Cape of Good Hope?"

"I have not," Ian replied.

"Good, I am going to take you there today. It is magnificent. Let's get ready. We will return sometime this evening."

"What do I need?"

"Nothing."

Michele pressed a buzzer and Ryker came up the elevator. "Good morning, Deputy Speaker. Your limousine is waiting, and all arrangements have been made." With that, the three descended and climbed into the limo. As they went up the ramp, the blackened windows were lowered. Ian was confused. He could see a crowd of people across the street shooting the limo with telephoto lenses. Michele gave a quick wave and a smile, then the windows returned to black.

"Michele, they just saw us together. I don't understand."

"Paparazzi, they will follow us for a while." That was all she said.

Ian could not leave it alone. "All day they will follow us?"

Michele smiled. "We will talk about it later." She quickly changed the subject. "I am looking forward to showing you the Cape and telling you its history, but first, let us get out of town. Tell me, how is Anton and his compound projects coming? You know, the 'Holy Ground'."

"Slowly, but forward. I will know more when I get there the day after tomorrow."

"It has been six months since the Dedication and almost three months since my dinner party. You scared my clergy friends with your 'Parenting' answer, Mr. Roberts."

"And you were ready to cast me out as well."

"Yes, I was ready to kick you out of the mansion. I do believe I would have asked you to leave had your explanation not been so precise. You absolutely startled me with your original response." They both laughed.

"I scared myself for a moment. I must tell you, sometimes God just throws it out there and leaves it up to me to explain it."

"Ian, you mean that was not rehearsed what you said?"

"Not at all. It just came out of my mouth. I know, Michele, it sounds incredible, but that has happened other times as well."

"Fascinating, everything I say in public must be well thought out. You know, politics. Give me another example."

"Well, when Anton and I first met, he wanted me to preach one Sunday morning. I looked at him and told him I was here to help him start businesses and I was not here to save anyone. That was his job."

"Okay, so you told him you were not a preacher, thank goodness." She smiled. "So, what happened?"

"On my third trip I was at the Sunday service. He was preaching to his congregation about what God wants his people to do. You know, help others, love, the usual. Then he looked down at me. I was sitting next to Esther. He said, 'We have a man in our presence today. A man who has been called to us by God. This man, without thinking about it, a man who is still unable to explain why he came to us, is here doing God's work. Uncle Ian, please come to the stage and talk to us.'"

"So, did you go up? You must have been shocked. What did you say?"

"I had no choice, Michele. Everyone was staring at me, and I had nothing. No thoughts in my head, not a clue of what to say. But as I walked to the stage, I was calm. The room was silent. All eyes were upon me. As I stood behind the pulpit and looked out over the congregation, I started speaking."

"What did you say?"

"I recited a quote I heard years before from an interview with Mother Teresa. The interviewer asked her about prayer. The quote went like this. 'God speaks in the silence of the heart, and we listen. And then we speak to God from the fullness of our heart, and God listens.'"

"I do not understand, Ian."

"I didn't either until that very moment, until it came out of my mouth from somewhere deep in my memory. And it was at that moment I realized how I came to be here. One doesn't have to hear a strong voice coming from a mountain top to know what God wants us to do. Take right and wrong as an example. We know inside what is right, and we know what is wrong. It is a feeling, not a list of rules. The scriptures are only important as a tool to reinforce our righteous feelings. I realize now, that is why I am not formally religious. It downplays feelings in most people. It discourages questions, but questions are what strengthens one's faith. That is why I am here. I keep stepping through the doors God opens for me. And when I do, he opens another."

"And that is what happened the night of my dinner party. You were winging it? We all thought, including Anton, you were about to insult an entire country of parents."

Ian chuckled. "I'm sorry about blurting 'Parenting.' I knew it would startle the room when I said it. And Anton nearly choked on his Cameroon."

"Ian, that night you exposed our health minister's claim that HIV could be cured with a mixture of African potatoes, garlic, and beetroot. I had heard rumors, but you exposed the reality of her claims; three hundred thousand lives have been lost due to it. That caused me to form a research committee. As of last month, educational material has been distributed nationwide to debunk that falsehood."

"Michele, that is wonderful. You are wonderful."

"I also made a connection with the World Health Organization to monitor those pharmaceutical companies who are performing HIV/AIDS clinical trials on our people. We will find out which of those are beneficial and which are using us as lab rats."

"Michele, I am impressed. I don't know what to say, except those were the words God put in my mouth that night."

"And Ian, had Esther not sat us together at the Dedication, none of this would have happened."

"And had the storm the night before cancelled the Dedication, and so on, and so on. This is what I am seeing for the first time in my life. It all connects for a reason." They both smiled.

Ian looked out the rear window. The cars and motorcycles were still following. "Will the Paparazzi be a problem for us all day?"

Michele gave a coy smile. Ian was confused by her lack of concern.

"Ian what are Anton's needs now that the Hospice is open."

"The Hospice has a problem we did not foresee."

"Go on."

Your government gives assistance to AIDS patients if their CD4 levels drop below 200."

"Yes, I understand and that is a controversial subject."

"We are taking in dying patients, but that has created a new problem."

"And that problem is?"

"We feed them, they rest, our people pray for them and love them."

"That sounds compassionate. Dying in peace is the goal, is it not?"

"Well, it should be, but in there lies the problem. Their CD4 levels rise above 200."

"Again, that is ...." Michele stopped herself.

"Now you are understanding the problem."

"I think so. Their levels increase above 200 and they lose their government assistance."

"Keep going."

"And then the Hospice loses the funding for the patient."

"It gets worse. The family who cared for the patient prior to the Hospice also gets nothing to care for them now."

"So, what happens?"

"The family refuses to take them back, so neither of us can afford to keep them. The patients are left in limbo and their levels decline once again. They go from sick to better to sick again. It is a terrible cycle."

"What do you do?"

"Anton did not foresee the cycle. He knew government assistance would not cover all the costs. Credence Community Church in the U.S. did not want to commit to unlimited funds for operations. That is where I came in. My business was to create jobs and kick off profits to help fund the difference. But I have been unable to grow it as I expected."

"Why is that?"

"Anton insisted the employees come from his congregation. The more jobs, the more people he can attract to his church and the more people he can bring to God."

"Sounds perfect. But why can you not grow the business."

"In the beginning I tried medical transcription. I had a market for that. Anton was specific as to whom I could hire. I took six young women to the States for training. Their typing skills improved, but their spelling and grammar from dictated voice files was not enough. So, I switched to data entry."

"Did that work?"

"Yes, they became proficient, but I cannot find enough work for them in the private sector, here or in the States."

"Okay. Any other problems?"

"Anton and I pushed to finish the second floor of the Hospice, but now the problems all tie together. Since the patients are getting better, the more

THE CAPE OF GOOD HOPE

we take in, the more we will place in limbo. We must limit our intake and can justify only one-fourth of the building."

"That is a problem. Let me think about it."

"Thank you, but I had no intention of burdening you with this."

"I asked, Ian. All is well."

The limousine pulled into a gas station with a small gift shop and snacks. Ryker went inside to secure the premise. He asked two patrons to kindly finish their purchase and leave. He waited inside as the driver opened the car door. Michele and Ian were cleared to enter.

"Come, Ian, let us see what they have."

As Ian climbed out, he could see cars and a motorcycle parked to the side of the road, keeping a respectable distance. Cameras were clicking. The entrance was now closed to the public.

Once inside, Michele grabbed Ian by the hand and led him to the back of the shop. In front of a small doorway stood a couple dressed exactly the same as Michele and Ian. Michele nodded to them. The couple walked around the story exposing themselves to the front windows. Toting a gift bag, they exited the front door, ducked their heads, and climbed into the limo. They drove off followed by the invasive swarm of reporters."

"Okay, time to get on with it, Mr. Roberts." She gave Ian a crafty smile. They bounced down a set of rickety stairs. At the bottom, a man in plain clothes and a shoulder holster opened the door.

"Deputy Speaker," was all he said as he opened the back door of an unassuming but comfortable Mercedes. They climbed in.

Ian began to belly-laugh. "Michele, that was wild. I had no idea what was happening. Now all those reporters are chasing the wrong people."

Michele gave a grin. "I love playing with them. They can be such a pain in the behind. They deserve to be tricked, but they will never know it."

"What about the shopkeeper? Won't he tell?"

"No, he is with our Secret Service as well. Like I said, I love doing that."

They both laughed. Michele slid across the seat and interlocked her arm with Ian's. "It is about two hours to the Cape. We can make a couple of stops along the way. You will love this trip, Mr. Roberts. I never get tired of it." They exchanged smiles laced with comfort and respect.

It was a picturesque drive on a gorgeous day. Reaching Cape Point, interlocked arm in arm, Michele took Ian to the 'Two Oceans' restaurant where they had a light lunch along with a bottle of wine from the Cape Point Vineyards. As they enjoyed themselves, they gazed out over the vast oceans. The contrasting hues of blue were magnificent where the Atlantic Ocean and the Indian Ocean melted mystically into one another. They strolled down pathways in the Cape Point Nature Preserve spotting a variety of wildlife including zebra, ostrich, and a multitude of baboon. As they strolled, Michele told fascinating stories of myths involving mermaids, sea monsters, as well as an array of paranormal ghost stories. And she did it so very well.

It was approaching late afternoon. They returned to the car to go back to Cape Town. But shortly after leaving Cape Point, they pulled into a gated community with a guardhouse like the one he passed the night of Michele's dinner party. Driving a short way, the Mercedes pulled into a semi-circular driveway paved with cobblestones. The car stopped and the door opened. Ian saw a sophisticated domestic woman standing on a pillared portico. Behind her in the tall double doorway was someone he had seen before. He wore a stylish lightweight tuxedo. "Good afternoon, Deputy speaker," the woman said as she bowed.

"And welcome, Mr. Roberts," said the man in the tuxedo. "It is a pleasure to see you again, sir." It was the butler from Michele's mansion.

"Hello, sir. It is such a pleasure to see you as well. That was such a delightful and enlightening evening. I am surprised to see you here."

"I go wherever the speaker needs me. How is Pastor Anton?"

"He is well, continually moving in some direction. We never know what is coming next with Anton." The man nodded his head.

Michele grabbed Ian's arm once more. "Come, let me show you the view. I thought a cocktail hour and dinner would be nice right here." She walked Ian through the exquisite house and onto the veranda. When entering, Ian noticed ten-foot razor wire spanning the few feet between homes. Now he knew why. The ocean spanned the horizon in a breathtaking panorama. The shoreline was five hundred feet straight down a sheer rock face. The house was impenetrable. Ian shook his head with a sigh.

"Michele, this is magnificent. It is one of God's finest works. I don't know what to say except thank you. This is one of the most memorable days of my life."

"Ian, I like you. You treat me like I am just a person. It is refreshing. I have not had a day like this for a long time. I feel so good."

They sat on the top of a cliff, having cocktails, more conversation, and a delectable dinner of prawn from Mozambique. They watched the sun be extinguished by the ocean. They exchanged adoring glances.

"It is time to head back, Ian. I have meetings I must attend in the morning or else we would stay here for the night." As she rose from her chair, she came around the table, bent over, and kissed Ian on the lips. This time she gave him a blank stare. "Ian, I should not have done that."

Ian stood up and reciprocated the kiss, only holding it much longer.

"We have a two-hour drive back to Cape Town. It will be late and time for us to go to bed when we arrive." She gave Ian a bashful smile.

"Yes Michele, I believe it will be time." Ian stared into her eyes. She grabbed his arm once more as they walked to the car. They cuddled in the back seat all the way to Cape Town.

AND HE ASCENDED INTO HEAVEN TO SEE THE LORD

The flight was two hours from Cape Town. Ian landed in Johannesburg at noon following a romantic and quixotic three days with Michele. Ezekiel was waiting for him in the rotunda. Mid-June was warmer here than in Cape Town, but it was apparent winter was approaching all South Africa.

Ian found it fun weaving through traffic in the city, but only if he was not driving. And riding with Ezekiel was almost as adventurous as riding with Anton.

They arrived at the compound in mid-afternoon. He tracked down Anton. As he approached, he was greeted with, "Ian, I can't meet with you now. I have meetings the rest of the day, but I need your Whiteness tonight." Anton looked concerned. It was a look Ian did not recognize.

"Of course, are you okay?"

"I must run, but we need to go to the hospital. My father is going to die tonight. You have met my father, have you not?"

"I know your father. Did you say he is going to die tonight? How do you know it will be tonight?"

"Because he called me and told me so this morning. Get some rest and take a bath. Eleanor will bring you back at seven o'clock." Anton turned and was off.

Eleanor took Ian to lunch at the Apache; ox tail was a must. She usually paid for lunch, but this time, she found her rand to be counterfeit. Ian paid. They gathered the children from school and made their way back to the house. Ian took a lukewarm bath and a nap.

At seven o'clock, Ian returned to the compound. Anton was running late. "Okay Uncle Ian, are you ready? The hospital is thirty minutes away depending on traffic. Hop in." Anton jiggled his keys in Ian's face. Ian gave a smug grin and proceeded to the passenger's side of the car.

As they pulled from the compound, Ian asked, "What is wrong with your father?"

"He is seventy-eight and has pancreatic cancer."

"That's not good, Anton. Do they have visiting hours?"

Anton stroked his goatee and smiled. Ian loved it when he did that. It meant something important happened or something important is about to happen. "How was your flight? How is your family?" Ian did not wish to lie. But Cape Town needed to remain a secret, so he avoided the flight question.

Traffic was heavy which gave the two extra time to debrief. Ian was unaware visiting hours would be over by the time they reached the hospital. Anton was not, thus the need for Ian's Whiteness. They arrived at 8:30.

Ian followed Anton through the revolving door of the main entrance. In the dimly light atrium, all alone, was a large middle-aged Black woman in a nursing uniform. She sat uncomfortably in a rickety wicker chair, behind a desk which appeared small compared to her. Her frown was not welcoming.

"Visiting hours ended at seven o'clock. They resume at ten o'clock tomorrow." She was curt. She resumed reading her magazine.

Ian knew Anton too well. That statement would not endure, especially with her attitude. Ian knew what was coming. He saw this scenario play out many times. Anton knew he had his weapon on his hip. It was Ian's Whiteness.

"I'm sorry Ma'am, but you do not understand. My father, Pastor Nikosi, is a patient in your second-floor ward and he is going to die tonight. I must insist I see him one last time." Anton gave his sweet smile and, as usual, stroked his goatee.

"I'm sorry you think your father will die tonight, but rules are rules. Visiting hours are over. No exceptions. Come back in the morning."

"No ma'am, you really don't understand." He glanced at Ian. Ian stepped forward staring unemotionally into the nurse's eyes. She stared back over her glasses. "This is a missionary that has come from America. He arrived just in time to pray for my father, who is going to die tonight."

"Sure, he is," she said.

Ian did not say a word but kept eye contact in a showdown. He then broke out a sweet benevolent smile of his own. "I am sure you would not turn away this man of the cloth who only wishes to see his father one last time. Or me, a man who has come all the way from America to pray for a father and his son in their last hours. I would not want to tell my American Embassy, who expedited this trip so I could pray for Pastor Nkosi and his son, that you blocked us. I am sorry, I did not catch your name."

She would have turned Anton away without hesitation, but Ian did what he needed. He was White and an American. The bluff always worked.

So, one and a half holy men walked through dark serene hallways, the silence broken only by an occasional cry of pain. Climbing the marble stairway, they proceeded to the second-floor ward where Ian assumed, he would find Anton's father resting quietly in his bed. As they entered, Ian was shocked. Twelve single beds were crammed tightly together: a small nightstand separating each. Some of the elderly men lie quiet, some sat on their beds reading their Bibles, but most were fixated on the man dressed in a pair of black slacks, a black shirt, and a white collar. Seeing Anton, the man shuffled towards him, his Bible clutched close to his heart.

"Anton, my son, you made it through the desk. I was afraid I would not see you before I leave." Anton hugged his father, stepped back, and gave him a unique smile.

"Father, do you remember my friend, Ian Roberts? You met him at the Dedication of the Hospice."

"I certainly do, my son. You are the American that helps my son in the township. It was your birthday if I remember correctly. You were with that pretty politician lady. She was interested in you, am I right?" Senior Pastor Nkosi had no inner dialogue. It was charming.

Ian gave a humble smile. "Perhaps, sir, and you are correct, it was my birthday."

"You did not answer my second question, Mr. Roberts. A man of my years can see those things." The Pastor's sly smile was adorable.

"Anton tells me you are going to die tonight, sir. Is that correct?" Ian smiled. He thought he would humor Pastor Nkosi. "Or did he tell me that so I would use my Whiteness to get him in here?"

"I taught him that old 'Whiteness' trick years ago, my boy. In the Apartheid days, whenever I had a White friend with me, I used it. Shoot, I still use it. Evidently, so does Anton." His grin went ear to ear. "Son, I am going to die tonight. That is going to happen. I am going to die tonight, no doubt about it. The Lord told me this morning during prayer."

Ian smiled again. "I would never challenge the Lord, sir, but you seem too healthy, and way too happy to die. You are filled with joy. You have such energy. You should be weak and scared?" Anton continued to smile. He knew Ian had no idea what was coming. But he did.

"Yes, young man, I am filled with joy. This is the happiest day of my life." The pastor raised his arms to the heavens, his worn tattered bible in his hand. He spoke as if the entire world was listening. He was dynamic. He was a bona fide preacher. The rest of the ward stopped to hear it again, what they had been hearing all day from the great Pastor Nkosi. Smiles dawned their faces and halleluiahs bounced off the walls.

Ian was confused. He never witnessed anything like this. In America, there was no happiness in a ward of death beds. No happiness in a hospice. But he was not in America.

"Tell him, Father. Let our Uncle Ian know why you are so happy. I want to hear it one more time." Anton stood back and watched his father. He was filled with absolute admiration. This was the man who introduced him to Jesus Christ. And because of Jesus Christ, and his father, Anton was Anton.

"Young man, let me tell you and anyone who wants to listen, I have been waiting for this day all my life, yes son, all my life."

A voice cried, "Why, Pastor, why have you been waiting for this day all your life?"

IAN AND ANTON

"Because tonight, this very night, I am going to see the Lord. I am going to look him in the eyes, smile, and drop down on my knees. My face will stream with tears. I will kiss his hand. I will kiss the hem of his garment. All my life, I have been talking with him and he has led me on the path of righteousness for his name's sake. In the darkest of times, the death of my beloved wife, this scourge of HIV, and the loss of Anton's brother, I always knew Fridays were a part of life. Jesus was crucified, dead and buried on Friday, but the Lord taught me to accept Fridays." The pastor went silent, along with the entire ward. "You know what I am saying, son?"

"I do not, sir," responded Ian. "Ian could not have answered the question better. And Anton could not wait for Ian to hear something he would never forget. Someday, it would tie all this together for him. It would all make sense. Ian would experience tough times in his future, but he would always draw upon this moment.

Looking skyward, then staring at Anton, he asked "My loving son, tell our American friend what the Lord tells us about Fridays."

"You tell him Father. I love it when you say it. One last time, let me hear it."

"On Friday, Jesus was made to carry his cross through the streets. They crowned him with thorns, they nailed his hands and feet to the cross, then pierced his side with a spear to be sure he was dead. He was buried. But was that the end, Mr. Roberts? Preach it out to our friend, Anton." Pastor Nkosi was grinning ear to ear.

"Tell him, Father. Tell him, why wasn't that the end?" Anton was excited like a school child.

"Because" he hesitated then exploded, "Sunday's Comin', my son. That's right, the Lord has promised us over and over, Sunday's Comin'. Jesus rose from the dead on Sunday morning. He taught us, no matter how dark in the tomb, no matter how bad the pain, Sunday's always Comin'. Someone can stick a spear in your side, someone can rip your scalp with thorns, someone can nail you to a cross, but the Lord has shown us, Sunday's Comin'. Praise the Lord, and tonight, my son, Sunday's Comin." He looked around the room and spun with his hands over his head, "Bless them all Lord with your Holy Spirit." Halleluiahs filled the room once again.

Tears ran down Ian's face. A tight sob welled in his throat. He remembered what Anton said to him on the first days of his mission, *'You will cry many times and for many different reasons.'* And this would be the only time he would see Anton with tears. For the rest of Ian's life, in his darkest moments, he would hear Pastor Nkosi's holy words, 'SUNDAY'S COMIN'.

After an hour of visitation, it was time to leave. Anton was saying goodbye to his best friend and mentor. He was on his knees, holding his father's hand. His father had his other hand placed gently atop his son's head. They prayed in Zulu. Anton wept. His father had a peaceful aura surrounding him. Ian felt he could see a light encircling the pastor. As Anton rose, his father wiped the tears from his son's face with his rough wrinkled palm. "You are blessed, my son. The Lord and I are proud of you. We love you."

"I am blessed, Father, because of you. I will see you in heaven."

Ian approached him with tears in his eyes. "I will never forget you, sir."

"No more tears, son. I am happy. Take good care of Anton and my people. You are blessed."

"Yes sir, I will. You are blessed."

Ian and Anton turned towards the door. As they walked out, they heard it one more time, only softly. "Remember boys, 'SUNDAY'S COMIN'." The ward was silent.

That night, as always, Anton prayed for all. He stared for hours at the ceiling as he reminisced, year by year, the time spent with his father. He fell asleep.

Ian joined the family at breakfast. Anton came down a few minutes later. He appeared solemn. "Anton?" asked Esther. Ian looked at the family.

"Yes, he left us last night."

"He looked so happy and at peace."

"He told me the Lord summoned him at sunrise yesterday. He knew you were arriving, Ian. The Lord wanted and needed you there. That is how it works." Anton smiled. He knew for Ian; each day was closer to understanding God's purpose for him.

Senior Pastor Nkosi saw the Lord that night. He left the earth doing what he was sent to do and what he loved most. Pastor Nkosi gave his last sermon to the weak and dying. Right to the end, he brought faith and hope to those nearing their judgment day. And with that faith and happiness, Ian learned, for the rest of his life, that SUNDAY'S ALWAYS COMIN'.

BOTSWANA

Ian went from Charlotte to Newark, Newark to Johannesburg, overnight in the airport hotel, and finally landed at the Maun International Airport in Northern Botswana. From there, he made his way to a small single engine prop-plane and headed for the Okavango Delta. Ian was last to arrive. All the other passengers were on the plane and ready to go. Walking onto the runway in the heat of September, he felt the tension building. But he must stay cool. He ducked his head as he entered the cabin. When he looked up, he smiled.

"Mr. Roberts, I saved you a seat." There was the face he longed to see.

Ian bent over and kissed her. He was still smiling. "Good day, De..." She grabbed his shirt and kissed him quickly."

"Hush, I am alone, no Ryker."

Ian looked around. "I can see why. We would never get off the ground with him in here." Ian sat. Michele put her arm through his. They were together once again.

"I have missed you terribly. It has only been three months, but it seems like forever. I thought the flight this morning would never land."

Ian smiled. "I left a day and half ago. But I showered this morning in Johannesburg. Can you tell?"

"With this heat, your freshness won't last long. But I adore your smell, Mr. Roberts." They kissed again.

IAN AND ANTON

It was a short flight to the Okavango Delta. September was the end of the dry season. The delta was now filled with watering holes, making it the best time to view the animals as they congregated for drinking. It was also the best time for predators.

They landed. Porters approached the plane and carried luggage to the open-air jeeps. Each was able to seat four passengers, the driver, and a guide with a rifle on his lap. Ian, Michele, and another couple were staying at the Abu Camp on the bank of the Okavango Delta. All the others were at the larger camps. Michele insisted on Abu for intimacy and safety, but mostly intimacy.

The ride was short. The last two miles were unpaved. The jeep stopped. The guide raised his rifle. Blocking them was a family of African elephants crossing the road. The Bull entered their path first, stopped and stared, while the mother and two calves crossed behind him. The driver backed up and turned the jeep around.

"Must we go another route?" asked Ian.

"No sir."

"Then why are you turning around."

"In case the bull charges."

"Are we safe."

"Yes sir, we are now."

Ian was puzzled. "What do you mean, we are now?"

"I mean, now we can outrun that bull. We could not in reverse." They all smiled.

Before unpacking, Ian and Michele got reacquainted. They took a cool bath in the outdoor tub. They requested room service this first evening. They sat on their wooden deck watching the sun set on the lagoon, enjoying cocktails, dinner, and conversation as the hippos splashed about.

The next day was exciting. The safari was breathtaking. Elephants, giraffes, zebras, wild dogs, and many more. The guides were well educated about the savannah. Ian's camera was having the time of its life. Ian and Michele could not have been happier.

That night, they joined the others for dinner in the lodge. The cuisine was incredible. Impala, wart hog, and crocodile; pap and vegetables as well.

After desert, they joined a couple from the United States for cocktails on the deck.

"Hello, my name is Franklin Meyers. This is my wife, Mary Ellen. We live in New York City. And you?"

"I am Ian Roberts, and this is…"

Michele jumped in, "My name is Michele Zuma. We live in Charlotte, North Carolina. I teach Sub Saharan African history at the university."

'Interesting Michele. What University?

Ian jumped in, "University of North Carolina."

"And you, Ian?"

"I have a medical administration business. We are here on vacation. And what do you and your wife do, Franklin?"

"My wife is an attorney and I work for the United Nations."

That got Michele's attention. "In what capacity, Franklin?"

"I am here gathering information on the success Botswana is having with their new policies regarding the HIV/AIDS epidemic."

"And what might those be, Franklin," asked Michele.

Franklin began to give Michele some background information, but Michele quickly interrupted. "Being a history professor, I am aware of those statistics in the Sub-Saharan. Unfortunately, they are all quite similar. Tell me more about Botswana's new policies."

"In 2003, the government began constructing primary care facilities with the goal of having no person more than five kilometers from care. In 2004, they began routine HIV testing on the public. If positive, they began free or cheap antiretroviral treatment for anyone who wished to participate."

"Who supplied the drug? Were the pharmaceutical companies giving it to them in return for clinical trials?"

"It was Merck and Bristol-Meyers. I am sure it helped in their research, but the drugs were purchased by the Botswana government."

"How could this small nation afford it?"

"Michele, Botswana is the largest producer of quality carat diamonds in the world, and they are in a 50/50 partnership with DeBeers of South Africa. Profits from three diamond mines and a coal mine give them sufficient funds to buy the drugs."

IAN AND ANTON

"Is it working."

"It has only been four years since implementation; however, they are treating 75% of infected adults and 98% of children. And due to the primary care facilities, we see a significant drop in infant and maternal mortality rates. And we have seen a 30% reduction in child infections."

"What are you concluding?"

"The government has a lot of money. Their corruption is the lowest on the continent. It is early, but it looks like the primary care facilities are detecting the virus early, and the centers are providing prenatal care and supervised birthing."

"Thank you, Franklin. I will watch your studies closely for my students."

"You are welcome, Michele."

The group continued conversation on several topics. Michele was careful not to expose her identity. Ian and Michele strolled home under a full moon. They heard an occasional crash as an elephant feed. They heard the frolicking of hippos in the lagoon and the eerie barking of the wild dogs. After a long day, they made their way to bed. Michele laid her head on Ian's chest. They snuggled tightly.

"Has Anton had any luck finding a use for the vacant space in the Hospice?"

"He has not. He still has a problem expanding his patient count. If they eat well and rest, the problem continues. Antiretroviral and prevention are the only answers."

"He has the High School to help with prevention through education. Now he needs early detection, medication, and obstetric care."

"Correct."

"Goodnight, Mr. Roberts."

"Goodnight, Ms. Zuma. I like that. It is much easier to say than your real name."

Ian and Michele visited two more smaller camps in the next week. They flew back to the Maun airport together. Michele's flight left three hours earlier for Cape Town than Ian's for Johannesburg.

As Ian walked Michele to her gate, he stopped, "Michele, I am in love with you."

"And I you, Ian Roberts. I will see you in January. I already miss you. Let us email every day, even if it is just to say hello."

They embraced. Neither wanted to let go. January could not come too soon.

CAMPAIGN INTERFERENCE

Ian rose from his bed. Charlotte was cold in the month of December and his feet felt it. This was Ian's busiest time of the year. As many took the end of the year to lighten their workloads and visit family, Ian had the arduous responsibility for closing his client's corporations with the IRS and determining bonuses for their employees. In addition, end of year holiday parties were numerous and as President of his company, his presence was required. And the final shopping for his own family in the crowded malls was his least favorite. January could not arrive too soon.

As his night's rest was continually interrupted by the task list in his head, he started his day reading and prioritizing his emails. Data requests, decisions, and Happy Holiday greetings were numerous. However, there was always one email he enjoyed. This morning he read it first, but it was disappointing.

Dear Ian,

I am sad to say I must ask you to cancel your visit to Cape Town in January. My workload is the same, however, as you know, I am up for reelection and will not be able to see you again until June. I yearn to see you, but I cannot give us the time I wish. My campaign manager has asked us not to communicate via email until after the election. Makeda will be in contact, and we can correspond through her.

It is painful to know I will not be with you for so long. Wish me luck.

May you and your family have the happiest of holidays.

Bless you my dearest,

Michele.

Ian sighed deeply. He understood and was not surprised, but he assumed this span would be after his January visit. His father was gravely ill and there were troublesome rumors pertaining to his own business. It was best for him as well to wait until June.

CREDENCE HAS NEEDS

Jordan West was shown into Mr. Wik's office by his receptionist. Without rising from his desk and no handshake offered, Charles Wik proceeded. "Jordan, have a seat, please. Allow me to get straight to the point. We have a problem, but nothing you cannot handle."

"Yes sir, Mr. Wik, how may I help you?"

Charles Wik was Chairman of the Board and a founder of Credence Community Church. He and six others made the decisions as to the direction of the church which was now bursting into mega territory. The board members were all prominent leaders of some of the largest corporations in Charlotte. And like the church, Charlotte was growing fast as well.

"Jordan, as you know, our current building campaign is estimated to raise one hundred million dollars over the next five years. And with those donations we plan to build branches throughout our suburbs and beyond."

"Yes sir, I am aware. It is exciting. As the Gospel of John says, 'I am the vine; you are the branches.' We are succeeding in following God's path."

"Yes, and to make this campaign more appealing, we have attached $200,000 a year to fund Pastor Nkosi's mission. That is $1,000,000 over the next five years."

"Our people love the thought of helping Anton and his people. It is Christian."

"Jordan, you have done a fantastic job of marketing our

CREDENCE HAS NEEDS

South Africa product and the fund raising reflects it."

"Thank you, sir. We have sent two large groups of 300 plus and four small specialty groups over there. Pastor Nkosi has visited twice with his music ministry. Our people view them as family."

"How are they doing? I understand the Hospice is having problems. Something about government assistance or something like that."

"Yes sir, it has something to do with CD4 rates. When they…"

Wik interrupted. "I understand they have a High School built and part of the Hospice is being used as a primary care facility."

"Yes sir. We sent one of our people, Dr. Joseph, over to report back. He said it is doing well."

"But the second floor is still vacant?"

"Yes sir."

"We want to keep South Africa as a tithing incentive, but if we are going to give one million dollars to them, we need to make this a formal business arrangement."

"I understand."

"Our legal consul believes if any of that one million was to be misused or some sort of fraud uncovered, our people would never fully trust them or us in the future. South Africa would be lost as a fund-raising tool and the damage to our reputation would be significant."

"Sir, I have worked with Anton since 2004. I trust him completely. During the building of the Hospice his appropriations were never in question."

"I appreciate your trust; however, your trust is irrelevant, Jordan. This is September 2007, not 2004."

"Surely, our accounting firm would require routine audit trails."

"Of course, but the lawyers performed a risk management matrix. The most disturbing thing to them is the immediate needs of Anton's people, like health, food, lodging. Our funds will be earmarked in a budget for Hospice operating expenses and his church's expansion, not immediate needs. With his corporation having complete control of expenditures, they think it would be easy for him to funnel funds elsewhere."

"I could see that. The immediate needs are endless. He might do that in a critical situation but is that a negative?"

"Jordan, stop right there. You are being too kind and too naive. The clergy part of you is showing. You told me Anton and a man named Roberts held our feet to the fire for $80,000 at the beginning of our relationship and another $100,000 for the vacant second floor of the Hospice."

"Well yes, we gave them more than we budgeted, but I wouldn't call it 'feet to the fire.' I was given bad information, Mr. Wik. I found out later those requests were legitimate." Wik gave a frown. He knew the bad information came from his daughter.

"You are missing the point, Jordan. Follow me. We are growing fast. We are to build three more churches around Charlotte, big churches. And with that, we are getting pushback from the Catholics and the Baptists."

"What is their objection? We are bringing new people to Jesus Christ, especially the youth."

"Not all of them are new Christians. This is a money issue. We are taking people from their congregations and consequently money from their offering plates. That is what we are doing."

"Okay, go on."

"Jordan, religion is big business. The churches many of us attended in our youth were lucky if they could afford a pastor. And now, our newly formed church is about to raise $100 million, and some from their coffers."

"Yes sir, I understand."

"So, I must ask you and your subordinates to stop stoking the fire."

"I don't know what you mean. Give me an example."

"Jordan, I love your competitiveness, as well as your staff's, but a bishop from Saint Matthews called me last week. He was upset. He claims someone from our stage was referring to former members of his church as 'Recovering Catholics.' Tell me that's not true."

Jordan turned his head to the wall and sighed, "Yes sir, that was me, but I did it in jest."

"Well, the bishop failed to see the humor. He felt it was offensive to all Christians and to Jesus Christ himself."

Jordan lowered his head like a child scolded. "Yes sir, I am so sorry. I will send a memo this afternoon to the staff."

"And did you also refer to our new Baptists members as 'Johnny's Boys'?" Jordan nodded again. "Help me son, stop the humor at our competitions expense."

"Yes sir. But may I ask? What does that have to do with South Africa?"

"Public relations, Jordan. As we attract more members and their tithes go to us, we make new enemies. We do use tithes as a measurement of our success; and nothing is wrong with that. And they calling us a cult is harmless. But our enemies would love to give the press a story involving embezzlement, fraud, or a juicy sex scandal. Anyone of those would cause some real damage. If we lose people's faith and trust, we lose their donations. Understand, Jordan?"

"I do. We must be careful how Anton uses our money. What do the lawyers propose?"

"They want us to place one of our people on the grounds to approve all expenditures; a person loyal to us."

"Someone from our congregation? Who would move to South Africa full time?"

"We are talking to Dr. Joseph, the optometrist. We can add him to the budget and pay him a salary."

"But, in the end, Anton will make the decisions on how the money is spent?" Jordan wanted to fully understand before talking to Anton.

"Well, sort of. We are preparing a proposal right now."

"And what does that proposal entail, Mr. Wik?"

"In order for Anton to receive the $200,000 per year, he must give up some control."

"What kind of control?"

"We will require him to dissolve his current corporation and we will create a new one. He will own 50% and we will own 50%."

"But he still runs the operations?" Jordan asked again.

"Not exactly. The new corporation will have a Board of Directors consisting of seven; four appointed by Credence and three by Anton. He will submit a budget and the Board of Directors will approve it or disapprove it. It is simple."

"Anton will be in charge of operations; things like expansion and personnel?"

"Jordan, you emailed me when you were there for the Dedication of the Hospice, and you told me the place was in chaos. You told me Anton and Roberts were incompetent to run the operations at any level."

"I did, but that was before I learned things work differently over there; a lot differently."

"Nonsense Jordan, business is business. The key is competent leadership and qualified personnel. We will hire a professional management firm out of Cape Town to run the corporation. They will perform the hiring and firing. That will allow Anton to return to preaching where he belongs."

Jordan shook his head. "Mr. Wik, he will never go for it."

"Are you telling me he will give up a million dollars; for what, power?"

"Mr. Wik, I can convince him of audits and invoice approvals, although he will be offended. He might even go for the management firm if it was a Black owned company. But unless he has total control over the personnel, he will reject our proposal. His doctrine from the beginning has been Black Empowerment. No exceptions, except Roberts."

"What is Black Empowerment?"

"From the beginning, he has proved to his people they can build a church and manage the compound themselves. He has proven to them, since Apartheid, they do not need Whites to succeed. He will not allow an all-White American church to change his doctrine."

"Jordan, this is business, and we are not all White. Watch, he will take the money and return to preaching. He will give up his outdated prejudicial doctrine. Call and make him see what a good deal this is for him and his wife. And remember, we want to keep him as a fundraising asset. Get back to me soon."

Charles Wik turned to his PC. Jordan West left his office.

REMEMBER SEPTEMBER MR. ROBERTS

It was August 2007. Charlotte was in the grips of a heat wave. And as usual, Ian hobbled through his first steps as he did every morning. The granite tile on his bathroom floor did not make the start of the day any easier. He found his way to his desk chair. He scrolled the senders to prioritize his responses. But this morning it was no contest. A sender was 'Anton Nkosi.' He opened it immediately. It read:

Dear Uncle Ian,

It will be a year since your last visit. I pray all is well and the Lord is giving you comfort over the passing of your father. Esther and I, along with a few others from the church are going to Mozambique in early September. My former assistant, Pastor James, has started a church on the beach. It is growing rapidly and in need of a roof. Are you able to donate the $1,800 needed for the project? We would like you to join us. Let me know as soon as possible.

You are blessed,

Anton

Ian smiled and responded quickly and briefly:

Anton,

You never have to ask me twice to travel. Let's make it happen.

You are blessed my friend,

Ian

Anton responded:

Amen

Ian and Michele planned their next rendezvous to correspond with Ian's trip to Mozambique. It had been a year since Ian experienced one of his mini vacations on the flight from Atlanta to Cape Town. The sleep was well deserved and most appreciated. Thanks to Ryker, he circumvented customs and was to be picked up curbside by his beautiful Deputy Speaker. But this time, Michele was not present to greet him. He was disappointed. Her greeting was one of the highlights of his visit. He was taken directly to the suite.

Ian was informed Michele was unavoidably detained at Parliament, so he took the time to wash the travel stench from his body. He made his way to the closet where he dressed himself in one of his favorite anti-Paparazzi outfits. And finally, feeling like a new man, he stretched out comfortably for a short nap. But just as his first illogical dream entered his head, he was awakened by a soft kiss on his lips and the delightful fragrance of Michele.

"Good afternoon, Mr. Roberts. I have missed you terribly since New York in June. It was nice to get away after the election from anyone who knows me. Our exchange of emails has been quite romantic, but nothing is as arousing as seeing you and touching you."

Ian reached up and pulled Michele firmly into his arms. "You take my breath away, lovely lady. I have missed you as well. You feel so good, Deputy Speaker." They both smiled as they kissed once more.

"The usual tonight, Mr. Roberts, cocktails and dinner while overlooking the lights of the city?"

"Perfect."

"Then entertain me with deep conversation after dinner?" Michele shot Ian a coquettish grin.

"Perhaps we should have conversation before dinner as well," replied Ian.

Michele beamed, arose from Ian's arms, closed, and locked the bedroom door. It was magical.

The next day of exploration was more than mere sightseeing. It was a daydream. With a secret service man on the cable car in front and one in the cable car behind, Ian and Michele had a spectacular five-minute ascent to the top of Table Mountain which overlooked the Cape Town area for miles. But Michele seemed uneasy about this visit. It was a malicious election; both parties attacking each other politically and personally. That is why she insisted on New York in June.

Michele also determined the national park in Table Mountain was too wide open and dangerous for them to stroll the nature trails, so a secluded corner of the restaurant overlooking the city was arranged by her protective and loyal bodyguards.

They drank wine from South Africa's vineyards and, as always, they laughed a lot. "It feels so good to be with you, Ian." She reached across the table and clasped his hand in hers.

"I love being around you, Michele."

"How is Anton?"

"First, I want to thank you again for referring the U.S Army to us. Anton tells me the high school is growing not only from his grade school, but from others paying a handsome tuition to attend. Anton's reputation has attracted quality teachers and allowed him to hire an excellent principal."

"And what does he think of his new primary care facility?"

"I don't know. He has not mentioned anything about it to me. I have been waiting, but I did hear about it from Dr. Joseph back in Charlotte. Knowing Anton, he wants to surprise me. Tell me more."

"From what I understand, it takes up half of the first floor of the Hospice. I am anxious to hear how he feels about it."

"He must love it. That justifies all the square footage on the first floor. Now for the second floor."

"Yes, I am aware. You told me of the vacancy problem the day we went to the Cape, then in Botswana, you reiterated the Hospice had stalled so we both thought a facility to take care of those in limbo would help, a facility with a testing lab."

"Are you telling me you arranged for that to happen, and he doesn't know it was you?"

"You defined the problem for me, and I told you I would think about it. Technically, I would say we both made it happen. I have been silent about our relationship as we agreed. He doesn't know we talk, and he certainly doesn't know we are in love." They both smiled. "I am glad to be of assistance, Mr. Roberts. And how about your business here in South Africa?"

"I am afraid I have failed."

"Why is that?"

"As I mentioned before, I needed a core of people with basic skills at the beginning to start the transcription business. I then needed to train them as trainers for growth."

"I remember you telling me Anton insisted you use people from his congregation, no exceptions."

"On my first trip, a person from the Credence church told his congregation from the stage, I would create a thousand jobs for them."

"That sounds like an unrealistic expectation. So, the lack of skills was typing?"

"There are transcription companies in South Africa, and they are proficient. The spelling of medical terminology was another, but also homonyms."

"Those are words that sound the same but are spelled differently?"

"Exactly, like won and one, like two and to and too."

"Go on."

"In medical transcription, the doctors have a zero tolerance for misspellings in their medical records."

"I understand."

"So, spellcheck takes care of routine misspellings, but it doesn't work for homonyms, and it certainly doesn't work for medical terminology."

"So, hire a proofreader?"

"We had one, but when a proofreader is required one hundred percent on every document, it costs more to prepare the record than we could charge, plus transcription is a global business. Anton's people cannot compete."

"So, none of our people can compete?"

"No, you have transcription companies here. But their early vocational training comes from places outside the township."

"What are Anton's people doing now?"

"Straight data entry. They read the word from a scanned image, then type it directly into a database. Mistakes are still made, but it is not a medical record."

"They can do that?"

"Yes, but that too is a global market, especially competing with India. The vocational training in the township schools is still deficient."

"What can be done?"

"I have suggested to Anton vocational classes be offered in his high school to teach typing, business English and business math. It would bring his people to a level where they could compete."

"Then why don't you do that?"

"It takes money, PCs, printers, teachers, space, plus security to protect the equipment. I, personally, cannot justify more capital investment straight from my pocket."

"Let me think about it. And the second floor of the Hospice is still vacant?"

"Still vacant and Anton is praying hard for the answer."

"Okay, I know I started the questions again, but I would love to change the subject." Ian eagerly agreed. Michele changed her demeanor and gazed into his eyes. "I have missed you way more than I should, Mr. Roberts." Michele reached across the table once more. They smiled as they held each other's hands in this private room on the plateau of Table Mountain.

Returning to the suite, their passionate routine of cocktails and dinner repeated once more. For Ian, this could only be a one-day visit. He needed to meet Anton for their trip to Mozambique. Michele arose from dinner and led Ian by the hand to her pedestal bed overlooking the lights of the city. After a while, they fell asleep in each other's arms.

As Ian awoke, Michele was snuggled into the small of his neck. She was awake. She placed her finger on Ian's lips. Kissing and caressing her hair he whispered softly, "I am in love with you."

"I am in love with you as well, Ian." A tear ran down her cheek.

Wiping the tear from her cheek he asked, "What is wrong, Michele. We just had the kind of night people dream of."

Michele snuggled back into Ian's neck. "You know what is wrong as well as I do, but neither of us want to say it. I am afraid this will be our last time together."

Ian gasped a short quick breath. "I don't understand?"

"Yes, you do, Ian. We both knew in our hearts this moment would arrive. We are intelligent people. I allowed myself to get way more attached to you than I ever expected. We cannot go on like this. I cannot go on like this. It hurts to much when you leave."

"But I always come back and always will."

Michele remained snuggled tightly into Ian's neck, not allowing their eyes to meet. "When you arrive, it is bliss, when you leave it is heartbreak. Our time apart has been part of our attraction. You are a busy man and travel throughout the world. I love that about you. And I am dedicated to my family and my country. You love that about me. We are perfect for each other."

"Why can't we continue the way it is?"

"Our sneaking around the Paparazzi is fun and our short intimate times have been magnificent. But one or two days is not enough for me."

"I don't understand. We are in love."

"Yes, you do Ian, you understand. I will be in pain when you leave today. I can't do it anymore and you are not going to leave the U.S."

Silence hung heavy as they embraced. Ian broke the silence, "Michele, we are not children. I want to tell you we can make this work. But we do live in different worlds. I love you. I will always love you. I will never forget you." They turned to each other and shared their tenderness one last time. Their tears intermingled.

When their final act of love ended, Michele stood at the bedside and stared at Ian, "Please go to your room and stay there until I leave. I can't say goodbye twice, my love. It's breaking my heart." Ian rose, they hugged, their bodies touched for the last time.

"I love you, Michele." Another tear ran down his face.

"I love you too, Mr. Roberts."

They then kissed for the last time. Michele went into her bathroom and shut the door.

Ian went to his room and prepared for his trip to join Anton. One new type of tear was on Ian's face, another one he never saw coming.

THE COMPOUND COMPOUNDED

Ian arrived at the compound mid-afternoon. His heart was in pain after parting ways with Michele only a few hours earlier. He had no one with whom he could share his loss. Like his relationship with Michele, that too must remain in darkness.

Anton's progress in one year was astounding. His vision, planted by the Lord, germinated as God's love showered down upon it. The vines of the Lord spread, the branches bore fruit, two of which were Ian and Michele.

Ian waited only a brief time for Anton's attention. He was anxious to show him what had transpired in the last twelve months. Three new structures were built in the compound, two orphanages and a home for disabled children. One orphanage lodged six boys, the other six girls. And in each resided an elderly couple serving as foster parents. Anton's creation of this social symbiosis between orphans and seniors was another stroke of brilliance.

The High School had grown quickly. Being feed by Anton's lower grades as well as transfers from public schools, it was a communal treasure. It would soon produce its first graduating class.

Anton led Ian past a new crop of preschoolers. Most had not yet met Uncle Ian, but the teachers remembered him well; the man who brought the children books and gave them endless hugs. The teachers had the children wave and shout 'Lacoua' in remembrance of those times. Anton smiled and stroked his goatee. Ian could not resist. He veered across the schoolyard to greet this new batch of little angels. The bell rang and the grade school children were dismissed for the day. Many remembered their Uncle Ian, the first and only White man who showed them love and respect. One boy charged him and attempted to jump into his arms as he did a few years ago. The boy had grown significantly. They both laughed as they stumbled and fell to the ground. Ian remembered those first days in the schoolyard. The tweak in his heart returned.

Ian and Anton walked to the Hospice. They made their way into the lobby. Ian knew what was coming, but he acted surprised. "What is this, Anton? Who are all these people?" The waiting room was filled. People overflowed to the outside where they sat on folding chairs.

Anton explained, "Shortly after you left last September, I received a call from The Department of Health in Cape Town. They heard I had vacant space available in the Hospice. They asked if I would consider turning part of it into a primary care facility."

"And then what?"

"I spoke with the Department of Health. I told them to submit a proposal. Turned out, they already had one drawn up. It was short and to the point. They expedited the permits, developed the space, and agreed to let me hire the clerical staff and medical assistants."

"And you did? You didn't want to save the space for more hospice patients?"

"We could not afford to expand. You know the problem. But Credence agreed to give us enough financial support to keep the Hospice open in a limited capacity. They do not want us to close completely."

"That is good to hear."

"And they are promising to keep that going for the next five years. It is in their new fund-raising campaign."

"That is perfect."

"And that's not all. They installed a government approved lab so we can test CD4 levels right here close to the HIV patients. And on top of all that, they gave us two minivans to shuttle those needing to be tested." Anton was excited to finally share this with Ian.

"How many jobs is that for your people?"

"Let's see, in the facility alone, six medical assistants, six clerical, three drivers, and two lab technicians.

"That is seventeen."

"And then we have six people preparing food. They cook, make sandwiches, and soups. Then our young people deliver the food to the health care workers and patients."

"Where do they prepare the food?"

Anton gave Ian a sheepish grin, "I thought I would ask your forgiveness rather than your permission. I moved your employees into an unused classroom in the High School and made your office into the kitchen. I thought you would be all right with that. And we are offering typing and computer classes at night with your PCs."

"Anton, that is fantastic, and this has all happened since I left last September?"

"Wait Ian, I have one more surprise." Anton led Ian down a small corridor to a tiny office. The office was just big enough for a desk. Next to the office was a room containing the necessary cleaning supplies and equipment for the entire compound, including a commercial washer and dryer. On the wall outside the office was a plaque:

Miriam Kasongo
Head of Janitorial Services

"Is that?"

"Yes, that's her. That is your Miriam."

Ian, once again, was touched. "That is why you had me stop sending money a year ago?"

"That's why. And she has three employees, one being her mother who does laundry. And little Ava, who is not so little anymore, helps her grandmother after school."

Ian turned to Anton. "My friend, this is a work of art. It is a beautiful work of God." He gave Anton a rare hug. "And I must ask one more thing, what about the second floor? Is it still vacant?"

"Yes, it is. I pray loudly for the answer. Thank the Lord we have the funds from Credence, or we cannot keep the Hospice open. The primary care facility is government owned. It creates jobs and cares for our sick but does not produce profits to fund the Hospice. But oddly enough, I received an email just before you arrived. It was titled, 'Office Space Available?' and it read:

> Please consult with Mr. Ian Roberts when he arrives.
> Return a list of your amenities."

"Who was it from?"

"The Department of Employment and Labor in Cape Town. Seems odd the email arrived just before you arrived today. Can that be a coincidence, Ian? How does the Department of Employment and Labor know who you are and stranger yet, how do they know you were arriving here today?" Anton shook his head and smiled. "Ian Roberts, my Uncle Ian, time to tell your Pastor Anton what is going on, but before you do, I think I know." Ian knew he and Michele were caught. "You went against my advice when we left Michele's mansion, did you not?"

"Yes, but how did you know?"

"I didn't know for sure until now. To start, you and Michele made friends way too quickly at the Dedication. My father even noticed it and mentioned it the night he died. After dinner, she pulled you aside and whispered something to you as we were leaving."

"Go on," Ian said with a childlike smile.

"When that Army Colonel mentioned you by name, I knew Michele arranged for you to give your AIDS Awareness speech to another American."

"Okay."

"Then, as soon as you left last September, the Department of Health contacted me about the primary care facility. Within three months we were seeing patients. It was too easy. Only someone with political power could cut through the bureaucracy that quickly."

"What was the final give away?"

"Today."

"Go on."

"I can read your emotions after years of being around you. When you arrived, you seemed sad. That is unlike you when you arrive."

"Good read."

"But before I saw you, Ezekiel came to me to tell me you were in the compound. He thought something seemed odd. You told us your arrival time, but when he checked it on the board, it was a flight from Cape Town, not Atlanta."

"Okay"

"Then the email today was the decisive factor. Tell me, Ian, what has been going on?" Anton knew.

Ian made it a short story. He told Anton about their wonderful times together. He told him about their conversations pertaining to his status and his needs. And he told Anton Michele's help was more than mere suggestions to her staff.

"Where is your relationship now, Ian. From your demeanor when you arrived, it does not seem good."

"Anton, it has ended on a tender, but sad note. We talked this morning. We could not go on, not because we don't love each other, but because we do. The time and distance were too much. If we were closer and spent more time together, perhaps."

"Ian, I warned you. Politics can be a rough game over here. But I was worried for your physical danger, not your emotional pain."

"I was safe. We had bodyguards nearby the whole time, and we stayed hidden."

"Ian, I should have known all this would happen."

"What was to happen?"

"The U.S. Army funds, the primary care facility, and who knows what this new email brings."

"I am confused. Why should you have known?"

"Think back, Ian. How did the two of you meet?"

"We met at the Dedication."

"Yes, but why did you meet?"

"Because Esther sat us next to each other?"

"Exactly, she knew what we needed, just not specifically. She knew God needed you and Michele to work together. And she wanted her Uncle Ian to find a wife."

"She did say that to me right before we were introduced. And she arranged to have Michele sit next to me."

Anton smiled. "And she made sure to get her attention by everyone singing Happy Birthday to you."

"Yes, she did."

"She asked me the morning of the Dedication if I thought you two meeting was a promising idea. At first, I said no. But I know better than to tell Esther no. She has a direct line to God, like Mother Theresa. She can feel what he wants, then she makes it happen. I am telling you; she can feel him. Having faith in her is the same as having faith in the Lord. I said no because I am protective of you, but she insisted and look at all that has happened."

"Yes, I can see it now, but it didn't result in marriage."

Anton stroked his goatee one more time and smiled wider than Ian had ever seen. Looking into Ian's eyes, he whispered, "Not yet."

Anton and Ian went to work on a return email to the Department of Employment and Labor. They wanted it sent the list of amenities before they left for Mozambique. The information was simply since the second floor was vacant. They gave them details of square footage, internet capabilities, food service, and daycare. The email was sent.

Dinner was delightful. The oxtail was delicious. Esther and the children brought Ian up to date on so many things. College courses, musical concerts, soccer standings. It was a family reunion, and Esther did not say a word about Michele, but she knew.

TRIP TO MOZAMBIQUE

The trip to Mozambique was a blessing. Anton was James's mentor. James was trained in the Nkosi style of faith; practicing Christianity both inside and outside the walls of the church, even though James's church had no walls. It was founded with HIV/AIDS as an educational pillar for the community. Nuclear families were taught to intertwine and bring comfort to those in crisis. He followed the Lord's vision inside of Anton. The blueprint was now being shared outside the compound. James was a true apprentice and devoted disciple of his Lord and Savior.

The congregation was diverse in age. James was charismatic. He was young, handsome, and his messages were dynamic and contemporary; many were written and sent to him by Anton. Young families flocked to him, followed by their parents and grandparents. The older population was predominantly women due to the Mozambican Civil War fought between 1977 and 1992. It was estimated one million of the fourteen million population lost their lives in the conflict. A noticeable trait among men who survived was a crutch and one leg caused by the multitudes of land mines buried by defeated soldiers fleeing the country.

Metaphorically, Jesus told Peter 'On this Rock I will build my church.' James built his church on a plot of sand in a small fishing village. The scent of sea water and fishing nets was biblical. Anton told James he approved because though the grains of sand were tiny, they were rocks. The church had only two dozen hand-made pews, an altar made from driftwood, and a pulpit. It did not have a roof. The rainy season was approaching, so it was time for the Lord to call upon Ian and Anton.

The team landed Friday night and readied themselves for the construction work on Saturday. The downpours were predicted to begin Sunday morning. That gave them a deadline of twenty-four hours. Early Saturday morning, Ian rode with James, Anton, and the team to gather the needed materials in downtown Maputo. His U.S. Mastercard was accepted with a welcome smile by the Mozambican merchants and eighteen hundred U.S. dollars later, the roofing materials would be delivered by noon.

As the group headed home, they stopped at the open-air marketplace to purchase food for the weekend. A Dedication brunch would be most appropriate. All climbed out of the van, but James stopped Ian. "Sir, I suggest you wait here in the van until we return."

"James, I will never be in Maputo again. I want to experience your city. Nothing will happen to me."

"I know you feel safe, and I know how you have no fear, but I am concerned for your safety." Anton listened.

"James, I go everywhere in South Africa and elsewhere. I have for years."

"We are in a dangerous part of the city. There is a lot of crime: drugs, robberies, prostitution."

"But it is before noon, James. I will be fine."

"I must be blunt. You are a White man. This country is different from South Africa. The Portuguese inflicted horrible atrocities and war crimes on these people, and that was less than fifteen years ago. And before that, these people were enslaved. Due to Mandela, the South Africans are much more forgiving. Anton's people know you are an American as soon as you speak. Other than my congregation, these people only know you are a White man in their inner city. They will assume you are Portuguese and assume you have money. My biggest fear for you is you will be kidnapped and held for ransom."

"That happens here?" Ian was skeptical. "Come on James, you have been watching too many American movies." Ian smiled. James did not. James looked at Anton.

Anton stepped in. "Ian, our driver is wearing a shoulder holster for a reason. Did you not notice?" Ian glanced at the driver. He saw it under his jacket. "Last night James told me he must hire him specifically to protect you. You will stay here in the van with the driver." Ian could tell by Anton's tone that negotiations were over.

Ian nodded his head and climbed back into the van. The group went down the block and into the market.

Ian sat in the van with the door open. The temperature and humidity were rising. It smelled like rain. The driver guarded the door. Ian saw him talking to a teenage girl. Her outfit and makeup made her purpose apparent. Ian assumed she was a friend of the driver. The driver approached him with the girl following close behind.

"Yes, what is it?"

"This girl says her mother is very sick and she needs money to buy her medicine. She wants to know if you will help her."

"How much does she need?"

"She wants one-thousand meticais. The is about fifteen U.S dollars. But, if you give her money, she will return with many friends. Do not give her money, sir."

Before Ian could respond, the girl rushed to the van and knelt on the step. She hugged Ian's leg and spoke in a language unfamiliar to him. "What did she say?"

"She said she will make you a very happy man for one-thousand meticais."

The driver grabbed the girl from behind. "No, go away."

She clung tight to Ian's leg. He was being dragged out of the van and into the street. She spoke again. The driver looked at Ian. "She now says she will make you happy for five hundred."

Ian managed to get himself free. "Block her from getting to me." The driver did. Ian pulled his wallet from his front pocket and grabbed two U.S. twenties hidden in his wallet.

"No sir, she said she will make you happy for five hundred, that is too much. I will close the door and let you know when I see the others returning, but you do not have much time. I will not tell anyone." The driver assumed Ian wanted far more than what five hundred would buy.

Ian looked at the girl. "Tell her she can have two twenties U.S., but she must stand over by the wall. You will give it to her as we leave. But, if she runs off to tell her friends, she gets nothing."

"Yes, sir." The driver was confused.

"And you say nothing of this to anyone, agreed?"

"Yes, sir. I will agree if you give me one of the twenties. Otherwise, I will allow her to keep harassing you."

The others returned from the market. They loaded the food into the van and were ready to depart. The driver walked to the girl now standing patiently against the concrete wall. Covertly, he slipped her one of the twenties and slid the other into his pocket. She scurried off without looking back. He climbed quietly into the driver's seat.

"Everything okay?" asked James. "Did our White friend behave himself?"

With no expression, the driver responded. "Yes Pastor, he behaved."

The trip was short by design. Neither Anton nor Esther wished to miss two Sundays in a row of preaching back home. Volunteers from James's parish swarmed the dune. Post holes were dug and set in concrete. The frame was constructed. By sundown, the thatch was attached, and the furniture returned and ready for the morning service. It would be another glorious day as all worshipped the Lord with their toes in the soft dry sand.

After the service, the congregation walked down the sandy road together, singing and praising the Lord for his blessings. At the Dedication brunch, Anton looked at Ian. "Thank you for your help."

"Anton, you know you don't need to thank me. It is why we met."

Anton looked at Ian, "James is hinting to me they need a floor. He wants me to ask you for the funds."

"Tell him no, and it is not the money. This is a special sanctuary. I won't be part of separating these people from God's earth."

"Separating?"

"You said it at the Hospice Dedication. You had everyone take off their shoes and stand barefoot. James should make his church shoeless. The sand makes this place another piece of Holy Ground."

"Ian, I agree. We again are standing on Holy Ground. It is beautiful." Anton smiled and stroked his goatee. "I am proud of you, Ian. I will tell James."

RETURN FROM MAPUTO

It was late afternoon on Thursday when the group returned to the compound. Except for Ian and Anton, all went back to their homes to unpack and rest. They made their way to their respective offices. Ian's employees had finished their work week and headed home. Ian logged into a PC. Since there was no internet service available to them in Mozambique, the backlog of emails was vast. Ian scanned the screen to begin his prioritizing routine. When he did, he saw an email from his largest client in the States. The email read:

> *Dear Mr. Roberts,*
>
> *We are sorry to inform you we have chosen another vendor for our business needs. We want to thank you for your many years of service to our corporation. We wish you the best in the future.*
>
> *The Medical Associates of Charlotte*

Ian gasped. He was stunned. Hundreds of thoughts ran through his brain, all intertwined with the emotions of shock and confusion. Like multiple lanes of traffic merging into one, thoughts came from every direction. Thoughts of financial consequences to his business in the States, and his business here in South Africa; then came the second tier. *How does this affect my very survival; my lifestyle; the lifestyle of my children and grandchildren? How does this affect the lives of my employees here and at home?'*

There was no doubt the ripple effect would reach the venture here in this room. The nausea in his stomach was pressing upward. He wanted to sprint to the bathroom and rid himself of the anguish. Like a frightened child, he wanted to run and hide where he could not be found, under his bed back home.

Ezekiel drove Ian to the house while Anton remained working. Perhaps he could escape with a nap, but that was not possible. Lying on his bed, his arms behind his head like a frightened little boy, he wanted to scream. He stared at the thatched roof. In the past, the roof served him well as a blank sketch pad for his creations. As he listened to the birds and rats scurrying throughout, he was fearful this problem was beyond his capabilities. He was drowning in a river of dilemmas; each one flooding his brain before a solution was acquired for the previous.

Then a voice from his early youth entered his head. It was angry. *'I can't get this. This is not going to work. Why did this happen? Give it up, Ian. Give it up!"* His throat was tight. He needed to breathe. He stood up and stomped around the room saying to himself. *'I am a failure.'*

The voice finally gave him a moment. "*Okay, go lie down, take a deep breath, and tell yourself about the tire. When you are finished, start over, and take it from the top. You will figure this out. You always do."* Ian did what he was told. He began a story he told to himself and others many times.

"*A man had a flat tire. He and his wife pulled over by the side of the road and got out of the car. He looked at the flat and started screaming and cursing. He kicked the tire over and over, all the time cursing the flat. His wife waited patiently and watched until he ran out of anger. She then went to the trunk and opened it. She stood there looking at him.*

"What are you doing? You can't change a tire?"

"I could but I won't. You are, as soon as you decide to quit blaming the universe, you will solve the problem. So, get on with it, my love."

The man changed the tire, and the couple continued their journey.

Ian used this exercise in times of mental and emotional chaos. It was a subconscious process for him. He knew stress was the belief one was unable to solve a problem. He knew his first reaction was to quit, run away, blame someone else, let someone else do it. But he could never leave anything unsolved. Once he removed the victim attitude, self-confidence was restored. The negative emotions drifted off like a child releasing balloons into the sky. He knew only then would the root problems emerge, and the solution arise.

He was deeply concerned for Anton, his people, his employees, and their families. But he needed to take care of himself before he could take care of others. He thought of Jesus' parable in Matthew, 'You hypocrite, first take the log out of your own eye, and then you will see clearly to take the speck out of your neighbor's eye.' He needed to remove his own fears. Unlike many around him in the township, his essential needs were not in danger. He knew he would never go hungry, never be naked, and always be sheltered. And now, with the teachings of Anton and Esther within him, he had faith in the Lord. He could hear Anton saying to him 'All will be fine, Ian, you are blessed.' With that, the real problem surfaced. He had failed Anton. His mission to fund the Hospice and create jobs had failed. He failed the patients in the Hospice. He failed to create a thousand jobs and he must tell the few he had created they were no more. And he was fearful of losing his newfound faith in God.

Back at the compound, Anton handled the problems needing his immediate attention. He planned his schedule for the next week, funerals, a wedding, business meetings. It was a long day for all. One that started at sunrise in Maputo and ending at the dinner table well after sundown. The children finished hours before. That left Anton, Esther, and Ian.

Dinner ended with Esther's delicious bread pudding. Anton looked at Ian. "Something is wrong with you, Ian. I can tell. You are never this quiet. You have a defeated look on your face. What is it?"

Esther glanced at both men and spoke, "You both look defeated. It could be fatigue, but it is not. We have all had longer days than this."

Esther turned to Ian. "Is it Michele? You didn't say much about her on the trip. Are you keeping the disappointment inside, Ian? We can talk about it after dinner if you wish, just you and me."

"That is kind of you, Esther, but that won't help." Ian turned to Anton. "We need to talk. I received some news that is crucial to my business both here and back in the States." But before Ian could continue, Anton left the table. When he returned, he tossed a ten-page document on the table in front of Ian. "What is that?"

"Read it. It's from Credence. I need to take a walk. I will be back." Anton rose from his chair and walked outside. Esther went outside with her husband.

The cover page read:

Dear Anton,

Attached is a proposal from us to you. As you know, we are earmarking $200,000 per year for the next five years to help operate and maintain the Hospice. To do so, we will need to have tighter accounting and auditing controls. We are sure you will understand. Please read our Letter of Intent summarizing the main points. If acceptable, we will draw up a formal contract. Please respond to us within the next thirty days with your acceptance.

In his name,

Jordan West

Ian read the pages quickly. Most of it was reasonable, however, there were two unsettling paragraphs. Ian now knew why Anton was upset. He waited for him to return. As he did, silence hovered over the room. He finally spoke. "Do you see what I see, Ian?"

"I do."

"Tell me what you see."

"I see their need for audits and accounting controls. I agree, they are necessary."

"No, no, let all that go. I understand they would like control over how I spend their money. But it is how they propose to do it."

Ian hesitated before responding. He took a deep breath, "They want you to dissolve your corporation and form a new one with them as your partner."

"And who runs this new corporation?"

"Anton, let's get to the point. They want the new corporation to be owned 50/50."

"But?"

"It is run by a Board of Directors consisting of seven, three appointed by you and four appointed by them."

"What else?"

"A management firm will be hired by the Board to make all operational decisions, including personnel."

"And where does that leave me, Ian?"

"You will be a puppet, an employee of Credence. They will hire the management firm and you will go back to being a full-time preacher. Is that what you see?"

"'Yes, and I am not against going back to preaching. Esther and I have spoken of it many times. I love saving people, just like my father. But now is not the time."

"I know, you have saved many souls. But that's not the problem, is it?"

"No."

"This contract ends your Black Empowerment doctrine. They will perform all hiring and firing. Remember, West called us incompetent when he was here. I would speculate that is what he relayed to the Board, thus the reason for the management company. You will become an African satellite of Credence Community Church."

"After all these years, a White church in America would become in charge of our church, our Hospice, our school, and our businesses."

"That is how they have it structured."

"All because of money." He looked at Ian and Esther. "I can't do it. I won't do it. We have come too far to let it end this way. I won't be a hypocrite to my people. I won't betray them."

Ian stayed silent. Anton knew his silence was his agreement. Ian was disappointed in Credence, but not surprised. He thought Jordan West respected Anton's Black Empowerment doctrine. He also understood Credence needed to protect their reputation with control. This could not be a Jordan West decision, he thought, it comes from higher up, the Board of Directors, and the Board underestimated the scars left by Apartheid.

Finally, Anton broke the silence. "Okay, they want four from their side and three from mine on this Board, correct?"

"Correct."

"How about you, Ian? What if I agree if you become their fourth?"

"You would want that?"

"Ian, you understand my philosophy and you support our mission."

"That is true. I do."

"You were here at the beginning. You challenged me in situations when I thought I was right, but I was wrong. Esther even takes your stance most of the time. We respect you. Other than my wife, I have no one else who will stand up to me. We need you."

"But isn't that having a White man with power over you?"

"No, people know you here. You are Uncle Ian. They saw you as a White man in the beginning, but that changed quickly. You taught us we can work as equals. You taught us Apartheid can go both ways. You would be perfect to make neutral decisions."

"You and Esther taught me to have faith in the Lord. But remember, Credence does not like me. We can give it a try. There is a reason I am here."

"Now, what were you going to tell me?"

"It can wait. It's been a long day."

Ian was lying on his bed looking for answers in the thatch above when he heard a knock upon his door. It was Esther. "May I come in, Ian."

"Of course, Esther. Are you okay? Is Anton okay."

"No, he is not okay yet. He is praying louder than I have ever heard him pray. He sounds angry and I cannot tell whether it is at Jordan or the Lord. He feels betrayed for a hand full of silver. He has these moments from time to time, but eventually he stops praying and he finds the answer in the silence. Then he moves on."

"It has been a trying day for him."

"And for you as well, Ian. You look so sad. Tell me what is happening with you. Is it Michele?"

"Some of it, but not tonight. I received an email from the U.S. today. My largest client is leaving, and layoffs will be necessary."

"Certainly, this is not a new occurrence. You can replace the client in time. You are a resourceful man."

"This is different. I will be brief. Health care in the U.S. is changing. Doctors are being hired by large corporations and hospitals. I have been successful because I have a close relationship with my clients. They trusted me and they knew I cared."

"I do not see the problem."

"As these large corporations hire more doctors, they need to hire corporate management firms. Those firms do what I have done for years only on a large scale. My market of the smaller groups of doctors is disappearing. Medicine is now big business. I have gone over this all afternoon in my head. It is time I must sell my business while it still has value."

"What will you do?"

"I will be fine, Esther. Someone will hire me along with the sale. I will be fine."

"Then why are you so sad."

"I must shut down the business here and the ladies will be out of work. I have failed them. I have failed Anton and all of you. I have failed the Lord who sent me."

"Are you going back to questioning your faith, Ian? After all you have seen and experienced, you are challenging your faith in the Lord?"

"I have failed, Esther. Why did he put me here to fail? I am embarrassed. I feel sorry for the employees losing their jobs. They had faith in me. You all did."

"Anton and I have been married for a long time. We were missionaries and preached in Namibia for eight years. When Apartheid ended, we moved back to grow our ministry and to raise our children. With the help of a friend, we bought this land where the compound sits now. We put a tent on the grounds. That was our first church. Like his father, Anton's preaching is passionate and inspiring. He said the Lord told him it was Holy Ground and gave him a vision. He told me the vision was not specific, but he kept hearing 'Knock and the door shall be opened unto you.' And he said the Lord wanted him to teach his people to practice Christianity both inside and outside that little tent."

"So, how did the church grow to where it is today?"

"The word spread quickly as to our tent. And as the township grew, the congregation grew. We built the sanctuary. People continued to flock to us. Soon after, we built the school, then started the HIV/AIDS ministry."

"That is when I arrived, but how did Credence get involved?"

"Anton and Jordan met at a seminary conference in Chicago. Anton shared with Jordan the idea for the Hospice and needed funding. Jordan never forgot about it. One day Jordan emailed. He said he took a position as the Senior Pastor of a growing church, and he wanted to talk. He flew here, they met, and we had the money for the Hospice."

"And that is how the Hospice funding came about. Sounds easy."

"No, it was not easy. Anton went from place to place, country to country looking for donors, but with no luck. This went on for years."

"He always kept his faith, correct?"

"He had his moments. He questioned whether his vision was inspired by the Lord or by his pride. If it was the Lord, for what was he waiting? People were dying, increasingly every day. One night he came to me frustrated and distraught. He said, 'Esther, I pray and pray and pray for the Lord to open the door. I am knocking, but if the Lord does not open the door soon, should I kick it in?'"

"What did you say to him?"

"I smiled and told him to keep praying and pray louder."

They both smiled at each other. "So, Anton had a vision, Anton meets Jordan, Jordan becomes a successful pastor, and the funds are available for the Hospice."

"Yes Ian, then you came."

"What does that mean, I came? I have failed."

"I want you to tell that to Anton tomorrow afternoon at the compound. Something is going to happen; I can feel it. See what he says." Ian was confused. "I knew the Lord sent you to us the first time you came to my prayer meeting. Do you remember?"

"I do. I remember being shocked when this soft-spoken preacher's wife began shouting to the heavens like the horns of Jericho."

"I saw you smile. But what I remember most is you closed your eyes and did not utter a word. You didn't know, but I did."

"Know what, Esther?"

"Unlike Anton, when I am alone and praying, I listen. You gave us the story of Mother Theresa from the stage one Sunday. Do you remember why you told us that particular story?"

"Because it is what came out of my mouth. I had no time to prepare. I told Anton before the service I was not going to preach because I was not a preacher. I thought he would respect that."

"He respected that, I didn't. I made him call you to the stage, no, I insisted. I wanted you to know how God works. I wanted you to say it. I wanted you to realize your silence in prayer was important. I wanted your faith to grow."

"Words have been put in my mouth many times since that speech."

"People chosen by God to lead do not need to hear a voice telling them what to do. Things happen when it is time. We are at a crossroads now. I have faith in you, and I have faith in Anton, but I mostly have faith in the Lord to deliver us from failure."

"You are telling me to wait, and the Lord will open the door when its time?"

"He has so far, has he not? You studied other religions. All of them are about feeling, not thinking. Many are about meditation in silence. Scripture justifies our actions and points us in the right direction through verse, but God is the feeling inside the silence that opens the door to the path we are to take. Satan is alive and well in many, but not in you. Continue to have faith. Recognize it. We are the only ones in your life that have made you see it. Follow what is inside. Seek and ye shall find."

Tears moistened Ian's eyes. I am sorry Esther. My tears over here flow so easily. It bothers Anton, so I try to do it when I am alone."

"He mentioned it the first time you were here. It worried him. So, I reminded him of the early nights he buried his face in my lap and sobbed over the death and sadness this place produces. He knew you were different when you asked him never to let you forget your first day in the township. Your tears are why the people here love you. Your tears are the outpouring of the Lord's love inside you."

Ian took a deep breath. Esther rose and placed her hands on Ian's head, "Good night, Ian, you are blessed."

Ian looked up and smiled, "Good night, Esther, you are blessed."

AND THE WORLD TURNED

Anton left for the compound before the dull light of the cloudy Friday found its way to Ian's bed. Many decisions still lingered waiting for his return. His day would show no mercy.

Ian awoke in a state of depression for many reasons. His appetite was gone due to his loss of Michele along with the sadness for people he must lay off here and in the States. Then intertwined was the probable sale of a business he built over thirty years. He went to the kitchen to force a bagel where he joined Ezekiel. They drove to the compound.

Ian stared out the window remembering his first ride through the township. People still walked on the parched road balancing broomsticks and water vessels on their heads. Children still walked holding their mother's hands, their faces covered in dust from the cars, trucks, and buses roaring past. As they pulled into the compound, Ian took the long way around the building to avoid the preschoolers. He entered the empty sanctuary and listened. He needed guidance. He felt nothing but grief. "God, please give me direction. Is this really over? Are you sending me home because I failed? I am so sorry." Deep silence reigned. He waited but felt nothing.

Ian made his way to the High School to give the sad news to his young ladies. He stopped and stared at the Hospice as people gathered around it waiting to be seen by a doctor. No tears this time. Nothing was sad or joyous this time.

IAN AND ANTON

The women were working steadily as Ian entered the room. They spun around in their chairs. With big smiles, "Good morning, Uncle Ian. How was your trip? How is Pastor James? Did you get the roof on before it rained?" They all had questions.

Ian did not answer. They glanced at each other. They knew something was wrong. "There is something I must tell you without delay." Ian explained the client leaving and the workload reduction. He explained he could not sustain the business any longer. He also shared with them his need to sell his business when he returned to the States. He informed them their compensation would continue until year end. He expected tears and concern, even resentment. He deserved it. He failed them, but once again, he was surprised.

"Uncle Ian, what will you do? You will lose your business? Where will you go?" They were concerned for him, not themselves.

"Don't worry about me. You have taught me the meaning of faith. You have taught me the phrase, 'All will be fine.' But I am worried about you. What will happen to all of you?"

"Pastor Anton taught us to have faith. And you taught us a skill. You gave us a safe, caring place in which to work. You took us to America. Not in our wildest dreams did we envision that. There is a saying, 'Give a man a fish and you will feed him for a day. Teach a man to fish and you will feed him for a lifetime.' Pastor Anton taught us the saying; you taught us to fish."

"I must leave Monday and not return. I am still worried about you."

"We have been offered jobs in the doctor building and in the Hospice. Kele is teaching typing to the High School children here at night. We have not taken those jobs because we did not want to let you down. The Lord will take care of us. We are not afraid."

Ian was speechless. The love was going both ways. "I am proud of all of you. I will never forget you. You have taught me much. I will see you on Sunday at service before I leave. You are blessed, my friends."

'You are blessed, Uncle Ian." The six of them took turns hugging him. Some cried, some projected their big, sweet smiles onto him; some did both. Ian's life in South Africa was fading, one piece at a time.

Ian proceeded to check his emails. He handled them one by one. Questions as to the status of his business were growing. His accountant needed to meet as soon as he returned. He could feel the stress eating at his insides. There was no way but straight through at this point.

Just as Ian finished for the day, one last email popped onto the screen. It was from Michele. His heart dropped. *'Please Lord, don't let us say goodbye again. Don't let her tell me she is having second thoughts now that my days are ending here.'* He opened it. It read:

Ian,

Have Anton check his email ASAP.

Michele

Ian forwarded the email to Anton and turned off his PC. Everyone had left for the weekend. He took his PC to the vault. Anton was performing a funeral and would return late for dinner. Ian went to find Ezekiel. He made one last walk past the preschoolers, but they were gone. He would never see them again. The emptiness was haunting. Ian returned to the house for dinner.

Ian cleaned up and sat with Esther at the table, waiting for Anton to return home. "How was your talk with our girls?"

"Better than I expected, Esther. They were not hurt or upset. They were fine."

"Ian, they all knew this day was coming. You had ideas to build that into something big, but the Lord brought you here for a different reason."

Ian was puzzled, "I don't understand."

"Anton called. He will not be home until late. He wants you to go with him tomorrow morning. He said he needs to talk to you at the compound."

Ian furled his brow and gave Esther a confused stare.

Ian awoke. It was a dreary Saturday morning. Rain fell lightly during the night. September was the beginning of springtime and that meant the rainy season. Ian did not consider three days a month a rainy season, but they did. The gray haze was not helping Ian's attitude. On the drive in, Ian asked Anton about Michele's email. He did not seem anxious to share it. They arrived at eight o'clock. The schools were closed, the office was closed, the church was empty. A few patients gathered at the primary care facility. The compound was muddy. It had a shadow of melancholy cast over it. Ian and Anton went to the kitchen to grab a bagel. Anton led Ian to the middle of the structures.

"Are you going to tell me about Michele's email, or are you going to torture me?"

"I will. But first, Esther tells me you have something to say to me. What is it?"

"I want to apologize to you."

"For what?"

"I am sorry I failed you and I am sorry I failed your people. My mission was to start a business, create jobs, and fund the Hospice. It was clear and I failed. I know you will have difficulty without the support of Credence. Maybe if I had worked with them a little closer, perhaps…"

"Stop. I decided to leave that partnership, not you."

"I knew one-thousand jobs was unrealistic from the start, but I only created six. I failed, Anton. I came here with an invisible hand on my back. You and Esther taught me to listen and have faith in what I was to do, and I still failed."

"Ian Roberts, after three years together, have you learned nothing. We are standing in mud, it is overcast. The Lord is sad you are leaving." Anton smiled at Ian and stroked his goatee. Ian attempted to smile back but could not. "Would you say this place looks different from when you arrived?"

"Of course, it is incredible. You have done God's work. I am proud of you."

"For a man as smart as you, you make me shake my head and wonder if you have been with me all this time. Look in front of you. What is that, Ian?"

"It is the Hospice."

"You played a major role in that."

"Go on."

"Remember at the beginning when I needed $80,000 in additional funds to start construction of the Hospice. I told Sam Bennet and Credence refused?"

"I do."

"You called him and explained the exchange and inflation rates to them in a way I could not have."

"It was simple math."

"Yes, but if you were not here, Credence would have refused me. But they knew you knew the facts. So, the Hospice was started."

"You would have found the money elsewhere."

"Perhaps. But the timing was important. And it kept you here."

"Go on."

"You supported me when I wanted the second floor to be built right away."

"And I talked to West, and he agreed."

"He didn't exactly agree, did he. He matched the one-hundred thousand dollar check you wrote to Credence on Jordan's desk, with his pen."

Ian smiled. "How do you know about that?"

"West told me when he was here for the Dedication. Until then I thought it all came from them."

"Who else knows?"

"Only Esther and me."

"But you still don't have a cashflow and Credence is pulling their funding." Anton ignored Ian and continued.

"Then you met Michele at the Dedication, and she invited us to dinner. A month later we receive money from the US Army to build our High School in the name of AIDS Awareness. That money would not have been approved without your speech at Michele's mansion and the two-story Hospice in the compound."

"Okay."

"Then came the primary care facility because Esther and the Lord put you and Michele together. You shared my problems with her. And because of that we added health care workers, clerical help, a kitchen, and a cleaning company. And the profits from the kitchen and the cleaning company allowed me to build two orphanages and the disability home."

"But now you are stuck. The Credence money would have filled the void that I was supposed to fill. Now that money is gone, and the second floor is still empty."

IAN AND ANTON

"Follow me to my office, Ian." They walked into his office. A six-page Letter of Intent lay on his desk. Anton slid it across the desk to Ian."

"You mean?"

"Yes, the Department of Labor wants to rent the second floor, which you made happen."

"It says here it will be a processing center for government health claims, as well as lab and clinical trial data from the primary care facility and the Hospice. The data will be used for research to treat and cure HIV/AIDS."

"You came here to create jobs and kick off profits to fund the Hospice. You say you failed. You only employed six in your business. No profits to speak of."

"Correct."

"But when the Hospice construction began, many construction workers had jobs for months. Then came the High School, and your offices, and the childrens' homes."

"Keep going."

"When the Hospice opened, it created ten jobs, the mortuary four. Then the High School thirty, the primary care facility twenty, the cleaning company eight, the kitchen eight, and my staff six more. It is not a thousand jobs, but it's not bad, Ian."

Ian looked up from the contract. "This contract says forty clerical, five managers, two IT people, which means more cleaning staff, kitchen workers, and IT people will be needed."

"And there is money in here to pay for two teachers to teach typing, business math and business English to the office workers and our High School children. One of the teachers will be Kele who you trained in the States."

"Are you saying you do not need Credence money any longer?"

"I do not. The rent will cover the Hospice and the ancillary businesses, food, cleaning, and the mortuary, will give me seed money for other compounds."

"Anton, you have the blueprint you envisioned from the start. The Lord planted the seed, and you made it happen. I am glad I helped even though I didn't know it. And Esther played a huge part."

"Because?"

"She put the people pieces together. And she taught me to pray by feeling what I am to do, not thinking."

"The only sad part of this is we will lose you. I am sorry your life will change upon your return home. I know you are troubled. But like he needed you here, trust the Lord will need you elsewhere. He will reveal it to you in time. The Lord says in Jeremiah 29:11, 'For I know the plans I have for you, plans to prosper you and not to harm you, plans to give you a hope and a future.' Be patient, my friend."

"I do not know where I go from here, but because of you, the journey will be easier."

"Do you remember the night my father left the earth.

"I do."

"He preached his favorite sermon just for you."

"I remember. He told me when all seems lost…"

Anton interrupted. "Yes, Ian, what happens when all is lost, and all seems hopeless?"

Ian smiled. His head nodded, "Sunday's Comin'."

"Yes, my friend. Today may seem like your life is over. You are in pain and depressed. You have self-doubt. Satan is watching you closely. He wants to destroy you. He is waiting. He wants you to die, like Jesus Christ, be buried and descend into hell. But God taught us, Sunday's Comin', my friend, Sunday's Comin'. Have faith in the Lord. He has faith in you and has blessed you, Ian Roberts. Without a doubt, you are blessed." They both smiled with tears yearning to escape, but this day was strangely joyous.

THE CHURCHES PART WAYS

Jordan West entered the office of Charles Wik. "I just talked to Anton."

"And he agreed. I told you he would."

"Not exactly."

"You told him the new corporation was not negotiable?"

"I did."

"And you told him no new corporation, no money?"

"I did."

"Out with it, Jordan, what did he say?"

"He said he would do it if Ian Roberts is our fourth Board member."

Charles Wik began to chuckle in an arrogant manner. "Now that is funny. This Roberts person has been a spear in our side from the beginning. He is not loyal to us. Kristin noticed that the first time she met him."

"You are right, your daughter was never a fan."

"She had her suspicions after a luncheon even before the trip. She described him as arrogant and power hungry. Then she reported it directly to me when she returned from the trip. She thought all along Anton and Roberts were planning a scam to use our Hospice money for their venture capital."

"Mr. Wik, I …"

"Now he wants us to make this con artist the king. We would relinquish all power, all control. Roberts would favor Anton on all decisions. That is funny, Jordan. Tell Anton, no way. Tell me what he says."

"Sir, I am afraid there is no deal. The partnership between us and Anton is at an end."

"How can he be so stupid. He needs our money."

"It is the Black Empowerment issue, sir. He said his people would lose all faith in themselves and in the Lord if he turned the entire project over to a White American church. He said our people and his people love each other from our mission trips together. We did a great marketing job, but I am afraid we must tell our people the truth."

"And what might the truth be, Jordan?"

"The partnership is ending because we must have control over Anton and his people in order to direct the use of our money and protect our reputation."

Wik hesitated and looked out his window before speaking. "Of course, we do. It is our congregation's money, and we need a solid reputation to grow. Your people must understand it is about protecting the future growth of my church, I mean…"

"But many will not see it that way. They could see it as colonial, or even a superiority issue."

"Okay, no one knows about this partnership proposal but us and our legal firm, and that is client privilege."

"Roberts knows. He is over there right now with Anton."

"So, put out a rumor that says we suspect Roberts of embezzling some charitable funds we sent to Anton."

"Then Roberts brings a defamation of character suit against us, you have no proof and Roberts exposes the proposal in court. The Press would love that. And I am positive Anton, and his entire congregation will defend Robert's innocence."

"I will talk to my legal staff and see what they say. We must find a way to stop Roberts from making us look like imperial White Americans. You are positive he refused the proposal unless we put Roberts on the Board? How about throwing more money at Anton? Promise him a big salary to just oversee his compound. How much will it take to break him?"

"Mr. Wik, I know Anton. He cannot be bought. Not when it comes to Black Empowerment."

"So, we either let him hire a group of incompetent uneducated Africans, to waste and embezzle our money, or we find a new mission to excite our people." Jordan stayed quiet. "So be it. Let's announce the end of our partnership. I will take care of Roberts."

"I will tell Anton it is over." Jordan West was disturbed and felt fear leaving the office of Charles Wik.

FARE THEE WELL

Ian and Esther drove to the church for their last prayer meeting together. As they approached the church, Esther turned to him, "I will miss you my Uncle Ian. I am missing you already."

"I will miss everyone, but especially you." Esther smiled. "You created the level of consciousness inside me I have searched for all my life. I would not have it if not for you."

"No Ian, I did not create it. It has been in your soul from the day God placed you on the earth. I only pointed you towards it. Your core would not allow Satan to attach to that void in you. Anton told me of your speech at Michele's dinner."

"What did he say?"

"You blurted the word 'Parenting.' And at that point you recognize God as the ultimate parent. When we first met, you told me you studied other religions. You told me most have similar traits as Christianity. I did not want to believe you, but I can see how the essential spirit of all is founded in love, and that love comes from the inner parent of all of us, which is God."

"In the States, I have my prayer room. That is unusual for a Christian. I saw them in Asia years ago. They are in most every home. I studied the discipline of Buddhism because I wanted to find that higher level. But, at the time, my silent meditation was only a way to relieve my stress."

"Did it work?"

"It did a bit, but until I met you, I did not realize what was happening."

"And what was that?"

"I was allowing myself to clear my mind of worldly things and subconsciously follow a path."

"That was the hand in your back, as you called it, that you could not explain."

"Exactly, before that, I was constructing my own path. I forced my life into my selfish vision, one that filled my needs, not others. I thought the only way I would feel peace was to control everyone and everything around me."

"And now?"

"As you taught me, I go where my silent prayer takes me."

"And you are now at peace?"

"I'm not right now." Ian chuckled. "Within a matter of days, a woman with whom I am in love, will be gone from my life forever. By the end of the year, the business I built over thirty years will be in the hands of another. And the African chapter of my life with my dear friends will be over. It is a lot of loss. I am in a lot of pain."

"Assure me, like the Book of Job, you will remain faithful to the Lord and kind to yourself. You must be patient."

"I am trying, but I find myself angry with him. I don't know what I did wrong, or." Ian stopped.

"Or what Ian?" Esther was afraid of what was coming.

Ian looked away then changed the subject. "I am looking forward to praying with you one last time."

"We will always pray together, Uncle Ian."

Word spread quickly of Ian's final attendance. The sanctuary was full. The service started gracefully late as usual. The teens played their instruments and sang, Anton danced across the stage and the elderly women threw the word of God from their Bibles. Then they turned and doused Ian. He smiled as he allowed the words to penetrate his soul. Magdalene, Miriam's mother, kissed Ian on the cheek. As the service continued, he fought to keep his thoughts from moving to his earthly problems. Then Esther joined Anton on the stage.

Anton had Ian stand. He gave a short but succinct history from Ian's arrival to this last day in the sanctuary. When he finished, Esther took the pulpit. She also gave a beautiful recap of Ian's spiritual growth and complimented the congregation for their part in Ian's development. But then she had Ian stand in front of the stage and face her people.

"This is our farewell to our Uncle Ian. He has given us much in these last few years. Uncle Ian is from America. He is a wealthy man. He has everything he needs. And God has everything he needs, but we give to God. As he is leaving us, we must give back to Uncle Ian. If you wish, you may now come forward and give him your blessings."

The organ began to play softly as people came forward bearing their appreciation. The tears once again swelled in his eyes. They gave him Rand, their handmade scarves from around their necks, and blankets from their backs. A young man gave him the watch from his wrist. And one boy gave him the ring his mother left him when she died in the Hospice. Ian attempted to refuse, but the boy said it was an honor. He said his mother always wanted to go to America, and now she was going. Ian embraced the boy and kissed him on the forehead.

The service ended. Others came forward and said their goodbyes. Esther told Ian Pastor Gladys was waiting outside to take him to the tent revival. As he walked through the door, angels appeared. It was a group of children. Many were older now, but their smiles were as innocent and endearing as ever. They gathered around him and chanted 'Lacua.' He took time to hug each one of them. When he finished, the boy who loved leaping into Ian's arms approached, the rest encircled him.

"Uncle Ian, we will miss you. We had the chance to know a White man and an American, and someone who loves and cares about us. You taught us a lot just by being you. Each visit you brought books to our Preschool. We want to give you our favorite to remember us by. We have all signed it. You are blessed, Uncle Ian, and we love you." It was a beautifully illustrated book called 'All the Little Children of the World.'

As Ian took it, the children cheered. Some cried. Some did both. Ian could not say a word. He waived to everyone as he got into the car with Pastor Gladys. As they drove off, another piece of his life was now in the rearview mirror.

RETURNING HOME TO THE WASTELAND

The day was excruciating for Ian. He had said his goodbyes. He did not want to do it again. Anton had a full schedule but would take Ian to the airport at three o'clock. Ian did not have the software he needed to begin work on the sale of his business. The children were in school. His alone time was left to his ability of problem solving without technology. He waited until noon to have Ezekiel drive him to the compound to check his emails one last time before his final thirty-hour portal-to-portal trek home. As he was finishing his emails, one last one popped up.

Dear Ian,

Please advise me of when you will be returning from South Africa. I will arrange to have you picked up from the airport so you can meet with us as soon as you return. We feel an immediate meeting is necessary regarding our partnership with Pastor Anton Nkosi.

In his name,

Jordan West.

Ian responded with his flight information and his expected time of arrival in Charlotte. Ian was curious. Completing his response, he made his way to Anton's office. Anton was on his phone with his feet on his desk, a habit he learned from Ian. "Anton, I just received a peculiar email from Jordan West."

"And what made it peculiar, Ian?"

"He wants to pick me up from the airport and meet with me immediately upon arrival. I am not sure that is wise."

"It is over, Ian, unless they are reconsidering. But the second-floor rental changes everything. Perhaps they want you to debrief them on my reaction. Just hear what they have to say and be gracious."

Anton drove Ian to the airport. It was a solemn time. Ian thanked Anton for the trips they took together. They spent time in Namibia, and Zimbabwe, in Mozambique and Mauritius. And they spent time in the U.S. going to sporting events and parties. But their favorite time together was shopping for Anton's preaching attire. The memories were numerous, but now, they carried with them a feeling of loss.

Ian looked at Anton. "I am so proud of you and what you have set in motion. Your blueprint is genesis. You listened well to the Lord. And now it will be used throughout all of Sub-Saharan Africa. I am honored to have been part of it."

"But I am worried, Ian."

"Worried of what, Anton?"

"I am afraid with all of these moving parts, I will not have time to preach. Esther tells me I will need to decide soon."

"Decide what?"

"Whether I will be a preacher or a businessman. I cannot do both. That means I may not get what I want unless..." Anton hesitated.

"Unless what?"

"Unless you become my CEO and I preach and fund raise."

Ian took a deep breath. "I have not felt the hand in my back for that one, Anton. But give it some time. I will return home and do what I must. Allow me to clear my mind, reenter the silence, and listen. In the meantime, Esther will let you know what the Lord wants you to do."

"She always does."

IAN AND ANTON

Anton pulled to the curb. Anton stayed in the car. They grasped each other's hands and said goodbye. No tears on either face. It was too real. They were both numb. Ian jumped out, grabbed his luggage, and went for the entrance of the airport. He told himself not to look back, just let it go. But before he could get to the door, he heard a thud. As he turned, Anton and a small bus had collided. An airport security guard was running towards them blowing his whistle and demanding they stop. The dent was small. Anton took off. The bus took off. Ian would miss everything about South Africa.

Ian landed, made his way through customs, then curbside of the arrival terminal at the Charlotte airport. It was eleven o'clock in the morning. Ian was lagged and fatigued. He saw a young man holding a sign that read 'Ian Roberts.' It reminded him of his days meeting Ryker and Michele in Cape Town. He was heartbroken knowing he would never see her again. The healing had not yet begun. But he knew they were put together for a reason, and that reason was accomplished. It was part of his sacrifice.

Ian approached the young limo driver. "Mr. Roberts?" he asked.

"Yes."

"Mr. Wik instructed me to pick you up."

"You sure I am the right person?"

"Yes, I am his chauffeur."

"I thought Jordan West was picking me up. Why Charles Wik?"

"Sir, all I know is I received a forwarded email from Mr. Wik instructing me to pick you up and deliver you to his office. Here is the email."

Ian looked at the email. It was his he sent to Jordan West with his arrival information. "Okay, is Jordan West with you?"

"No, sir. I don't know that person."

"He is a Pastor at Credence Community Church."

"I heard Mr. Wik has something to do with that church. Can we go now, sir?"

"Yes." The driver carried Ian's luggage to the limo. Ian followed. He climbed in and they left the airport. His mini-vacations on the flight to and from South Africa were over. Another ending.

The limousine pulled up to the entrance of a skyscraper. The sign read 'Ballister Corporation.' Exiting the driver's seat, he instructed a young door attendant to take Ian and his luggage to Mr. Wik's office.

A private elevator took Ian and the door attendant to the forty-ninth floor. Like Michele's suite, the elevator opened directly to a reception desk where a female welcomed him. "Mr. Roberts, please have a seat. Mr. Wik will be with you shortly. Can I get you anything?"

"How about a pillow. I just finished a thirty-hour trip from South Africa." Ian smiled.

"That is a long time. I travel a lot, but never out of the country. I don't have a pillow, sir. I'm sorry."

"I get a little silly after those flights. The jet lag, you know. But I could use a bathroom."

Ian went to the bathroom, threw cold water on his face, and slicked back his hair. He returned to the couch."

"Mr. Roberts, Mr. Wik will see you now."

Ian entered the office. It had a panoramic view of Charlotte. Charles Wik came from behind his massive oak desk to welcome Ian with a handshake and a smile. "Mr. Roberts, it is a pleasure to finally meet you. I am Charles Wik and for your purposes I am Chairman of the Board of Credence Community Church."

"A pleasure to meet you as well, sir. I was under the impression I was meeting with Jordan West. Will he be joining us?"

I thought it best for the two of us to speak in private. Have a seat, Mr. Roberts." Ian sat low in a deep side chair in front of Wik's desk. Wik took his seat in his high-back leather chair, where he could look down on Ian. "I want to thank you so much for coming directly from the airport. Have you spoken with anyone since you have returned?"

"Yes, I called my daughter to let her know I was back in the country."

"Did you speak to anyone else. Have you sent any emails to anyone regarding the unfortunate ending of our relationship with Pastor Nkosi?"

'No sir, I have not.'

"Good. I would like our conversation to stay in this room."

"Go ahead." Ian was sensing something. He would drop the 'sir.'

"Ian, I understand you have spent over three years with Pastor Nkosi."

"Yes, that is correct."

"And you have worked closely with many people there, and your relationships have been more than just business."

"If you are asking me if I made close friendships with many people, I have."

"And you know many people in our church also feel close to those people."

"Yes, they write to each other, share photos of their families, some of them have shared their homes with them here in the States."

"Credence has done a wonderful job intertwining the two churches. But I don't have to tell you, we are uneasy giving Pastor Nkosi control over our money."

"I read your proposal and understand the deal. He was not opposed to your audits and controls at all. It was the management company, and the hiring and firing power Credence would control that broke the deal. Anton would become an employee, a puppet if you may, to Credence and their Board of Directors. And his people would be at your mercy for employment."

"You are speaking of that Black Empowerment thing."

"Yes."

"Mr. Roberts, you are a businessman, I am told, and business is business. This is a money issue. We are not going to give him a million dollars and let him squander it or worse."

"What makes you think that might happen.?"

"Because West and another pastor told me you and Anton are, well I'll just say it, incompetent."

Ian sat quietly although inside his anxiety was moving to a breaking point. He knew the other pastor was Wik's daughter. He was tired, he was hurt, he was grieving over many things. Although he knew anger would be a natural response, he must remain quiet, but finally, he spoke, "So, why am I here?"

"Mr. Roberts, I assume Pastor Nkosi will not reconsider our proposal as written, is that correct?"

"That is correct."

"And we will not accept you on the Board as the swing vote."

"I understand, because of my incompetency." Ian stared into Wik's eyes."

"So, you are here for one simple reason."

"And that is?"

I must silence you. I must keep you from telling our congregation the partnership terminated because we want to have total control of him and his people."

"Does sound a bit colonial, doesn't it Charles?"

"Your attitude toward this situation will not be good for the expansion of our church."

"Maybe you should reconsider your proposal and become true partners."

"You can stop there, Mr. Roberts. We will not reconsider anything. That partnership is done, and Jordan West will announce it on the stage next Sunday."

"Okay, I assume it will have a pro Credence twist? The truth will not come out, will it, Charles?" Ian had dropped the respect.

"And you will not dispute our message, Mr. Roberts."

"What makes you think I will not expose you?"

Wik stayed silent for a moment. Then sitting up tall in his chair and with a sinister grin, he began.

"Mr. Roberts, I understand you are single and have had two previous wives, is that true?"

Ian frowned. *Where is he going with this? He thought.* "Yes, that is true."

"And we understand you had a Black girlfriend a few years ago before you went to South Africa."

"Yes, I did. We were both single, about the same age and for what it is worth, she was vice president of Publix floral division."

"And after her you went to South Africa where you have been seeing another Black woman."

"Yes, her name is Michele. She is the Deputy Speaker of Parliament. What is your point?"

'When you brought your little South African girls to the States to be trained, one of them was pregnant. You paid for prenatal exams for her. I have been told you were quite friendly with all of them."

IAN AND ANTON

Ian's face became red. "If you go there, no one will believe you. When people find out you are lying, it will be worse for you."

"Maybe you went to South Africa because you like Black woman. Maybe they rejected you over here and you wanted to try a more vulnerable type."

"You would not lie. You are a church. Nobody will believe you."

"I don't have to lie. A few strategic people with a rumor. Come on Roberts, nothing like a juicy sex scandal I always say. That would spread like wildfire. Your children would be embarrassed and ashamed of their father. The church people will love it when we ask you to leave the church. They might even think Nkosi knew and kept it secret. And that is what I want."

Ian sat stunned. He took a deep breath. "What do you want, Wik."

Wik stared into Ian's eyes. It was evil. "I want you silenced. I want you to be gagged. I want you to come to the service on Sunday and hear Jordan's message to the congregation. Then I want you to leave the building without saying a word and never come back. I promise you, if you do that for me, I will not destroy your character."

"Does West approve of this arrangement?"

"No one will know of this conversation except you and me. If you talk, I talk. And if I talk no one will ever trust you again. It will follow you wherever you go." Wik nodded his head and rose to his feet. "Good day, Mr. Roberts."

Cued by a buzzer under his desk, two security guards entered the office. They escorted Ian and his luggage to the sidewalk in front of the building. Ian hailed a cab.

THE MESSAGE

It was a peaceful Wednesday in late September. Jordan West was preparing his message for the weekend services. He would inform a curious and disappointed congregation of the reason their relationship with Anton and his people was ending. He would praise the congregation for the achievements resulting from their donations and thank them for the righteous love they gave to a vastly different culture far away. He would ignore any business details as stipulated by Charles Wik. He would tell them Anton appreciated their help and how God had blessed him with success so he could go forward without their financial support. He would also tell them Anton wanted them to find the next benevolent cause in the name of Jesus Christ. And finally, he would encourage people to continue their friendships and pray via email with their South African brothers and sisters. He would end with a prayer blessing Anton and his people and thanking everyone for their devotion to God. Jordan felt comfortable ending with a compassionate message. Finishing his first draft, he took a satisfied sigh of relief. He checked his emails. One was from Charles Wik. It read:

Dear Jordan,

Our marketing department finished its appraisal of the Anton Nkosi situation. They feel we must burn the bridge in case the real reason is exposed, and our congregation wants us to reconsider. His integrity must come into question. Attached is a list of talking points you must share with the congregation this weekend. I trust you can create a credible message convincing your people we are doing what is in the best interest of our stewardship.

Thank you for your dedication and loyalty,

Charles Wik/Chairman of the Board

Jordan opened the attachment. The marketing department was professional. The talking points were perfect for the purpose of Charles Wik. He would portray Credence as a righteous and caring paternal figure, protecting the church and its flock from abuse. Anton would be depicted as selfish and thankless. Jordan leaned back in his chair. He folded his hands behind his head. He looked to the heavens and prayed aloud:

"Dear Lord, give me wisdom. I will not utter these words. By giving our people half-truths and insinuations, I am bearing false witness against my neighbor. I promised Wik I would not reveal any business details. But I will not wrongly vilify Anton. He is dedicated to his people and their livelihoods. I understand the split is to protect our reputation and thus the expansion of our church. I understand our expansion will save souls. But not this way. Give me wisdom, Lord. You are pointing me to James 4:17, 'So whoever knows the right thing to do and fails to do it, for him it is sin'." Jordan ended his prayer; however, he went to work preparing the message as Charles Wik instructed.

Credence promoted the weekend message aggressively. They described it as the reason behind the dissolution of the relationship, but it was to be the reason according to Charles Wik. Jordan worked well into the night. He waited for the Lord to give him the wisdom to somehow avoid Anton from character assassination and still appease Wik. But every path he followed failed. He finished with the best he could do. He was unable to sleep. The next morning, he sent an email with both messages attached:

THE MESSAGE

Dear Mr. Wik,

Attached is my message including the talking points you suggested. I have also enclosed an alternative message which I feel would be more appropriate and end our relationship on a Christian note. Please advise.

In his name,

Jordan West

It was an hour when the response arrived.

Dear Jordan,

I considered your messages. You may proceed with your alternative message. I would also like you to have Jim Bennet and Dr. Joseph on stage with you. They have spent significant time on the grounds in South Africa. They can help document our achievements and share their individual experiences. Have a good weekend.

Charles Wik

Jordan leaned back in his chair. "Thank you, Lord."

The weekend arrived and Jordan felt at peace. The marketing department and the lawyers were overruled. He was proud of Charles Wik.

Ian decided to attend the Saturday night service. He was anxious to hear what West would say. The service was crowded. Ian took his usual seat, the third-row aisle. He avoided contact with friends and colleagues. He did not want to be interrogated. The service began with music, then Jordan West welcomed all with prayer. When he finished, three chairs were brought to the stage, one for Jordan, one for Sam Bennet, and one for Dr. Joseph. All sat and Jordan began to speak.

"As many of you are aware, our relationship with South Africa is ending." A veil of melancholy fell over the sanctuary. "It is sad for all of us. As a group, I want to begin by sharing what we achieved with Anton and the Lord. I have asked our outreach minister, Sam Bennet, to join us and share a bit of our history with South Africa."

Sam prepared a three-minute slideshow for the congregation. It was done well. It instilled a sense of pride for the church and created fond memories for those who became directly involved in friendships. At the end, he spoke of the never-ending needs for clothing, shelter, and medications." Sam finished.

Jordan then introduced Dr. Joseph. "Dr. Joseph is an optometrist. He went to South Africa by himself to perform eye exams for both the children and the elderly in Anton's congregation." A small applause was heard. Ian felt snubbed but it summed up his whole relationship with Credence. "He also visited recently to inspect the new primary care facility that opened in our Hospice. Dr. Joseph, please share your experiences with us."

The audience was silent. Joseph began. "As Sam reported, immediate needs of the people are endless. HIV/AIDS is rampant, but also diabetes, cancer, and birthing mortalities. Even the basic need for heat in the winter is a luxury. We helped where we could, but the need remains endless. That is why we found ourselves in this dilemma."

An eerie feeling came over Jordan. He thought, *'That is the message I wrote, word for word, the one Wik told me I did not have to give. But I am not giving it, am I? Joseph is. Wik is the only one who had that message, and he is making Joseph present it. Wik double-crossed me.'* There was no way to stop Joseph. Jordan was helpless.

Joseph looked at the audience with a sad face. "Due to those immediate needs, we are uncomfortable giving Anton one million dollars without any control of our funds. We are not inferring Anton would misuse our funds, but the temptation to help those in need could be overwhelming. Pastor Anton loves his people, and they love him. So, we proposed a formal partnership between the two of us which we felt reasonable. We would be 50/50 partners." The crowd listened intently. "This would allow us to continue to work together. We would volunteer our management expertise to him. With our management team in place, Pastor Anton is free to do what he does best and that is preach and spread the word of Jesus Christ throughout his township and all of Africa."

Jordan felt a pause where he could stop what he knew was coming. "Yes, we all thought that would be a wonderful solution for him and his people, but…"

Joseph jumped back in. "But Pastor Anton refused our offer. He told us he would not give up control to us, not any. He was willing to take our money, your money, but he refused to commit to us. The young people among us know of the term, 'Friends with Benefits'." Whispers and chuckles were heard throughout the sanctuary. "If any of you have experienced that kind of relationship, it is disrespectful and can be very hurtful. We felt abused. Pastor Anton agrees to take our money, but he will not commit to us. He does not want to be our partner. We helped him build his Hospice. We helped him with his start-up expenses. We visited his community to build houses and sow gardens for his people. We shared the sacraments with him. And now, he will take our money but refuses to formally commit. We will find another worthy cause with which we will partner. We refuse to be 'Friends with Benefits.' "Joseph concluded.

Jordan looked at the congregation. He did his best to finish on a loving note by thanking Anton and his people for their friendship, but the damage was done.

Jordan asked the congregation to rise. He led them in prayer and for the success of South Africa. It was heartfelt. As the prayer ended, all sat down except Ian. Jordan saw him standing alone. Ian stared at Jordan. Jordan thought *'Is he going to challenge us in public. Would he expose the truth about the Black Empowerment issue so conveniently left out of the message? Was as he going to expose Credence's power play?'*

What seemed like an eternity was only a moment in each of their souls. Ian turned and left the sanctuary unnoticed. Ian would say nothing about the message. Wik had him gagged.

As he reached the vestibule, he removed his name tag. He helped himself to one last cup of coffee. He remembered the first day when the young marketing student retrieved the coffee for him. That day he was intrigued that Credence had such a well-thought-out business plan. Now he realized, for the Chairman of the Board and his corporation, it was

Machiavellian; to stay in power, the end justifies the means. Credence inferred Anton was breaking a commandment, 'Thou Shalt not Commit Adultery'. Anton wanted something but would not commit. The twist was diabolical.

Ian left the building and would never return. He would stay angry for years.

Three Days Later.

"Hello."

"Hello Anton, it's Ian."

"Hello, Ian. I was expecting a call from you."

"You saw the service on Credence' website?"

"Yes, I watched it right after I received your email."

"After everything you did for them, Anton, the people, the friendships, the money you raised for them. Now they infer you are an adulterer. I am furious."

"Did you confront them?"

"They threatened me if I revealed the truth."

"How did they threaten you?"

Ian explained his conversation with Charles Wik. He also made sure Anton understood that Jordan knew nothing about the secret meeting.

"Anton, I want to expose this. This is wrong."

"Ian, you must remain silent. To taint people's faith in their church and in God and Jesus Christ is not what the Lord wants. It is not your place. And to allow Charles Wik to destroy your life and your family's reputation accomplishes nothing. Only the Lord can judge, and he will. Matthew: 25,26, my friend."

"Tell me."

"Woe to you, teachers of the law and Pharisees, you hypocrite! You clean the outside of the cup and dish, but inside they are full of greed and self-indulgence. Blind Pharisee! First clean the inside of the cup and dish, and then the outside will be clean."

"But many people here have lost faith in you, Anton."

"I have another for you, my friend."

"Go ahead." Ian smiled into the phone. He knew the preacher in Anton would not let this go without a lesson in wisdom.

"Ecclesiastes 12:14, 'For God will bring every deed into judgement, including every hidden thing, whether it is good or evil.' Ian, this is for God to judge, not you. Has he failed us, or failed you, in our relationship?"

Anton could hear Ian sigh on the phone. "He has not."

"You did what God asked of you, otherwise we would have never met."

"Yes, you are correct. But I am angry at the church."

"No, only one man, and he is not the church. Ian, it could be worse."

"Go on."

"Jesus rode into Jerusalem on a donkey for Passover. The people praised him and laid palm branches in his path. Three days later they nailed him to a cross." Ian remained silent. "Ian, Jordan is a good man. He loses his way at times due to his pride. He is a powerful man now and he does not want to lose that. God has a plan for him and it is a righteous plan. Many will be brought to the Father and to jesus Christ because of him. In the end, he supported what you and I were doing. He told me so. I am sure this troubles him. It will be a long time before he is at peace with it. Pray for him, Ian."

Ian took a moment. "But I cannot pray for Charles Wik."

"Then pray for his soul to be saved. Satan's greed has a hold of him."

"I can, but it won't be easy, and it won't be soon."

"I will pray for you, my friend. Have faith that the loss of your business, the loss of Michele, and the loss of your church are all a part of God's plan. He has a new plan for you. Feel it. Let us remain friends in his name. You are blessed, Uncle Ian."

"Thank you, Anton. You are blessed. Give Esther and the children, and everyone, my love."

The call ended. Ian turned around in his desk chair. He rose and went to the other side of the room. He lit the seven colorful candles on his Jewish Menorah. He sat on a small Persian rug in front of a pad displaying a Buddhist Dharma Wheel. He wore his Christian cross around his neck. He laid the ring on the rug given to him by the young boy whose mother died in the Hospice.

The day had passed. An era of his life had passed. It was nighttime. He closed his eyes, watched his breath, and quieted his mind. He returned to the silence from where it all began. From where he met God.

www.ingramcontent.com/pod-product-compliance
Lightning Source LLC
LaVergne TN
LVHW091533070526
838199LV00001B/44